BANTAM BOOKS BY SANDRA LEE

Love at First Sight
Falling for Her

FALLING
FOR
HER

SANDRA
LEE

BANTAM BOOKS

New York Toronto London
Sydney Auckland

FALLING FOR HER

A Bantam Fanfare Book / October 2000

ISBN 0-553-58011-6

Published simultaneously in the United States and Canada

PRINTED IN THE UNITED STATES OF AMERICA

OPM   10 9 8 7 6 5 4 3 2 1

For dear Ole,
a legend in his own time,
with all my love.

PROLOGUE

England, September 1066

ROSCELYN EYED the unconscious man who lay on her father's bed. Draft-borne candlelight and shadow wavered across his face, lending a snakelike undulation to his dark, bearded countenance.

Man?

Nay, Roscelyn thought. Cerdic was an abomination.

None but a demon would force his attentions on his bride's sister at his wedding feast. Only a cloven-hoofed beast would slaver for the flesh of a child not yet ten.

Unable to bear the sight of him, she lowered her gaze to the rush-strewn floor.

She should have heeded her instincts, the sense of

disquiet that e'er plagued her when Cerdic visited Cyning. Instincts she'd ignored for the benefits her marriage would bring her family and people. With her vows, Cyning's wealth now rivaled King Harold's, as did its strength on the battlefield.

Shivering, she hugged herself, her cold fingers curling into the fine embroidery of her bridal tunic.

For the moment Cerdic slept hard, courtesy of a sleeping potion she'd secured from the village witchwife. But dawn was not far off, and Cerdic would soon wake.

She grimaced. There was nothing for it. She would have to murder Cerdic, for she could never bring herself to lie with him. Nor would she allow him ever again to threaten her sister.

Poison. Aye. Men grew sick and died every day of mysterious ailments. None would know—

Abruptly the candle sputtered, sending darts of light and shadow to course over her tunic. 'Twas as if Satan wished her to know he awaited her immortal soul.

A fulsome shudder tore through her body, leaving her weak and shaking. Conceal the deed from mortals she might, but she could not escape God's all-seeing eyes.

"Cease," she whispered at her despairing thoughts.

Surely God understood her dilemma. To say aught to her father would result in war. Instead of one man's death, many would perish. Nor was there any guarantee that her father and brothers would survive. Cyning's fields would fall to the torch ere the harvest was complete. The village folk, her people, would be burned from their homes and left to starve. And Wulfwyn . . .

Her lips puckered. Had she not discovered her sister and Cerdic in the granary, Wulfwyn would no longer be a maid.

Nay. She would not tell her father. Her sister had suffered enough at Cerdic's hands. The child did not deserve to have her reputation tainted by what many men would consider a drunken indiscretion on Cerdic's part.

Consumed with her thoughts, Roscelyn was frightened near senseless when a pounding came on the door. Ere she could find her voice, Gunderic, one of her father's housecarls, burst into the cramped bedchamber.

"Rouse yourself, man!" The wiry, dark-haired warrior fair leapt on Cerdic, shaking him violently. "We go to battle for England."

Roscelyn's breath caught.

Battle? Cerdic would be leaving?

Reprieve!

She turned her head when her husband rose and vomited on the floor. 'Twas the least he deserved. And should he not return alive . . .

Her eyes rounded. What was she thinking? If Cerdic went down in battle, 'twould be one less man protecting her father's and brothers' backs.

Lifting the hem of her rumpled wedding gown, she hurried from the bedchamber into the adjoining great hall where men were arming themselves.

God forgive her sinful thoughts. If only He would keep her father and brothers safe, she would never again wish harm to another. She would be God's faithful, obedient servant, meek and biddable as He commanded women should be. And if He meant for her to lie with Cerdic, to take his seed into her womb, so she would. If only He would return her menfolk unharmed.

"Ros." Her father beckoned her aside and she went to him.

"Your marriage . . ." He raised a hopeful reddish-gray brow. " 'Twas consummated?"

She lowered her gaze and shook her head, embarrassed to speak of such to her father.

"Ah, well. 'Tis no fault of yours. For now, you must see to our needs."

She nodded and hurried from the hall. Flour, cook pots, pigs, lambs, fodder, kegs of ale. Racing to and fro, she ordered, directed, and instructed until she feared her tongue would fly from her mouth.

At last she and Wulfwyn stood at the entrance to the manor grounds where the men prepared to set off.

As always, she was struck by apprehension at the sight of so much food leaving the manor. Though the men usually returned with more than they carried away, there had been occasions when they'd returned home empty-handed.

'Twas e'er the peasants who suffered under such circumstance. She would immediately begin hoarding food against such a possibility that the village folk would not starve.

Keeping her thoughts to herself, she kissed a smile line that grooved her father's cheek.

" 'Tis blessed I am to have such fine daughters." He ruffled Wulfwyn's hair, then tugged Roscelyn's braid, which he claimed e'er brought him good fortune.

"Cease slobbering on me," Roscelyn's eldest brother

teased when she kissed him, his merry green eyes along with his curly red hair a mirror of her father's.

More tempestuous, her younger brother made a great show of waving his sword at her. "No weeping fits either."

He cast her a stern look, though the effect was ruined when a strand of blond hair flopped over his light brown eyes. Eyes the color of hers and her mother's.

"What say you, Wulfwyn?" Her younger brother continued slashing the air with his sword. "You have a birthday nearing. Shall I bring you a severed head?"

"And some bloody guts, please." Wulfwyn's grin was forced, her tone subdued.

Roscelyn winced. 'Twas a game they played with the intention of making her queasy.

"Dolts," she sniffled, and swiped at her eyes. "You will not—" Grabbed from behind, her words ended abruptly.

She twisted about to stare into Cerdic's dark, red-rimmed eyes. In an embrace that would appear affectionate to any who watched, he crushed the breath from her.

Powerless to escape, her insides shriveled as he hissed accusingly in her ear. "You dare to poison me?"

She gasped for air. "You dare to force yourself on my sister?"

He ground his lips hard against hers and she near gagged at the stench that emitted from his mouth.

Gripping a handful of hair, he held her head immobile and slid his lips across her cheek to her temple. "By all that is holy, once I am returned, you shall suffer the remainder of your days."

"Your pardon, my new son." Her father's cheerful voice sounded behind her. "If I might borrow my daughter a moment, there is a matter I would discuss with her ere we leave."

Released from the bruising embrace, Roscelyn felt her legs shake as she followed her father away from the assembled housecarls.

The consequences be damned. She would tell her father what Cerdic had dared.

But the words never came. So great was her shock at hearing what her father had to say, she could not bring herself to speak.

ONE

ROSCELYN INHALED the odor of decayed vegetation that rose from the freshly turned earth. Considering the rich, loamy soil, this hedged section of ground beside the orchard might well serve as a garden.

Except for the graves that crowded the area.

She shivered against the damp wintry afternoon and eyed her father's headstone. 'Twas a hasty effort that nowhere near matched the finely wrought design of her mother's headstone. But that would change.

In a matter of months, she would be able to build a monument worthy of her father.

The secret scroll he had left unto her care not only provided her the means to control her own destiny, but the means to free England from the butchering Normans.

At the thought, she realized she was pacing. Halting mid-stride, she glanced down, then released her pent breath.

At least she had not stepped on any graves, praise the Blessed Virgin.

She had no desire to incur the wrath of the dead in addition to the misfortunes that currently plagued Cyning. Half the village folk sick with a catching fever, scarce enough food to last the winter, a late sowing of the winter crops that would feed the village in spring—none of which compared to the Norman threat.

With her father and brothers dead, there would be no protection from the wretched Norman curs should they visit Cyning.

But Cerdic was dead as well, God forgive her sense of relief. Gunderic had seen him fall early on in the battle. And according to Gunderic, the remaining Saxon armies—friends of her father's, men she knew and had entertained at Cyning—had retreated to the fens of northeastern England. Even now they forged an alliance with the Danes in hopes of driving the Normans from England.

Meanwhile, she possessed the scroll.

For the moment she'd buried it beside her father's headstone. 'Twas the safest place she could think to hide it.

She shivered with anticipation, then caught herself before she could begin pacing anew. Faith, 'twas difficult to keep still when she held proof that the Norman Duke William had deceived the pope.

Her lips curved in a grim half smile. The Bastard Duke William thought himself clever, no doubt. He'd received papal blessing for his invasion of England by claiming the Saxon King Harold had sworn over sacred relics to serve him.

Lies. The word sizzled in her head like fat dripping into the flames of an open cook pit.

In truth, King Harold had given his oath under duress, had been forced to swear allegiance while a virtual prisoner at William's court in Normandy.

As for the sacred relics that Harold had held while making his pledge to the greedy Norman duke? They were in fact no more than the bones of a goat.

Again she fought the urge to pace.

The truth was sworn and attested to in the scroll by the bishop of Rouen and several of William's barons. The pope could hardly deny the document's authenticity.

His Holiness would withdraw Church support for William's foray into England. Saxons would again rule the land. And for her efforts in delivering the Saxons from the Normans, she could name her price.

She hugged herself beneath the folds of her gray cloak. She would demand riches enough to make certain her people never again suffered from hunger or cold, wealth enough to pay hundreds of housecarls for protection that Cyning would never again be left to the mercy of an invading army.

And as Cerdic's widow, she would demand his lands and give them to her sister.

Abruptly, a sense of desperation crept over her and she clutched the material of her cloak in her fists.

Prithee, God, speed the remainder of Gunderic's recovery.

The only housecarl to return from battle, Gunderic's loyalty had near cost him his life. Badly wounded, he'd scarce possessed the strength to carry her father's remains home, much less those of her brothers', whose bodies still lay on the battlefield—along with Cerdic's.

She took a deep breath and held it. 'Twas yet difficult to grasp that her father would never again tug her braid for luck, that her brothers would never again tease her over slobbery kisses and weeping fits.

They would never sit in the great hall again. Never challenge one another to a game of dice after the evening meal. Never again tell gruesome tales, then laugh gleefully when they made her half sick.

She stared at her father's headstone.

How many nights had she dreamt they were alive and well, only to awake and experience the loss anew?

She exhaled and swiped at her eyes.

In the next few days, Gunderic would be well enough to deliver the scroll to Saint Dunstan Abbey. 'Twas only the elderly abbess at Saint Dunstan whom she could trust to see that the document reached the pope— or rather a portion of the document, enough that the pope would recognize the document's contents and its authenticity.

Meanwhile, she would keep a portion for herself until she'd secured her future and the right to care for her people.

She would also send Wulfwyn with Gunderic to the

abbey against the chance that a Norman lord would be appointed to govern Cyning before the scroll could reach the pope. 'Twas an idea Gunderic endorsed, though the housecarl argued that she should seek refuge at the abbey as well.

Not that she would consider such. She would never leave her people alone to face a Norman threat. As well, the village folk were dependent upon her counting skills to see that the dwindling food supplies were evenly distributed.

Her lips puckered as her thoughts moved to her sister. She had mentioned nothing to Wulfwyn. She could well imagine her sister's reaction to the idea of living in a cloister. Like as not, she'd have to truss—

The sudden, quarrelsome landing of a crow in a branch snatched the thought from her head.

Death's companion.

Her breath caught. When had she begun pacing again?

She glanced down and her eyes rounded. *Great toads!* Had she just walked over her great-granduncle's grave?

The crow screeched, raising the hair at her nape.

Had she cursed herself?

Had the bird been sent by her brothers? Did their immortal souls yet haunt the battlefield? Would they never find peace for lack of a Christian burial?

What if Gunderic had been wrong? What if one of her brothers yet lived? What if even now he lay calling for aid?

Her glance skittered about the brittle, dark

branches that surrounded the crow. 'Twas almost as if she could hear her name being called, carried on a cold, spectral draft.

"Roscelyn!"

She near fell over the hem of her cloak as she spun about. Expecting to see a ghost, fear prickled her flesh even as she realized 'twas only her sister.

"Must you shriek?" Her quavering voice scarce cleared her throat.

Wulfwyn's mass of auburn hair danced like flames about her head as she shook it. "Thuri Priest is going to burn Lufu's home!"

Roscelyn frowned, then smiled at her own scrambled musings. "Faith, for a moment I thought you said—"

"Thuri Priest says Lufu's witchery has brung evil elves to Cyning." Wulfwyn hopped from foot to foot, her great gray-brown dog, Poppit, circling her. "The elves are wot got the villagers sick. And God won't protect Cyning 'til Lufu's gone."

Roscelyn's smile crumbled. What was Thuri Priest thinking? With so many sick, the ancient village witch-wife and her healing tonics were needed more than ever.

Raising her skirts, she trotted off toward the village as fast as her stiff leather boots would allow, Wulfwyn and the overgrown dog at her heels. Halfway down the frost-burnt hill from the manor, she spied the knot of peasants assembled before Lufu's cottage.

Her steps slowed to a halt and she swiped at wisps of dark blond hair that had escaped her braid. Faith, fully half the village must be present, upward of two-score people. Even from this distance she could hear their angry rumblings.

"'Od rot!" Wulfwyn snapped. "You are slower than a lame snail."

"And you speak like the most common of churls," Roscelyn retorted. Then she jerked her hand from Wulfwyn's reach as the girl made a grab for it. "I must collect my thoughts if I am to reason with Thuri Priest and the peasants. I am not Father, and I do not possess a contingent of housecarls to impose my will."

"You have me," Wulfwyn declared. "If the old goat hurts you or Lufu, he'll rue the day."

Roscelyn felt a sudden urge to tear the braid from her head. "A fortnight has scarce passed since the old goat caught you putting that leech in the holy water. Faith, but I worry for your immortal soul. You will swear to do nothing more that might jeopardize your entrance to Heaven."

"I swear!"

As if echoing her sister's angry sentiments, a cheer rose from the gathering below and several torches were held on high.

"Great toads!" Roscelyn hissed. "Get yourself back to the manor and do not leave until—"

Her words ended abruptly as Wulfwyn ignored her directive and charged off toward the village. Though Roscelyn struggled to keep pace, by the time she reached the gathering, Wulfwyn was nowhere in sight.

". . . wretched crone," Thuri Priest was saying. "I've

no wish to harm ye, but ye have brung evil to Cyning fer the last time."

Several in the crowd called aye-ayes, while others simply grunted, though whether or not in agreement was unclear. Judging from the sour smell of ale that hung in the air, many were sotted.

"Lady Ros!" Afled, the dairymaid, spied her. Separating herself from the fringe of the crowd, the plump woman hurried toward her, carrying her baby daughter on her hip while her toddler son clung to her skirts. "Ye must do something!"

Roscelyn nodded, gulping air to catch her breath.

"Ye are a fool, priest-man," the witchwife's son-in-law called. "Lufu delivered yer babes of yer woman, same as ever' other man here. It's her potions wot's eased ever'one's misery."

Though Roscelyn would have chosen her words so as not to antagonize the priest, Lorstan's arguments were well made. Yet as she opened her mouth to second his opinion, Thuri Priest responded.

" 'Tis God wot delivers babes and good health. This hell-borne place invites naught but the mischief of Satan's minions."

"Thuri Priest is right," seconded the village toolmaker. "Them wot's not sick is busy takin' care of them wot are. I ar'nt had nothin' but cold gruel fer a week 'cause me wife is down."

"All the more reason to—" Roscelyn began at last, but the yellow-eyed, gore-bellied miller cut her off.

"Ar'nt nobody able to tend their plow strips. Won't be no food come spring."

"Ar'nt no food now!" another man shouted. "We'll starve long afore spring."

"Unless them Normans kills us first!" came a shrill, female cry.

A round of guttural fury rose from the crowd and Roscelyn was bumped backward.

Good lack. She must stop this nonsense. But where was Wulfwyn? Her sister was like to be trampled by the unruly mob. Tiptoeing, she skirted the edge of the noisome crowd, hoping to spot a mop of unkempt auburn hair.

All she saw were the spread of shoulders and the backs of men's heads. Indeed, the only other thing she could see was the uppermost point of Lufu's thatched—

Her breath caught as an idea struck.

Just as quickly, she grimaced. Nay. 'Twas daft to think of attempting such a feat.

Yet what better way to spot Wulfwyn? At the very least 'twould gain her the peasants' attention and keep them from burning the cottage.

Before her resolve could again waver, she scurried around the crowd to the side of Lufu's cottage. The thatch hung low, plenty low for her to grasp. There was even a pail upon which she could stand to begin her climb.

She paused. Small as she was, she was still a full-grown woman. There was little guarantee that the roof would hold her weight. If she fell before anyone noticed her, and the enraged mob torched the cottage . . .

"Hie yerself off, witchwife, or burn!" Thuri Priest's voice boomed above the fractious clamor.

Without another thought, Roscelyn scrambled up the thatch, cursing her skirts, her stiff boots, and, God forgive her, Thuri Priest.

⟿❦⟿

SEATED ATOP a hulking gray destrier at the head of a dozen liegemen, Varin de Brionne shifted his helmet in the crook of his elbow. Glaring down at the squire who stood panting before him, he despaired. "I send you to gather information, and you return a lackwit who babbles more than yon river."

He nodded at the River Ouse, then turned his attention to his giant underlord, Arnulf. "Can you understand a word the boy speaks? Witches and elves and people astride houses. One would think he is daft. Either that, or he is afraid of a few puling Saxons."

Arnulf's hazel eyes rolled heavenward in his great ugly head before he leveled a look of strained patience on Varin. "Unlike you, Sir Stalwart, we weaklings require breath to speak. Give Adam a chance to catch his wind."

Varin's voice cracked as he raised it to mimic his big friend's uncommonly high pitch. "We weaklings require breath to speak."

An exaggerated sneer twisting his tanned countenance, Varin turned to look beyond the river's ford. Would that he could hear above the spill of water where it cascaded over the rocky shelf's rim. Armed men e'er made noise, whether 'twas a whispered command or the soft clink of mail.

His gaze narrowed. The few dilapidated huts he

could see were suspiciously deserted. 'Twas the reason
he'd sent young Adam into the village. A nameless boy
would go unnoticed by a contingent of Saxon housecarls.

Or Danes.

He shook his head. There should be few, if any,
housecarls about. Cyning's Saxon lord and his sons had
died at Hastings.

But the Danes . . .

The Danes made no secret of the fact that they welcomed what was left of the defeated Saxon armies.
United, a Danish-Saxon alliance presented an immense
threat to William's tenuous hold on England, especially
at strategic locations such as Cyning's. And Cyning's
deceased Saxon earl had a daughter whose husband was
reported to be alive and well and conspiring with the
Danes.

". . . no Saxon housecarls," Adam was saying.

Varin returned his attention to the boy.

"'Tis naught but a Saxon priest. Says the village
witch is evil, and he will burn her hut. Only there's a
woman standing atop the witch's roof, trying to stop the
priest."

Varin rolled his eyes. Why would anyone defend a
witch to a priest? It made no sense. But then what fool
would stand on a roof that was about to be set ablaze?

"Very well, Adam. You may return to your duties
with the oxcart," he ordered.

As the boy moved off to do his bidding, Varin
cocked his head in the village's direction and raised a
brow at Arnulf, silently asking his friend's opinion on
the possibility of an ambush.

The giant cast him a crooked smile, his ruddy complexion deepening beneath carrot red sprouts of hair on his head. "Surely you do not fear a few puling Saxons?"

Varin narrowed an eye at the giant's mockery of his earlier words to Adam. "'Tis a wonder your bull's wind does not blow your poor, bowlegged mount from beneath you. The Saxon who cleaves your ugly head will doubtless receive papal dispensation."

"You dare to call me ugly?" Though the giant's features reflected savage brutality, his melodious voice ruined the effect. "I was most handsome until you broke my nose these many years past."

Varin burst into laughter. How fortunate he was to call Arnulf friend. Indeed, had he a brother, he would wish him to be Arnulf.

At the thought, he sobered. He had no father or mother, much less a brother.

He yanked his helm over his head. William had shown great trust in bestowing Cyning upon him, a decision William would not regret. No Saxon-Danish force would find a foothold here. He would discover from the earl's daughter what her husband and his Danish cohorts intended. Then he would cut the head from the Danish-Saxon snake before it could strike Cyning.

He adjusted his seat in the saddle. Ere he was finished, Cyning would be known far and wide as a jewel in William's English kingdom, and Varin would never again be a landless pauper. Nor would any dare refer to his father's cursed treachery.

He would marry one of William's many nieces, as William's wife, Matilda, suggested. His loyalty to

William would be secured not only by deeds, but by blood, and his honor would never again be questioned.

Signaling his men to gather 'round, he issued his final instructions. "Armed resistance is to be met with death. However, the peasants will be most knowledgeable in village affairs. Though they will be frightened and resentful, they can be of great assistance to us. As for the Lady of Cyning, she likely knows much concerning her husband. She is mine to deal with, and I will brook no untoward advances."

He looked each of his dozen men in the eye to make his point. Satisfied with the nods he received, he turned and spurred his mount across the slick ford.

Chickens squawked and feathers flew once he and his retinue gained the opposite riverbank to ride along a winding, muck-filled lane. Adam was forced to abandon the oxcart to chase snarling dogs with his staff. One in particular, a great grayish-brown cur . . .

Varin craned his neck to stare at the dog, his heart suddenly pounding. 'Twas not possible, yet—

At the rumble of angry voices, he snapped his attention forward. That the sound was muffled by distance was no comfort. An entire Saxon army could have charged him just now, catching him unaware while he ogled a stupid dog.

Annoyed with himself, he rounded a bend in the lane and was confronted with several women and a number of small children. Upon seeing him and his men, they alternately gasped, screeched, grabbed babes, and scurried for cover—with the exception of one woman, who froze in her tracks.

"Lady of the manor?" Arnulf queried in a hushed tone, drawing up beside Varin.

Varin nodded, for clearly this was the earl's daughter. Her blue cloak was spun from fine wool, not the drab gray-brown of goat hair. Where her feet peeped beneath her hem, he saw leather boots, not the splintered, wooden-soled shoes that peasants wore.

He waved Arnulf behind him as he approached the woman, then halted several horse lengths in front of her. Not bad to look upon, he decided. Her dark hair was clean, as was her light complexion. Though she was a bit lean for his taste, the thought of gathering information from her regarding her husband was hardly unpleasant.

"I am Varin de Brionne, new lord and master of Cyning by King William's command." His tone reported more harshly than he intended for he had to raise his voice to be heard over the increasingly loud dissension that carried from around the next bend.

"What is all this hue and cry?" He inclined his head in the direction of the noise.

The woman rushed toward him. "You must do something before the entire village is burned!"

"Hold!" Varin commanded the foolhardy wench as his destrier, Rok, tensed and laid his ears back. Stroking the animal's neck, he affected his best minstrel's voice. "Bite or kick the lady, and I will slit your mean-tempered throat."

Realizing her jeopardy, the woman halted and covered her mouth. "Your forgiveness, mi'lord." She spoke through long, slender fingers. "'Tis just that I am so grateful to see you." She dipped her head, as if embarrassed that she'd made so bold a statement.

Even as Rok settled, Varin frowned, his brows rubbing the inside of his helm. She was grateful to see him? Grateful to see a Norman who'd come to claim her home? Grateful to see a man whose brethren had killed her father and brothers? 'Twas not to be believed.

When she raised her head, tears had pooled in her blue-green eyes. "Everyone is sick. We have little food. Now Thuri Priest threatens to burn Lufu's cottage, and fire spreads quickly, and, and—" Her shoulders shook with a sob. "What if my home burns? What will become of me?"

She choked, unable to continue, and Varin's suspicions of her gratitude melted. Though he knew not this Thuri Priest or this Lufu, 'twas clear that the lady was distressed beyond reason. It was understandable that she would be glad to see a man who could resolve her difficulties.

"Come." He beckoned her closer. "Easy, lest my horse behaves brutishly."

The woman edged toward him, sniffling, as another outburst resounded from around the bend.

"There, now." He flipped the side of his cloak over his short-sleeved byrnie and leaned to cup her chin in a gloved hand. "I know you have suffered greatly, and for that I am sorry."

Arnulf cleared his throat with all the discretion of a bleating goat, and Varin shot a menacing glance over his shoulder. The great oaf had the audacity to cast him a simpering look.

Returning his attention to the lady, Varin asked, "What can I do to ease the misery of one so beautiful?"

For all her demure looks, the woman reached up and placed a hand on his thigh, a blatant move that bespoke more than sisterly interest.

"You must stop Thuri Priest." She squeezed his thigh.

Varin's brows near soared through the top of his helm. Clearly the wench thought to manipulate him with the unspoken promise of fleshly rewards.

'Twas all he could do to keep from chortling while she continued to babble. He'd cut his teeth on such sexual games. Though he could not decide which he preferred, the earthy lust of a serving maid or the jaded sophistication of a prurient baroness, one thing was certain. The lady would happily tell him all she knew of her husband before he was through.

" 'Tis Roscelyn's fault," the promiscuous woman was saying. "While everyone goes hungry and sick, she hoards food that could ease our suffering."

As she chattered on, Varin eyed her fingers where they crept up his thigh. Roscelyn, he mused. The name was familiar. Where had he heard it?

Lady Roscelyn?

The Saxon earl's daughter Roscelyn.

He clapped his hand over the woman's wrist, interrupting her mid-sentence. "You are not Lady Roscelyn?"

She blinked. "Nay. I am Elswyth. My father was housecarl to—"

"Where will I find the lady?"

The woman's tone grew cool. "You will find her perched upon a roof 'round yon bend."

Varin's spirits soared as the dark-haired wench pulled her hand from his grasp. Bloodygore. Why could she not be Lady Roscelyn? Secrets would doubtless slip from her mouth with the ease of melted butter, and he'd so anticipated sampling her charms.

'Twould not happen now. He dare not allow a meaningless dalliance to spoil his chance of charming information from the Lady Roscelyn.

The Lady Roscelyn who would defend a witch to a priest while standing atop a roof that was about to be torched.

Without another glance at the brunette, he urged Rok forward when the clamor from around the next bend suddenly abated.

Again, he drew rein.

TWO

PESTILENCE OF THE BODY," Thuri Priest intoned in the stillness that finally claimed the crowd, "is God's punishment fer sin, and them wot denies God's will is in league with the devil."

Half dizzy from the height, Roscelyn clutched her thighs beneath her cloak. Cease! she commanded her shaking legs as she balanced upon the narrow splits of wood that supported the roof's thatch. Though she had yet to spot Wulfwyn, she'd had measure in full of Thuri Priest.

"You are a good man, Thuri Priest." She affected a humble tone and nodded thoughtfully, concealing the fact that even her head shook with fear when she looked down. "Cyning is abundantly blessed to have you."

The portly priest fair preened at her compliments and she cast him a beseeching look, hoping to gain his sympathy. After all, Thuri Priest's discontent with Lufu was not unfounded. The witchwife delighted in bedeviling him.

"You have e'er shown great compassion in your godly works. Instead of burning Lufu's cottage, might you not perform a blessing to rid the place of any demons foul?"

Abruptly Lufu's voice cracked from below. "Enough of this blather. Get off me roof, girl, afore ye breaks it."

Hoots of laughter followed the witchwife's strident demand and Roscelyn's face warmed with irritation. She glared down at Lufu. "Your roof is about to be set afire, and you worry over me breaking it?"

Lufu scowled until it appeared her wrinkles might swallow her entire face, leaving naught but a coarse tuft of thick, white hair atop her neck. "Thuri Priest will not be burnin' me place. Once the poison ivy wot's caught on the hem of his robe raises blisters, he'll be needin' me poultices."

Even as fresh peals of mirth burst forth, so did the peasants clear from around the priest. "Evil hag!" he roared, his pink double chin quivering with rage.

The harder he shook his fine green robes, the higher they flapped—and the more pasty-fleshed leg did he display. It soon grew evident that he had not accidentally come by the poison ivy, for it clung too tenaciously.

Holding his robes as far from himself as his short

arms would reach, he leveled a hateful look on Lufu. "Ye shall burn in hell everlastin' fer this."

"Cease exposin' yerself at me," Lufu quipped.

Roscelyn pursed her lips to keep from giggling. As lady of the manor, she should not encourage such irreverent behavior by joining in the merriment.

Yet words of admonishment for the witchwife deserted her. Instead a smile broke across her lips.

Thuri Priest looked like a great, green apple trying to escape a pack of hungry worms.

Her mood lifted further when she spied two heads as they bobbed through the midst of the crowd. One bright auburn, the other raven black, they could only belong to Wulfwyn and Golde, Lufu's great-granddaughter of thirteen winters.

Not that Roscelyn need worry over Wulfwyn being accidentally injured. The drunken mob had lost its deadly sting to gusts of tear-dripping laughter. Still, she was glad Wulfwyn was nowhere near Thuri Priest and the poison ivy.

The two girls wiggled from the edge of the crowd, peeling woolen mittens from their hands as—

Roscelyn's smile thinned and her eyebrows slashed down.

Cold though it was, Wulfwyn hadn't bothered with shoes, and Golde likely wore none either. What need had they of wrapping their hands?

Great toads. 'Twas the two imps who'd fastened poison ivy to the priest's robes, doubtless at Lufu's behest.

As if Wulfwyn could hear her exasperated ruminations, the girl glanced up. She cast Roscelyn an angelic smile, then made a show of waving farewell to Golde.

Roscelyn's lips puckered. 'Twas well and good that Wulfwyn would soon abide in the safety of Dunstan Abbey, she thought, watching her sister skip off in the direction of the manor. The child needed discipline, else she would never learn—

Cries of alarm rose over the crowd and Roscelyn blinked, her attention refocusing. At the nearest bend in the lane, there appeared to be . . .

Men. Astride horses. Armed to the teeth.

Her heart tumbled from her chest to her belly.

Normans!

She took an involuntary backward step as the torches meant for Lufu's cottage were thrown at the riders. Horses whinnied and shuffled, inciting the village dogs to snarl and bark, Poppit in the midst of the frenzy.

'Od rot! She must calm the villagers ere the Normans butchered—

The thought was left dangling when her foot went through the unsupported thatch between rafters. She shifted her weight, only to have her other foot follow.

Down she dropped. Gasping, she clawed at the prickly roof rushes until her forearms found the beams on either side of her. Her shoulders wrenched when she caught herself.

She grimaced as the area about Lufu's cottage quickly emptied of village folk. Had she broken a bone?

Dear God, it mattered not. She must free herself that she might reason with the Normans on the peasants' behalf.

Swinging her legs below the thatch, she felt one foot connect with a rafter. She pushed hard against it while levering up on her elbows. Just as her waist cleared the roof, her foot slipped.

Again she dropped, only this time 'twas her ribs that caught between beams. Breath gurgled from her lungs as a rough-edged, deep voice invaded the sudden quiet left by the villagers' retreat.

"This is no battle to be won in a single day."

Roscelyn stilled, eyeing the mounted group of men. Never had she seen such huge horses, such oddly shaped shields . . .

Her jaw dropped.

Never had she seen such an ugly man as the orange-haired giant who near dwarfed his mount. He was the only rider who did not wear a helmet, and Roscelyn could see the reason for it. Just looking at his scarred forehead and misshapen nose would likely kill those with faint hearts.

". . . indulge the peasants' defiance for the moment," the deep voice was saying. "I am no longer a simple knight. As new lord of Cyning, I am dependent upon these people for provender, as are they dependent upon me for protection."

Roscelyn blew at a strand of hair that had escaped her braid to fall over one eye. The new lord of Cyning?

Plague take her toenails! The lowly worm was here to steal her home. She squinted, trying to determine who was speaking. Except for the giant, noseguards shadowed everyone's mouths.

"If yer finished with yer fine speech," Lufu interjected, "there's a great silly girl stuck up yon. I'd be in yer debt if ye'd fetch her afore she brings me whole roof down."

Embarrassment dashed across Roscelyn's face and she sucked air.

Blowing at the hair that continued to hang in her eye, she resumed her struggles with the thatch. Faith, but there were times when she could cheerfully strangle Lufu.

VARIN EYED Roscelyn's gray-cloaked shoulders atop the roof, the strand of dark blond hair that flopped over her eye, the pieces of thatch that sprouted from her head.

This was the woman from whom he hoped to charm information? Bloodygore 'twould take a mighty effort on his part. She did not look to have the wit God gave a goose.

But perhaps this was one instance where appearance was indeed deceiving. He'd halted upon rounding the last bend in the lane long enough to hear the lady's address to the priest. Judging from her facile tongue, she had wits aplenty.

Might you not perform a blessing to rid the place of any demons foul?

The gall. She would dare ask a priest to bless a witch's den?

The question gave him pause. If this was an example of what she would do to protect a witch, what might she do to protect her husband?

"Well, boy," the witch challenged from where she stood near the cottage door. "Will ye just sit and stare?"

Varin cast her a sour look. The last man who'd

called him boy had lost his front teeth. Not that the old crone possessed any.

"Adam!" he commanded, and the squire came forward to hold Rok's reins while he dismounted. Arnulf made to join him, eyeing the witch suspiciously, but Varin declined. "I would that you remain mounted lest we yet find ourselves at the sharp end of a Saxon threat. I will call if I have need."

Striding forward, he announced to the head and shoulders on the roof, "I am Varin de Brionne. Allow me to assist you."

"I need . . ." the head panted while the cloaked shoulders continued to thrash about, "no aid . . . from a Norman."

"If you'll pardon my saying so," he persisted, "it appears you do need assistance."

"Nay!" the head fair shrieked.

Varin halted, grinding his teeth. The head's high, tight voice pealed through his ears to jar the length of his spine.

In the next instant, a great weight struck his shoulder blades, the momentum carrying him forward a pace.

Ere he could draw his sword and turn, a warm, slobbery tongue ran up the back of his neck.

"Poppit!" the head shouted. "Down!"

Realizing 'twas naught but a dog's paws on his shoulders, Varin shrugged away from the animal.

"Please do not hurt him," the head implored. "He means no harm."

An eerie sense of disbelief settled over him as he turned and found the great grayish-brown cur he'd noted earlier.

" 'Tis Lack," Arnulf pronounced in a thin voice.

Varin glanced to see the giant's gaze dart between the dog and witch.

He returned his attention to the overgrown animal as it wagged its tail and looked up at him, its slobbery, pink tongue hanging happily from its great, square head.

"Nay, 'tis not Lack," he said, more to himself than to Arnulf.

Though he could find nothing in looks that would indicate 'twas not Lack, this was not the pup he'd once rescued after it had fallen into a well. 'Twas not the pup that had grown into a clumsy, gargantuan beast that ate more than his horse. 'Twas not the pup he'd dubbed Lackwit, and later shortened to Lack.

'Twas not possible.

Despite all manner of restraining devices, Lack possessed a stubborn penchant for following him into battle, a loyal habit that had finally got the fool animal killed.

Shaking off the disturbing memory, Varin scowled. While he stood pondering impossibilities, there was a lady in need of rescuing.

His determination restored, he strode to the cottage, pausing at the door to remove his helm and gloves. The old crone stood aside, watching, then had the audacity to wink at him.

He raised a brow. "If 'tis your intent to frighten me, hag, you had best get in line. There are a host of demons ahead of you."

Lips drawing upward in what could have been a smile or a grimace, the old woman spoke. "Saw yer demons in me runes. They'll take ye if ye lets 'em."

Ignoring her, Varin started forward, then held up a hand when the witch followed. "I need not your flapping gums in my face. You will remain here."

With that, he ducked inside the cottage, slamming the door shut when the dog, too, tried to follow.

The animal immediately set to baying and Varin rolled his eyes.

Bloodygore. Witches and ghost hounds and—

The helmet and gloves slipped from his grasp. Slender, bare legs dangled amidst musty clumps of dried leaves that hung from the ceiling.

Faith, but it appeared Lady Roscelyn wore nothing but her boots.

Lowering his head to avoid the rafters, he moved to inspect the situation. The dangling legs occupied his attention well enough that he was not tempted to glance inside a small cauldron that hung nearby. God only knew what contents it held.

The lady might as well be nude, he decided, drawing up beside her. Her chainse and tunic were caught above the roof. Her underdrawers would be up there, too, were it not for the crux of her . . .

Christ's bloody bones. Mayhap 'twas the uniqueness of the situation, or mayhap 'twas his lack of bedmates these weeks past. Whatever the reason, his sex rose beneath his braies.

Clearing his throat, he swallowed hard and spoke over the dog's howling. "Can you hear me?"

At the lack of response, he called louder. "Can you hear me?"

Tremors rippled over the sleek legs as the head above responded. "Aye."

"Let us try to push you up."

More violent tremors raced over the legs. He tossed his cloak back over his shoulders and licked his lips, trying to decide where best to place his hands.

There, just above the knees? Would that provide the leverage he needed? Petite as her legs were, the skin above the knees appeared firm. Though not nearly as appealing as the intimate flesh higher on her thighs.

Would the thighs provide a more solid hold? A firmer base of support?

The more he looked, the greater grew his anticipation of touching her. And so did his randy sex respond. At last he reached for the nearest place.

His reward was a knee to the head.

"Cease your kicking," he bellowed, clutching a small lump that quickly rose over his brow.

"Idio—y—you," the head stuttered from above. "Your hands are cold."

Varin rubbed his hands together to warm them and took a deep, calming breath. He would hardly charm aught from the lady if he did not control his temper.

He again reached for the more appealing thighs. "Better?"

If she answered, he did not hear. Indeed, he could not say whether or not the dog continued to bark. He was too engrossed with the impression of tender flesh against the rough skin of his hands.

Her woman's core faced him at eye level, her underdrawers drawn so tight where they were caught overhead that the bud of her sex was clearly defined, as were the pouty lips that surrounded it.

He inhaled, capturing her scent. Would she taste as sweetly as she smelled? Would she feel smooth as pearl on his tongue?

Grunting, he shoved upward. If he weren't careful, he would waste himself in his braies, a feat he'd not managed since his youth.

He paused as groans drifted from above. "I am hurting you?"

"Hur—shh. Aye. Nay. I—I mean . . ."

Aye and nay? "A single answer will do, mi'lady."

The thighs trembled beneath his hands, though the skin felt most warm. Indeed, if legs could blush, hers were doing just that, for they held a most charming rosy glow.

He gritted his teeth impatiently. Did the wench think a man could hold her enticing little thighs the entire day long without appeasing his lust?

"Can you not determine whether or not I have hurt you?" he demanded at last.

"Foo—aith. Your hold is wrong."

Varin frowned. Must the woman stutter thus? 'Twas difficult to understand her. "My hold is wrong?"

"The angle!" The head's voice again approached a shriek.

Varin glanced up. The thatch's pitch was indeed awkward. Mayhap if he moved around to the lady's other side, the angle would be better. At least he would no longer have to wrestle with the temptation of her sex staring him in the face.

A mistake, he realized the instant he reached her backside. Her round derriere was as exposed as her front, a firm juicy peach, split in perfect halves, accentuated by the taut draw of material where her underdrawers rode upward. 'Twas the most inviting bottom he'd e'er laid eyes on.

He grimaced at the discomfort of his straining shaft. Bloodygore.

Planting his hands on the silky little rump, he pushed up.

TORN BETWEEN RAGE and mortification, Roscelyn near screamed her frustration. Like an eel trap that allowed entrance but no exit, the harder the Norman pushed, the greater grew the thatch's resistance. Meanwhile, was there no place on her lower body that the toad-eating thickwit had not groped?

She winced. Judging from the pool of material about her chest and the frosty nip of air on her skin, her body was completely exposed below the rafters. The cold invaded her privacy everywhere—except the heated spots where the Norman's large hands spanned her bare rear, and where her underdrawers chafed between her thighs.

'Twas the last that made her feel so . . . so . . .

Squirmy was the only word she could think of to describe the sensation that gripped her. And this Varin de Brionne did naught but aggravate the condition. Not knowing where next his hands would move sharpened her focus until she was little more than a quivering, expectant mass of disturbed flesh.

At least Poppit had ceased his howling before someone killed him.

" 'Tis not possible," the man called at last, his tone exasperated.

His voice alone irritated her skin, Roscelyn thought. It was coarse as a saw blade, deep as the purr of a tomcat, gritty as dirt. When he released his hold on her rear, the skin he'd touched was left sore and achy.

Not that he was treating her ungently. Still, 'twas as if his every callus, every curve in his splayed fingers, the cups of his large palms, left welts on her flesh.

"Raise your arms over your head," the Norman ordered from below. "Let us try to pull you down."

Roscelyn grimaced. "But my ribs-s-s—"

The word ended on an indrawn hiss as the frigid iron rings of his byrnie pressed against her bare skin. His arms wrapped about her thighs and the expanse of his chest bore hard against her bottom. Above that, the beard stubble along his jaw prickled the small of her back. Judging from the warm moist breath that bathed her hip, his mouth was pressed to her waist.

The mucker. How she longed to heap curses on his head. Not that she dared. Who knew what the man would do if she angered him, and she'd near called him an idiot and a fool already.

"Prepare yourself," the Norman ordered.

She scarce had time to raise her arms before he yanked hard. Her ribs caught for the barest of moments, grinding against the rafters. Then down she flew amidst a hail of thatch. Bending beneath her, the man absorbed her fall, setting her down on her feet.

Roscelyn doubled forward to clutch her ribs, praying she might live to draw another breath.

De Brionne clasped her about the waist, his front pressed to her backside. "You are hurt?"

She opened her mouth to berate him, but the most she could manage was a groan. The stings on her rear and thighs where she'd been pinched by the rings of his byrnie were naught compared to the pain in her chest. Faith, it felt as if the rafter had skinned her alive. 'Twas a miracle her breasts had not been ripped from her body.

"Where are you hurt?" The man's fingers slid under her folded arms to probe her ribs. "Can you breathe?"

Realizing her bottom was shoved flush against his groin, Roscelyn forced herself erect. "Leave go," she croaked.

"Are you able to stand?"

She swatted his hands away and shuffled forward a few paces before angrily turning to face him. "Never," she spat, "have I . . ."

Her tirade withered before she could vent it, parched by a sudden dryness in her mouth.

Never had she seen such a handsome man. His deep-blue cloak was thrown over his shoulders, and even did he not wear the short-sleeved mail byrnie, he would be broad of chest. His arms bespoke the raw strength of a powerful warrior, while the seamed leather of his chausses only emphasized the muscular length of his legs.

But none could compare to the beauty of his face.

Eyes more blue than his cloak . . . generous nose and lips . . . 'twas striking how the dark stubble of beard on his square jaw contrasted with his blond hair.

Suddenly aware that she was ogling the bumptious

clod, heat scorched her face. Worse, she was holding her aching breasts.

She jerked her hands down, then adjusted her skirts, which she noted belatedly rode far too high. "I . . ." Her gaze was captured by the ooze of blood from a cut on her arm. "I . . ."

The ground seemed to tilt beneath her and she swayed.

'Od rot. She would not be sick before the Norman, she vowed. Nor would she faint. She certainly would not sit on the floor and stick her head between her—

She plopped to the ground. "Cease," she hissed at the darkness that encroached upon her vision. "I will not have it."

Clutching her shins, she jammed her knees against her temples. "Nay," she whispered over and again.

'Twas not fair. Not fair that she should fall through Lufu's roof. Not fair that half her body was exposed in the process. Not fair that she could not tolerate the sight of blood.

"Easy." The Norman's boots appeared in her line of vision, then his knees as he crouched before her. "All will be well."

His deep voice sounded suspiciously soft around the edges, almost as if . . .

Before she could decide whether or not 'twas pity she heard in his voice, his hand stroked her hair.

She jerked her head up and scooted backward in the same instant. What was the man about?

"Do not be frightened." He remained crouched, his hands held palm out near his shoulders. "I will not hurt you."

Faith, did he truly hope to gain her trust? 'Twould not happen so long as she drew breath. Yet his tone was most concerned, his look quite sincere.

He pointed at her arm. "You are bleeding."

She shook her head, then caught herself before she explained aught of her sickness. She would not reveal any weakness to the man.

He frowned. "Did you strike your head?"

"Strike my head?" she repeated. The question made no sense.

"Allow me to look."

He placed a forefinger under her chin and tilted her head up, his blue gaze roaming her face . . .

Suddenly she was tired.

So very tired.

Tired of fearing for her people, tired of fearing for her sister, tired of fearing an uncertain future.

'Twas as if his touch drained her of strength. How she longed to close her eyes, just for a moment, to rest her cheek in the man's big, callused palm.

A man who would worry whether or not she was hurt. A compassionate man?

She could not prevent the note of wonder in her hushed tone. "There is naught wrong with my head."

The moment the words left her mouth, it occurred to her what he was seeing.

A grown woman who sat on the floor with her face between her knees while talking to herself.

She stiffened. The toad-eating Varin de Brionne thought she'd been knocked senseless by her fall through the roof.

"I am sorry to disappoint you, mi'lord," she snapped, "but I am in full possession of my senses."

She surged to her feet. Fighting the dizziness that assailed her, she staggered past the Norman as he rose. Would that she could kick him, but like as not the motion would cause her to fall in her light-headed state.

When she paused at the door to catch her balance, de Brionne clasped her elbow.

"Aye, I can see you are in possession of your senses." His tone was glib. "Only a sensible person would risk God's eternal displeasure by defending a witch to a priest."

"Witch*wife*," she emphasized, "not that 'tis any of your—"

"Only a sensible person would climb about on roofs that were about to be burned."

"Lufu's home was saved."

A growl rumbled in his chest. "Only a sensible person would refuse aid after falling from a roof."

"I need no aid from a Norman."

She jerked her arm from his grasp and yanked open the door. Reeling outside, she ignored Lufu and the Norman men-at-arms who awaited their liege.

Poppit followed as she struck out for the manor.

Gunderic had no more time to heal. He must see Wulfwyn and the scroll to Saint Dunstan Abbey without delay.

THREE

NOT AN AUSPICIOUS beginning, Varin
reflected later as the cloudy sky grew purple with twilight. He'd not meant to antagonize Lady Roscelyn by
remarking on her lack of good sense. Casting insults at
her would hardly gain him information about her husband or her husband's Danish allies.

But by all that was holy, the woman was stubborn.
Worse, her petite size, her big eyes, honey-colored like a
fawn's, her lack of regard for her own safety—all served
to prey on an absurd protective instinct he'd not realized he possessed.

Nor could he erase the image of her sitting on the

floor, talking to herself. 'Twas as if the lady were moon-struck, despite her claim to the contrary.

At the idea, his inwit squirmed. Regardless of the importance of learning all he could about her husband, it did not seem fair to elicit secrets from a woman not in full control of her wits.

"What think you?" he asked Arnulf as they made their way from the stables to the great hall. "Is the Lady Roscelyn daft?"

Arnulf shrugged. "I don't know what to think. She is so small, had I not heard her speaking to the priest, I'd have thought her a child."

"Small," Varin muttered, rubbing the sore spot on his head where she'd kneed him. "She is stubborn as a full-grown mule. Climbing about rooftops as if she had wings."

"It does seem peculiar. But as you said, she did save the witch's hovel."

"Witchwife," Varin corrected sourly. "And I did not say she saved the witchwife's hovel. That is what *she* said."

"Witch, witchwife, what is the difference?"

"Indeed," Varin agreed, "though clearly the lady sees some difference—enough to take on a priest. And what of her sudden stuttering?" He gestured at Arnulf. "I tell you, I could scarce understand the woman while trying to loose her from the roof."

The giant snorted. "Even you will admit that the circumstance of your meeting was unusual. Most women have delicate sensibilities when caught in a state of . . . half dress."

"Pff. You did not see the vacant look in her eyes

when she sat on the floor and began talking to herself. Then up she stands and off she dithers as if naught has occurred."

The giant frowned and shook his head. "Mayhap the lady is like old Lord Robert. Remember the sudden fits of madness that struck him? Afterward, he could recall nothing."

Varin rubbed his grizzled jaw. Mayhap Arnulf was correct. None would dispute Lord Robert's intelligence or skill as a leader on the battlefield. Yet none would dispute the fact that Lord Robert suffered moments of madness.

Varin inhaled, then wrinkled his nose, distracted. "What is that smell?"

"I believe 'tis the sheep pen," Arnulf offered. "Either that or 'tis the dovecote."

Varin squinted at the tumbledown dovecote that leaned precariously close to a sheep pen. "The stench from those two eyesores alone would weather timber."

He grimaced, recalling the afternoon he'd spent inspecting the manor grounds—the ramshackle penfolds, the dilapidated barns, the rickety buildings. "I am not certain whether to fortify this place or leave things lie until the Saxon-Danish threat is done. One look at these wretched conditions and the Danes would likely retreat beyond the sea."

He quieted as a matronly servant approached, followed by two young boys carrying pails. The maidservant bobbed a quick curtsy, then pulled the boys along from where they'd halted to gawk.

"An ogre," one of the boys whispered as the trio hurried away in the twilight.

"Did ye see his face?" the other gushed. "Look't like he wanted to have me fer his meal."

"Hush," the matronly woman admonished. "If we don't fetch them eggs . . ."

Despite his sour mood, Varin grinned. Come morn, his giant underlord would be known far and wide as a one-eyed, fire-breathing, baby-eating ogre. "I see you were able to locate some servants," he remarked.

"Peasants. I sent Roger to the village."

"Did you put Simon to the task of following the lady?"

Arnulf nodded in the direction of the hall and Varin looked to see the dark-complexioned young liege-man hovering near the entrance doors.

"Anything?" Varin inquired, drawing abreast of Simon.

The slender young man shook his dark head.

A sense of disappointment lowered over Varin. Not that he truly expected the lady's husband to be any-where near. Rather, 'twas quite possible she might send a message alerting her husband to the fact that Normans had arrived.

"I'm sure you have needs to attend," he said, dis-missing the liegeman.

Arnulf opened one of the hall's two splintered doors and Varin entered, then drew to an abrupt halt upon crossing the threshold. Though he'd glanced inside ear-lier, he'd been too busy to note the complete lack of amenities.

No rushes covered the dirt floor. No tapestries hung on the windowless, soot-blackened walls. A hole had been cut in the roof above the central hearth fire where blazing logs alternately popped, crackled, and wheezed smoke.

And amidst the grime, amidst the smoke that floated in yellow-gray layers before the dull glow of rush-lights, amidst the sodden chill that seeped through cracks in the walls, stood Lady Roscelyn.

She'd been watching him, Varin realized, for her gaze darted away the moment he looked at her. A lit taper to hand, she turned to kindle a rushlight set in a sconce along the far wall, the hem of her white chainse showing below the brown material of her tunic.

Varin frowned. Where were the lady's servants that she was left with the task of lighting the hall?

And why, he wondered, exasperated, should he care?

"Yer sister's busy. Fetch me a pail of clean water and have that ne'er-do-well, Ricberht, bring some ale."

Varin's frown deepened to a scowl at the familiar voice.

The witchwife.

"Bloodygore." He turned to share an annoyed look with Arnulf, only to discover his fearless, hulking under-lord was preoccupied with crossing himself. And did his eyes deceive him, or was the one-eyed, fire-breathing, baby-eating ogre mouthing silent prayers?

'Twas not to be borne. Squinting, he tried to locate the hag through the haze and smoke, to no avail. Judging from her voice, she was somewhere on the opposite side of the hearth.

He marched forward. "Begone, witch."

His march faltered as a young girl rose to stand in the circle of light that ringed the central fire. Her auburn hair was a tangled mess, her green tunic stained near black in places.

A grimy little serving maid, he decided. Nor should he be surprised to see the big dog rise beside her. 'Twould be interesting to discover which of them possessed the most fleas.

His features twisted with distaste as he imagined the girl serving his dinner. Her fingernails were doubtless encrusted with dirt.

Without warning, the child shrieked, causing the dog to bay, resulting in a high-pitched combination of sound that near rattled the teeth from his head.

Then the girl flew at him, a churning ball of dirty red and green, the dog bounding along behind her.

"Wulfwyn!" Lady Roscelyn shouted. "Nay!"

Varin blinked. 'Twas not to be believed. The girl held a dagger that gleamed before the rushlights, and it was pointed at—

He captured her arm as she plunged the blade toward his chest. Grunting, she twisted and writhed in his grasp, kicking at his shins and clawing at his hand, the dog barking and bounding to and fro.

"Enough!" Varin bellowed at last. Grabbing her other arm, he affected his most threatening look. "You will cease this nonsense this instant."

The dog immediately sat and the child's head snapped up, her green eyes fearful. Her arms grew limp and he relaxed his grip, prepared to take the dagger from her. "There, that is—"

Quick as a striking snake, she sank the blade into

his forearm. Blood spurted and pain shot through his bones clear to his shoulder.

"By the bloody wounds of Christ!" he roared, tearing the dagger from her hand.

"Hurt her . . ." Lady Roscelyn panted, "and you will not live . . . to see the morrow."

Varin looked to find the petite woman struggling to free herself from where Arnulf held her about the waist, her feet dangling in the air. Meanwhile, the dog sat and howled.

"Cease!" he bellowed at the animal, relieved when the dog obeyed.

He turned his attention to the girl. "To whom does this misbegotten brat belong?"

"She is my sister," the lady hissed.

Switching his grip to the scruff of the child's neck, Varin removed her to arm's length. Sister? The two bore no resemblance.

As if it mattered, he railed at himself.

He had land to defend, information to gather, a worthy reputation to secure that would win him a king's niece. Yet here he stood with a surly child and an overgrown cur.

"Release them," came a man's thin, hoarse voice from the shadows beyond the hearth fire.

Varin rounded. A Saxon housecarl? Had he and Arnulf walked into an ambush?

Even as Arnulf drew his sword and spun, Varin jerked the girl against him. Crushing her arms to her sides, he held the dagger level with her throat.

Not that he would kill her, nor even beat her as she so richly deserved. But the thin-voiced man could not know such. Lady Roscelyn and her sister would make excellent hostages, ensuring his and Arnulf's safety until he could determine how many housecarls might be present.

At last a lone man shuffled forward in the circle of illumination offered by the hearth fire. Emaciated, his graying hair limp, he held an unadorned broad sword at the ready.

"Hold, Gunderic," Lady Roscelyn cried.

"Release them," the housecarl repeated from a mouth that appeared more sunken than his eyes.

"Shall I kill him?" Arnulf inquired.

"Nay!" the child and Lady Roscelyn squealed in unison.

Varin winced as the dog raised its voice to join in the head-splitting noise. "Quiet!" he roared.

Silence descended and he glared at the lady. "How many other men have you?" he ground, his tone deliberately low and even.

"None," she gasped. "I swear it."

Varin eyed the housecarl. A slight breeze was apt to blow the man down.

He lowered the dagger and loosed the girl, pushing her forward. "Lay down your sword—" He inclined his head at the housecarl. "—and my underlord will release the lady."

The housecarl hesitated, and the witch stepped from the shadows, a scowl puckering her wrinkled features. "If yer done scarin' the wits from ever'one, ye might wish to see to yon taper that her ladyship dropped afore the whole hall burns to the ground."

Varin spun. Smoke and small darts of flame rose from a trestle table where it leaned against a wall.

He sprinted toward the spot, shoving the dagger in his belt. Then he near strangled himself in an effort to tear the cloak from his back. That the dog grabbed the hem of the garment in its massive jaws, shaking it, slowed him even more.

Free at last, he wrestled the cloak from the dog and tossed the heavy folds of material over the spitting flames. Arnulf joined him and together they pounded on the cloak until it appeared the fire was smothered.

"Get that end of the table," Varin directed, his arm throbbing. "Let us carry it out—"

He gasped at the sudden icy wash that splashed him broadside.

"Daughter of Satan!" He rounded on the demon child, who smiled sweetly, an empty pail in her hand. Beside her, the housecarl drew a bead on Arnulf's head with his broadsword, his grip on the hilt double handed.

Varin's gut knotted and he froze.

Still holding the table, the giant glanced at the housecarl, then back at Varin. "Shall I kill him now?"

"Strike him, and your suffering will know no end," Varin threatened the housecarl, his voice little more than a rasp.

The man smirked and drew his blade farther back, prepared to swing.

"Gunderic! Lay down your weapon." Lady Roscelyn trundled forward, carrying two pails of water that looked to weigh more than she. "We are vastly outnumbered."

The housecarl hesitated. "Better to die and take two of the cursed bastards with me than take another breath in their foul company."

The lady plopped the buckets on the ground and fair leapt to stand between Arnulf and the housecarl. "I am your lady and you will obey my command. Put aside your sword."

The housecarl flushed and his hands shook where he held his blade.

Varin dropped his hold on the table and jerked his blade from its sheath. The man burned hot to deliver a deathblow and was unlikely to be dissuaded by a woman's words.

"If you must kill the man—" The lady's voice held firm. "—then kill me first. I have no wish to suffer the consequences that will result from your actions."

Varin clenched his jaw against an inane urge to throttle the woman. Her unyielding courage was like to get her killed.

He'd taken but one step toward the housecarl when the man snorted and threw his sword on the ground at Arnulf's feet.

Varin continued forward and near collided with the lady when she picked up a pail and turned. "Your forgiveness, mi'lord. If you would, step aside." She made to throw water on the table, which yet smoldered.

Even as Arnulf lunged to subdue the housecarl, Varin halted.

"Step aside?" he repeated.

Noting that Arnulf had secured the housecarl's hands behind his back with the man's own belt, he gave his full attention to the lady.

"To what purpose should I step aside? I am already drenched. If I do not catch my death of cold, I am like to bleed to death." He stuck his weltering forearm in front of her face as proof.

"You will get that unholy demon sister of yours from my sight this instant," he continued, "and rid the hall of that beastly cur."

He waited for her to comply with his command, though she made no move to do so. Instead she stared fixedly at his injured forearm where he held it away from his body.

Her slender throat worked with the effort to swallow, and her full lips parted, as if she would speak. She blinked, and for a brief moment, her gaze met his.

Then her honey-colored eyes rolled back in her head. The pail she held thumped to the floor and she collapsed.

Guilt swelled to drown his anger. Plague take him for a Sodomite. Had he frightened her into a fit? Would she now froth at the mouth like Lord Robert?

Should he pick her up or leave her lay until she recovered?

Before he could decide, the demon rushed to the lady's side and dropped to her knees. "Wake up, Ros. Oh, please." The girl patted her face.

When the child got no response, she glared at Varin. "Look to what you've done."

"I have done naught," he snapped. "'Tis no fault of mine that the lady suffers from thick-comings."

"Thick-comings!" The demon's green eyes grew venomous. "She has fainted, dunghead. Seeing blood makes her sick."

Varin raised a brow. Surely the girl had not dared refer to him as a dunghead. "What did you call . . ."

His words trailed off and his focus shifted to the prone lady. Blood made her sick? A woman who would brave the torch to save a witch, who would risk eternal damnation to argue with a priest, who would place her life in the hands of a housecarl bent on murder?

A little blood made her sick?

He recalled her vacant stare at the witchwife's hut. She'd been bleeding from a cut. He'd pointed it out to her.

Plague take him for the *son* of a Sodomite. He scowled at the demon. "Do not give me that accusing look. If blood makes her sick, then 'tis your fault for stabbing me."

The girl's pointed chin jutted forward. "You kill't our father and brothers. You steal our home. You call my sister senseless when she is a hundredfold smarter than you, dunghead."

Varin's nostrils flared. "Refer to me by one more foul name and I'll stuff a rag in your mouth and tie you in the latrine."

A sharp rap on his shoulder caught him unaware and he jerked around.

"Cease this foolery," the witchwife ordered, pointing a stick at him. Before he could say aught, she jabbed the stick in the demon's direction. "Ye apologize to his lordship. Then ye and that wretched cur hie yerselfs to the village. Have Golde fetch me basket of salves and me needle and thread. And be quick. Won't do no good to stitch the man's arm once he's bled to death."

"Nay, Lufu." Lady Roscelyn's strained voice scarce

carried from where she'd risen to a wobbly half crouch. "I'll not have Wulfwyn charging about the countryside unattend—"

"My apologies," the demon snapped ere the lady could finish. Scrambling to her feet, she dashed around Varin and out the door, the big dog at her heels.

"As fer ye—" The witchwife turned the stick on Arnulf where he held the housecarl prisoner. "—go to the dairy. Ye'll find a man called Ricberht, likely slobberin' drunk. Tell him I says to haul some ale over here."

"You will shut your flapping mouth, crone." Varin finally found his tongue. "I am lord and master here."

He gasped as the witchwife clutched his aching arm.

"Come along." She steered him toward a rushlight. "I can scarce sees that hole in yer arm."

Varin tried to pull from her grasp, which was surprisingly strong. "My underlord will do naught unless I order—"

"Use the side door over yon," The witchwife gestured at the giant, who was dragging the housecarl toward the hall's entrance. "'Tis nearer the kitchens."

As if he were a pithless puppet, Arnulf reversed direction and headed for the opposite end of the hall, shoving the housecarl before him.

"I did not give you leave," Varin snapped.

"By your leave?" Arnulf squeaked as he continued to toward the side door.

"Cease your moaning, girl," the witchwife groused at Lady Roscelyn, distracting Varin. "Gather your wits and have a bath prepared for your new lord."

He watched the lady struggle to stand. Not until

she'd gained her feet did he realize he'd allowed the hag to lead him along.

He halted. "I have had measure in full of your she-goat ways, crone. Take yourself off, or I will order Arnulf to . . ."

His threat died when he glanced back in the giant's direction. His underlord was nowhere in sight. Indeed, was that the bang of a door shutting somewhere beyond the hearth fire?

"Come along, boy." The old woman tugged him forward. "Me eyes ar'nt as good as they once was."

"Leave go. 'Tis but a scratch."

"Tsk. Men," the witchwife muttered. "Gleefully throw theirselfs into battle, never blink at a sword slash or a mace to the head. But let an old woman threaten to poke them with a needle—"

She halted to narrow an eye at him. "Yer not scare't are ye, boy?"

Wondering if he'd somehow managed to cross an invisible barrier into hell, Varin shook his head, unable to speak. When the hag led him forward, he followed, docile as a lamb being led to slaughter.

'Twas useless to fight. Arguments and threats were a waste of breath. A melee on the battlefield was an orderly affair compared to the chaos that ruled Cyning.

He swallowed a sudden wild urge to laugh. Deserted by a cowardly one-eyed, fire-breathing, baby-eating ogre. Bested by a foul-mouthed child, a girl no less. His wound left to the mercies of a toothless old hag and a young lady who fainted at the sight of blood.

The witchwife halted beneath a rushlight to examine his arm. "Ye won't be needin' stitches. 'Tis not wide, but 'tis deep. I'll make ye a poultice so's to keep it from putrifyin'. Ye should be fine."

That said, the witchwife loosed his arm and trudged off in the direction of the hearth fire.

Varin offered a silent prayer of thanks. Henceforth, he would stay far beyond the witchwife's reach.

"If you will follow me," came an anxious feminine voice, "the kitchen is warmest and best suited for bathing."

Lady Roscelyn.

Who was in full possession of her senses? Who was a hundredfold smarter than he?

More aware than ever of the pain that gnawed at his arm, the raw cold that penetrated his body where the demon had doused him, the hunger that feasted on his belly, he leveled a contentious look on her.

With the exception of her eyes, which shone remarkably like gold in the hazy light, the lady's countenance was devoid of color. Her small shoulders were bunched up almost to her ears, and she hugged her chest. When she shivered, he realized one side of her tunic was wet, doubtless from where she'd spilled the pail before collapsing.

He caught himself as an impulse to comfort her sneaked up on him.

Her forlorn appearance be damned. He could scarce imagine the disasters that would result from her seeing to his bath. The skin boiled from his bones by scalding water, if not apurpose, then certainly by accident. Knocked in the head by a bucket and left unconscious to drown. At the very least, soap in his eyes.

"If you will direct me to the kitchen and a tub, I will see to my own bath."

The lady blinked, then frowned. "As you will, though I would be most happy—"

"'Tis not necessary." Varin held up a hand before she could offer any more help. "I will manage."

"Very well."

As she gave him directions, he noted how she had no trouble speaking. Indeed, her generous lips moved with a sensual grace. He forced his gaze up. Though she appeared tired, her eyes were focused and clear, surrounded by thick, dark lashes.

"Mi'lord?" She interrupted his thoughts.

She regarded him with lifted brows and he realized he was staring. With a slight bow, he turned for the hall's entrance doors.

"Your pardon, mi'lord, but you are going the wrong way. As I said, the kitchens are beyond that door."

He glanced over his shoulder to see her pointing in the direction Arnulf had taken earlier. And was that a droll quirk curling one side of her lips?

Bloodygore. He'd not heard a word she'd said and the lady found it amusing.

"If it meets your approval," he responded evenly, "I . . . I intend to fetch my squire ere I bathe. And some fresh clothing," he added for good measure.

With that, he strode to the main doors and outside, congratulating himself on his facile tongue. The lady would think twice ere she again amused herself at his expense. And plague take the disquieting sense that this was but the beginning of the lady's amusement. 'Twas absurd that he should feel thus.

He was a man, was he not? A powerful man with a strong body and a keen intelligence. The petite Lady Roscelyn could not possibly hope to compete against him.

A chill rattled his bones as he walked along. 'Twas blasted cold and he hadn't a clue where his squire might be.

He scowled. How difficult could it be to locate the cursed kitchens anyway?

FOUR

❧

'**O**D ROT THE TOENAILS of a hound," Lufu grumbled the following morn, setting a candle on a stand and pulling a black tattered shawl over her shoulders. "The sun ar'nt yet rose. Can I not have a moment's peace?"

Wulfwyn plopped on a stool at a table near the door and Roscelyn relaxed now that they'd gained the safety of the witchwife's hut.

While walking in the dark from the manor to Lufu's, she'd been struck by the crawling sensation that someone was watching her and Wulfwyn.

A foolish notion, she chided herself. Poppit would have set to howling had something been amiss. Judging from the way he bounded off to greet his fellow dogs in the village, he'd felt nothing untoward.

On the other hand, 'twas passing strange how Poppit so readily accepted de Brionne. Indeed, the dog had cornered several village boys just last week when they'd dared to aim their slingshots at Wulfwyn. Yet the animal sat on its haunches while the Norman lord held a blade to Wulfwyn's throat?

"Your forgiveness for the early hour." She dipped her head at Lufu. "I could wait no longer. The Normans will soon arise."

"And ye couldn't stand the thought of me sleepin' when ye was up?"

"Please, Lufu." She rubbed her temples. "Could we not forego your clever quips? I have been awake all night."

"Ar'nt no fault of mine."

"I suppose you would sleep well surrounded by your enemies." She struggled to maintain a level tone against the flush of anger she felt. "You would not worry over being attacked at any moment. You would not concern yourself with your sister's safety after a man held a dagger to her throat."

"I ar'nt got no sister." The witchwife shuffled about to kindle a fire. "And if I did, I wouldn't be draggin' her about in the middle of the night so's she could fall asleep at other folks' tables."

Roscelyn glanced over her shoulder to find that Wulfwyn had indeed fallen asleep at the small, rickety table, her cheek resting atop her folded arms.

"The child is exhausted, Lufu. And 'tis not the middle of the night. 'Tis early morn."

As if to prove her statement, a rooster crowed.

Lufu snorted and filled a small cook pot with water. "Wot is it ye wants?"

Roscelyn puckered her lips against a smile. The witchwife's ill-tempered nature was in truth an endearing trait. It only meant that Lufu cared. Indeed, the deeper the witchwife's feelings ran, so did her sourness grow.

"I ar'nt got all day," Lufu prompted.

Shaking out the folds of her gray cloak before the spreading warmth of the hearth fire, Roscelyn inclined her head. "I would like a sleeping potion, enough for a dozen men and one giant."

"Have ye lost yer wits?" The witchwife looked much like a ruffled bird about to peck a fat worm.

Roscelyn drew back from the old woman's threatening countenance. "How long do you think the Norman lord will allow Gunderic to live?"

"He ar'nt killed him yet."

"Nay, but he has him bound and tied to a post in the stables. 'Tis only a matter of time. Short of killing the Normans, putting them to sleep is the only way I know to free Gunderic." She glanced at Wulfwyn and lowered her voice. "I need Gunderic to provide escort to Saint Dunstan Abbey."

"Ye listens to me, girl." Lufu's tone grew peremptory and she shook a finger. "Yer future lies here at Cyning, not in some abbey."

"Shh!" Roscelyn glanced at Wulfwyn, grateful her sister was a sound sleeper. "Calm yourself, Lufu. 'Tis Wulfwyn and the—"

She caught herself before she mentioned the scroll.

Not that she didn't trust Lufu. Rather, she feared the old woman might insist on reading her runes to see the outcome of her plans with the document. 'Twas a practice that had grown far too dangerous for Lufu at her advanced age.

Roscelyn cleared her throat and spoke in a low, soothing tone. "'Tis Wulfwyn and Gunderic who concern me. They will be safe at the abbey. I shall remain at Cyning to make sure the villagers' needs are met."

"O' course," Lufu slapped her forehead. "Them Normans won't bother theirselfs a bit when they wakes up spewin' their guts and discovers ye give them a sleepin' potion. Yer pardon if I cover me eyes against yer blindin' brilliance."

A lump rose in Roscelyn's throat and she swallowed hard. Judging from her invective, the witchwife was worried nigh unto death on her behalf.

"I will manage," she assured the old woman.

Lufu's eyes rolled heavenward. "Sweet Blessed Virgin, may ye protect this idiot child."

"Cease." Roscelyn held up a hand. It hurt to see the elderly witchwife worry herself thus. "There is nothing else to be done. I'll not risk Wulfwyn's safety."

Nor would she risk the scroll, she silently vowed. Though she yet fretted over its hiding place, she could scarce imagine anyone finding it. Surely even the Normans would not be so depraved as to rob graves.

". . . is naught else to be done!" Lufu's exasperated voice intruded on her thoughts. "There's plenty else to be done, girl. If ye be smart, ye'll concentrate yer efforts on the new lord."

Roscelyn eyed the woman, then frowned. Try as she might, she could make no sense of the witchwife's words. "Concentrate on the new lord?"

"Aye," Lufu snapped. "Me runes says the boy has more of a passion fer ye than he yet knows, and 'tis with him yer future lies."

Roscelyn's lips thinned as the witchwife's meaning grew clear.

Lufu was not consumed with worry for her. She wanted her to . . . to . . .

Rage shot up her spine. "Think you I would betray my Saxon heritage for wont of a paltry Norman future? My father would—"

"Yer father would want yer and Wulfwyn's futures secured."

"A pox you say!" Roscelyn's voice shook and she clutched the folds of her cloak in her fists. "I would die ere I sought succor from the man responsible for the deaths of my father and brothers. My father would spend eternity in hell ere he would see me bind myself to a Norman."

"Bah," Lufu sneered. "Think ye the boy wielded the very blade that kill't yer menfolk? 'Twas war, girl, a man's war, and it's done. Ye've gots the chance to secure a fine future fer yerself and Cyning, and yer father'd be right glad to know ye and yer sister is safe."

'Twas on the tip of Roscelyn's tongue to tell the witchwife that she would indeed secure herself a fine future, one that did not include an ill-bred Norman lout.

But even as she opened her mouth to speak, the thud of horses' hooves from the lane outside prevented her uttering a word.

Apprehension constricted her chest. Upon arising and finding her absent, did the Normans now search for her? Would they bind her hand and foot as they had Gunderic?

"A sleeping potion," she hissed lest she be overheard. "If I am unable to fetch it, you must see that it is served to the Normans."

"I'll do no such thing." The witchwife made no attempt to lower her voice. "Did ye not hear a word I said? And wot is all that racket?"

Lufu marched past her to the dull thump of fists pounding on doors down the way.

"You will not disobey in this, Lufu," Roscelyn persisted.

The witchwife ignored her from where she pressed her ear to the door.

"There are matters at hand that go beyond your knowledge. I have in my possession—"

A sharp knock sounded against Lufu's door and the witchwife jerked her head away to clutch her ear. "Wot is it?" she demanded.

"His lordship summons all persons to the village well," came a masculine voice.

Lufu flung the door open. "Wot fer?"

Silhouetted by a pink sky, a lanky Norman man-at-arms took several backward steps and crossed himself. "He wishes to present himself as your new lord."

With that, the man fair flew to the next cottage, where Roscelyn could hear him repeat the summons.

She released the breath that had frozen to clog her throat. The Normans were not looking for her? They had not concerned themselves with her absence?

"Are ye coming?" Lufu interrupted her musings.

"Aye," Roscelyn muttered, reaching to shake Wulfwyn, who had yet to stir.

So, the toad-eating de Brionne would present himself to the villagers as their new lord. "Hmph." She could well imagine what such an introduction would entail. Demands for food and money, as if the village folk had aught to give. Orders for labor, as if half the peasants weren't too sick to work. And what of the young village women? Would they be commanded to serve the Normans' baser appetites?

"Wulfwyn." She shook harder. Faith, waking her sister was like raising the dead.

"I'll just be on me way." Lufu's tone dripped with affected patience. "The two of ye might not reach the well afore eventide."

Roscelyn scowled at the witchwife's back as the old woman set off.

Concentrate her efforts on the new lord, indeed. She would concentrate all right. Concentrate on destroying de Brionne's reign at Cyning.

Until then, she would protect her people and ignore Lufu's remarks concerning the *boy's passion* for her. And plague take the fact that Lufu seldom erred when it came to reading . . .

Her runes?

Roscelyn whipped around and stared out the open door. A few villagers trudged past in the lane outside, but the witchwife was gone from sight.

Lufu had been reading her runes?

What was the elderly woman thinking to place her life in such jeopardy?

A dash of cold water was finally required before Wulfwyn roused, and then 'twas only to complain. "I don't wish to see the dunghead present hisself."

"If I again hear that word from your mouth—"

"But he's already presented hisself to me."

Roscelyn pulled her sister to her feet. "These are *our* people and it is *our* duty to attend this occasion on their behalf. You will cease your whining and behave like the nobly bred lady you are."

She narrowed an eye at Wulfwyn, daring her to object as she steered her outside.

Then Poppit appeared and the girl's mood lightened. "Did the dung—er—the new lord command yer presence, too?" She scratched the dog's ears as she walked along. "Poor boy."

'Twas impossible to argue with Wulfwyn's sentiments, Roscelyn conceded as they fell in behind the fuller Hogarth and his family.

"Is it true, Lady Ros?" Hogarth's youngest boy asked. "Is there an ogre wot serves the new lord? Does he eat small boys?"

"Aye," Wulfwyn spoke before Roscelyn could respond. "He grinds up their—"

Roscelyn jabbed her with an elbow. "Pay Wulfwyn no heed. There is a big man, an underlord, but he does not eat small boys."

"Did ye really stab him, Wulfwyn?" the fuller's middle boy asked, a note of reverence in his tone.

"Nay. 'Twas the lord hisself I stabbed. And next time 'twill be his throat I slit."

"Wulfwyn!" Roscelyn gasped.

"Wot of the new lord?" Brunhilde inquired, her face

flushed. At thirteen, she was Hogarth's eldest. "Is it true that he is the handsomest man to e'er grace Cyning?"

"Hush, girl," Hogarth's wife hissed. "Yer brazen tongue is like to be yer ruin."

Faith, but gossip spread quickly, Roscelyn thought. Uncomfortable with all the questions and her sister's bold remarks, she clutched the back of Wulfwyn's cloak, slowing their pace until the fuller and his family outdistanced them.

The moment they were out of earshot, she gave Wulfwyn a stern look. "Listen well, sister. I know not why this de Brionne did not kill you yestereve, but you will not tempt fate a second time with your unruly tongue."

Wulfwyn cast her a petulant look. "Ye . . . You wish me to cower before the Norman pigs?"

"Until you reach the safety of Saint Dunstan Abbey, that is precisely what I wish."

Wulfwyn gaped. "Abbey!" She shook her head and tried to free herself from Roscelyn's grasp. "I ar'nt going to no abbey."

'Od rot, Roscelyn cursed herself. She'd done it now. There would be no appeasing Wulfwyn.

Dragging the child to one side of the lane, she sought the privacy of a vegetable patch beside the toolmaker's cottage.

"Be still a moment," she whispered, her gaze lingering on the impish face, the pointed little chin, the upturned nose, the green eyes that had seen far too much misery in such a short life.

What to tell the child?

A child now ten and on the brink of womanhood,

her inwit whispered. 'Twas time and past she told Wulfwyn of the scroll. And if she twisted the truth a bit, she might gain Wulfwyn's cooperation.

"Know you how great is my love for you?"

Wulfwyn narrowed an eye. "Ye'll . . . you'll not be tricking me into going to no abbey."

"I seek not to deceive you," Roscelyn lied. "I need your assistance, and there is no other I would trust. I've but waited for Gunderic to heal to say aught that you would not grow over-anxious."

At last she had Wulfwyn's attention.

Roscelyn glanced about to make certain they were alone, then returned her attention to her sister.

"There is a secret document," she began, her tone hushed and hurried, "a scroll that will rid England of the Normans . . ."

Wulfwyn's features reflected excitement at first, but as Roscelyn continued, the girl's face grew solemn. By the time she'd explained her plan for freeing Gunderic, her sister's countenance reflected distress.

"Are you daft, Ros? The Normans will think you've poisoned them, just like Cerdic."

'Twas twice her wits had been questioned this morn, once by Lufu, and now by Wulfwyn. "A catching fever runs rampant in the village," she snapped. "Should the Normans grow sick, 'tis no fault of mine."

At Wulfwyn's wounded look, she chided herself. 'Twas not her intent to hurt her sister with sharp words.

She moderated her tone. "I will not leave our people alone to face the Normans. Nor dare I trust the scroll to any other than you and Gunderic. 'Tis important that you have a care for yourself and cease risking the Norman lord's displeasure with your prattle on how you will slit his throat. If aught should befall Gunderic, all of England will be dependent upon you alone."

Wulfwyn lowered her gaze. "You are very clever. I should have trusted you would have some plan that would benefit Cyning."

Roscelyn eyed her sister's downcast features. Since her wedding feast, Wulfwyn had adopted the coarse language of a commoner, as if the girl thought herself unworthy of aught that was noble. But now . . .

"Faith, 'tis a blessing to hear such proper speaking from you," she whispered around the bittersweet lump that rose in her throat.

Wulfwyn cast her a fierce look. "Fear no more. I will take great care with myself, and I will not fail you. The scroll will reach the abbey or I will—"

Her mouth clamped shut at the thunder of approaching horses' hooves.

Within moments, de Brionne swept past them. Bedecked like a king in a fur-lined cloak of scarlet, he was accompanied by his giant underlord.

Roscelyn grabbed Wulfwyn's arm and hurried to join the few village stragglers at the rear of the crowd, praying the Norman lord would take no notice of her and her sister.

Wulfwyn squeezed her hand. "Does Gunderic know of your plan?" she whispered beneath the low buzz of agitated conversation that vibrated the air like a mad swarm of bees.

"Nay," Roscelyn murmured, distracted by what her eyes beheld.

The sun had risen over hollow-eyed mothers who

held babes in tattered swathing. Gaunt-faced fathers and sons glowered, thin lipped and sullen. Children who wore rags on their feet huddled in clumps around their parents.

Roscelyn lowered her gaze, unable to bear the swamp of sodden misery that surrounded her.

'Twas obscene that de Brionne would strut about in such finery amidst such deprivation, especially when the Normans were to blame for such grim conditions. Had England been left in peace, Cyning would not be reduced to such pitiful circumstances. The peasants would be well fed, their clothes mended, their huts repaired against the coming winter. And she would have gone about her business—

The thought died abruptly. Had the Normans not invaded England, she would have been forced to kill Cerdic and Cyning might well be at war with his family.

Unbidden, Lufu's recent words swirled in her memory. *Think ye the boy wielded the very blade that kill't yer menfolk? 'Twas war, girl, a man's war, and it's done.*

Truth tell, 'twas most unlikely that de Brionne had engaged her father or brothers on a field that hosted thousands of men. Nor could she fool herself that Cyning would have stood untouched by war had the Normans not arrived.

A sudden chilling gust swirled over the crowd, stealing any warmth the sun might provide. Pulling her cloak snug, Roscelyn glanced up to find de Brionne's intense blue eyes regarding her from where he'd climbed atop the well wall.

Elevated above the peasants, his red cloak billowing

around him, he looked like an avenging angel just delivered by the wrathful hand of God.

Her lips parted and she could not look away. The same disturbing will-snatching weakness that had assailed her at their first meeting at Lufu's returned to fill her with longing.

To again feel his gentle touch on her face, to give herself unto him for safekeeping.

Abruptly his gaze grew forbidding and shifted to sweep from peasant to peasant, singling them out, until each in turn grew silent.

When at last he spoke, his voice carried hard with authority. "As lord and master of Cyning, it is my will that you shall prosper. It is by my commandments that you shall live, and by my sword that your enemies shall die."

Murmurs of approval wafted over the gathering and he paused. Again he eyed the peasants one by one, his deliberate gaze lending credence to his words.

'Twas the promise of a powerful warlord. A man who possessed the strength and the intelligence to see his will done. Inexplicably she longed for him to look at her, to declare to her with his eyes that he would vanquish her foes the same as he would the villagers'.

That he did not so much as glance her way again did nothing to cool the longing. Rather, her desire for his attention grew tenfold. Did she not know better, she'd think herself elf-shot.

The handsomest man to e'er grace Cyning.

She struggled for a reasonable denial, to no avail. Indeed, de Brionne might be the most handsome man to e'er grace England.

And he would have some passion for her?

She rolled her eyes at her errant thoughts.

Common sense dictated that de Brionne was no untried youth where women were concerned. Why would he develop a passion for her when his looks alone would provide him with his pick of Norman women?

Fast upon the question came another. Had he a wife?

The thought was more appalling than any she'd yet entertained.

Bad enough that de Brionne had appropriated her father's bedchamber for his own use. That he would lie in her father's bed and forge Norman offspring was not to be borne. But neither possibility compared in bitterness to the idea that a Norman woman would take her place as lady of the manor.

The squall of a babe intruded on her wretched musings and she looked to see Dunne, the widow of a housecarl, wrestling with her toddler.

A greater sense of despair lowered over her.

How long since she'd seen Dunne or even inquired after her?

Despite the woman's efforts to the contrary, her son seemed determined to get his feet on the ground. Roscelyn shuddered when the statuesque woman smacked him on a leg that was far too thin.

The child screamed all the more, and unable to soothe his temper, Dunne finally gave into tears herself.

Roscelyn hurried to help. 'Twas not at all like the even-tempered Dunne to treat her beloved son thus.

Long before Roscelyn could wend her way through

the knot of peasants, the giant underlord reached the crying woman.

"Nay," Dunne pleaded as he attempted to take the babe from her. "He will quiet, I swear."

Roscelyn's heart leapt to her throat and she charged forward, bumping and bouncing from one peasant to the next. If the fearsome man dared to hurt the child—

"I mean no harm," the giant piped in his incongruously high voice, prying the babe from Dunne's arms.

"Hear, hear." He spoke in a singsong voice and carried the child toward his mount, Dunne yet clinging to the boy's foot. "What is all this howling from such a fine fellow? Come and pet my horse. See how soft?"

As if by magic, the boy quieted, and Roscelyn halted mid-stride.

"He is most pretty for a horse, is he not?" the big man asked as the toddler reached to stroke the animal. "Perhaps you would like to sit in the saddle, eh?"

A hum rose from the crowd where Roscelyn now stood surrounded, and she searched the giant's ugly visage for signs of madness. No man she knew would care for his own screaming child, much less the screaming child of another.

"By your leave, Sir Gallant," de Brionne interjected, an exaggerated sweetness to his gruff tone.

At the giant's nod, de Brionne's tone again grew commanding. "In exchange for my protection, every able-bodied man and boy will submit themselves to my underlord for direction." He gestured at the giant. "A trench must be dug around the hill where the manor stands and a wall erected."

All sounds of approval at once grew stifled, while Roscelyn wondered if she'd heard aright. Did de Brionne intend to use all the village's available labor to dig ditches and build walls?

"In addition, we are in need of maidservants. Every woman, young or old, will present themselves to the manor for service."

Clearly the lord knew not what he was saying. His orders precluded any work in the fields, a fact that would not be lost on the peasants. There would be no food come spring, for the winter crops would not be sown.

"Mi'lord," she interrupted before he could continue. "Might I have a word?"

De Brionne scarce glanced her way. "Later." He focused his attention on the crowd. "Every man shall bring—"

"Your pardon, mi'lord, but this is not an issue that can wait," she persisted.

Deliberately ignoring her, he continued to address the crowd. "Every man shall—"

"Your forgiveness, sir, but the good folk of Cyning will hardly appreciate your efforts on their behalf when they are dead of starvation."

To her immense satisfaction, rumbles of agreement rippled through the crowd, though the villagers nearest her sidled away, leaving a ring of empty space around her.

"These defensive works," de Brionne ground, "will provide each of you sanctuary in the event of an attack."

"Yours is the only invading force in England," she pointed out evenly. "Do you mean these walls and ditches will save us from you?"

"They will save you from Danes and any other threat that presents itself."

The man was referring to a Saxon threat, though for the moment she would not pursue the obvious. Instead she crossed her arms over her chest. "So everyone will survive, and then what? You will feed them?"

"Aye," de Brionne snarled.

She inclined her head and spoke in a most reasonable tone. "And what, prithee, will you feed them? Grain from your fields? You realize you will have no crops. No one will have sown them. You are aware, as well, that even in the most abundant of seasons, the fruit and vegetables from your orchard would not provide enough to serve you and your men.

"I suppose, however—" She tilted her head, affecting a thoughtful look. "—there will be meat aplenty. Without vetch for fodder, you will be forced to slaughter everything with hooves ere it starves, including your own horse."

De Brionne's blue eyes blazed with enough heat to boil the skin from her bones and she took an involuntary backward step. No avenging angel, 'twas Satan himself who stood before her.

She swallowed dryly. By all that was holy, she would betray no trace of the fear that clattered down her spine to rattle her knees. She returned his regard with what she hoped would appear cool assurance.

Abruptly de Brionne tilted his face to the heavens and . . .

Roared with rage?

Nay. 'Twas the deep roar of laughter that issued from his mouth. Roscelyn ground her teeth against the foreboding sense that she'd made some foolish error.

A grin continued to etch grooves along his cheeks when he finally looked back to her. "If you would allow me to finish, Lady Honking Goose, you would know that your concern is misplaced."

Lady Honking Goose?

Fury sent blood pounding in her ears. Ere she was through, de Brionne would rue the day he was birthed. She would—

She would . . .

Even as she puzzled over what she could possibly do to exact vengeance on the toad-eating thickwit, the villagers' muffled merriment penetrated her ears. Glancing around, she noted the gazes that shifted before her perusal, at the hands that quickly covered smirking mouths.

She refused to lower her head. Let the peasants enjoy themselves for the moment. They would remember her words when they had naught but a ditch and a wall to fill their empty bellies.

"Enough!" De Brionne raised a hand, his tone menacing. "Your lady argues hard in your favor where most nobles would not concern themselves. While her tongue may run ere she thinks, 'tis naught but your welfare to which she attends. I will consider any mean remarks against her the same as if such were directed against me."

Roscelyn stiffened as appreciation for his defense tried to worm its way into her feelings. She would not be appeased by a few kind words after the man had made her appear the fool.

". . . no miserly Saxon," de Brionne was saying. "I have wealth aplenty, and none who serve me will go hungry."

"Mi'lord!" came a feminine appeal.

Roscelyn wrinkled her nose at the familiar voice.

Elswyth pushed from the crowd and scurried to bow at de Brionne's feet. "I would be honored to serve your needs."

Roscelyn rolled her eyes. She could well imagine the needs Elswyth would serve. Not that she cared.

"Bless yerself, yer graciousness." The haymaster bowed and scraped his way forward. "Me and me motherless children, six in all, yer lordship, we ar'nt had nothin' but watery gruel fer the past fortnight. I'd be in yer debt if ye'd find it in yer heart to spare us a bit of meat in exchange fer our service."

"Of course," de Brionne conceded easily.

"Me as well, yer lordship." The trapmaker edged toward the well, his head lowered. "Not that me wife ar'nt done her best. But wot with her bein' sick an' all, I was forced to sell me flour and ale to buy medicine from the witchwife."

De Brionne narrowed an eye. "The witchwife?"

Before he could say aught else, the crowd surged forward. Pleas for succor arose from all corners, the peasants vying with one another to be heard.

Roscelyn's lips puckered. An avenging angel delivered by the wrathful hand of God?

More like a lowly worm about to be pecked to pieces by a screeching flock of hungry blackbirds. Every peasant in the village would now claim some pressing need, whether or not 'twas true.

Not that she could blame the peasants for taking advantage of de Brionne. He'd brought it upon himself with his easy acquiescence to their demands.

But what if his professed concern for the villagers was a façade? Would de Brionne remain so generous once he had his ditches dug and his walls built? Or would he decide to keep his great wealth to himself?

She grimaced. 'Twas a stupid question. He was a Norman and the peasants were Saxon. Of course he would keep his wealth to himself.

She looked about for Wulfwyn.

With the Norman thus occupied, 'twould be a good time to speak with Gunderic.

If only she could convince Lufu to provide her with a sleeping potion.

FIVE

UNDER COVER of darkness, Cerdic crept along a ditch that bordered the village fields. He carried no lamp or torch. To be spotted would destroy his plans and could well mean his death. But his need for information and food was beyond desperate. He had no choice but to approach Elswyth.

By all accounts, only Gunderic had survived the battle at Hastings. Thinking to secure the secret scroll and Cyning before Normans could lay claim to the manor, Cerdic had gathered ten men and raced home from the fens of northeastern England.

His lip curled. 'Twas all for naught.

Not only had he arrived this afternoon to discover

Cyning fair crawled with Normans, he knew not what had become of the scroll his father-in-law had given to his wife for safekeeping—had no idea if his wife lived.

Worse, when using the forest where it bordered the fields to conceal himself, he'd noted the activity around the manor hill. The Normans were already digging a trench and would soon erect a wall. 'Twas a Norman strategy for defense that was sweeping the entire south of England, one that would make the taking of Cyning near impossible without help from someone inside the manor.

Abruptly he stumbled over a protrusion, then staggered several steps before catching himself. God be damned. He was like to break his neck before he gained the village.

He picked his way forward. For now, he and the ten men he commanded were weak from empty bellies and he must secure food. Ultimately . . .

His blood heated at the thought of vengeance. While the scroll would discredit the Normans' claims to England and provide him with a king's riches, the Normans were unlikely to relinquish England without a fight. Ultimately he must recapture Cyning that Saxon and Danish forces would have a secure base from which to beat the Norman scum back across the channel.

Impatient to reach Elswyth's, he searched the darkness. Surely he must be close to the village.

Nothing. Not even the moon or stars were visible for the cloud cover.

'Od rot, but he'd counted on finding Roscelyn and Wulfwyn alone at the manor. Matters would have been so simple. The scroll would have been his for the taking.

He would have sworn fealty to the wretched Norman king while secretly providing a haven for rebellion. And Roscelyn would have paid dearly for poisoning him.

A barking dog interrupted his thoughts. Ahead loomed several village huts, their outlines barely discernible despite his nearness.

He squinted, skirting a half-fenced croft. Old man Ansel's, he realized, smelling the buckets of urine that the tanner used to cure hides.

His bearings set, he continued a half-dozen doors down to Elswyth's where he paused to draw his sword. Should the dimwitted slut have chosen to share her bed with a man this night, the man would die.

He eased his hand through a hole in the wattle and daub and lifted the inside door latch, letting himself in. Though the hut's interior was black as pitch, well did he know the direction to Elswyth's bed.

Crouching, he felt for her pallet, found her alone, and clamped a hand over her mouth. " 'Tis I," he hissed at her muffled cry.

"Cerdic," she breathed when he removed his hand. Covers rustled, then her arms went around his neck. "Gunderic said you'd died."

"Gunderic is well?"

"He said you fell to a Norman sword."

Cerdic sneered, the memory kindling the embers of his rage. "The sword did little damage. 'Twas a kick to the head that laid me out. What news of Gunderic?"

"He is being held prisoner in the stables."

Cerdic rose to stand, hauling Elswyth to her feet where she yet clung to his neck. "What of my wife?"

Abruptly her body stiffened. "You come to my bed and ask after your wife?"

He clutched a handful of hair and jerked her head back before she could pull away, pleased by her gasp of pain. "You will have a care with your shrewish tongue and tell me of Roscelyn."

"What care you?" She pushed against his chest. "'Twas never your wish to wed her."

He pulled her head back until she whimpered, then traced her exposed throat with a finger. "You dare much to test my temper," he intoned silkily, "especially knowing as you do of my appetites."

"Ros is alive and well," Elswyth whispered, her body suddenly trembling.

"What of Wulfwyn?"

"She, too, is well."

Cerdic smiled in the dark. 'Twould appear that fate had not deserted him after all. Now all he need do was compel Elswyth to help him, a simple task he greatly anticipated.

He released her. "Fetch a light and some ale," he ordered.

Within moments flint struck and he moved to seat himself before a candle at a small table. Elswyth turned away to pour a cup of ale and he eyed the braid that hung down her back, a dark arrow against the white of her chainse.

"I was sorry to hear of your father's death." He forced a sympathetic tone, knowing his words would aggravate her.

She spun and delivered his ale, slamming the cup

on the table with enough force to slosh half the brew over the cup's rim. "The old fool is dead, and look what I am left with." She gestured at the room. "This hovel, a few strips of land."

"Take your ease, mi'lady," he soothed. 'Twas to his advantage that Elswyth bemoaned holdings most peasants would envy. "Your poverty shall not long last."

She crossed her arms over her chest and pouted. "Why is that?"

He stroked his dark beard. "Let us just say that William will not live to be crowned Christmas Day."

"You are going to kill him?" Her eyes rounded and she gaped.

Changing the subject, he inclined his head. "Have you some bread and cheese to spare?"

He'd scarce blinked before food was placed before him.

"You are going to kill the Norman king?" she asked again.

Not deigning to answer, he took his time eating, chewing slowly, aware that each bite he took served to increase her curiosity tenfold—along with her annoyance.

"When will you kill him?" she demanded at last.

He licked his fingers and waved aside her question. "I can say no more, other than Cyning will soon be the most powerful and wealthy of kingdoms in all England."

"A kingdom?"

"Unto itself. And I shall be its ruler."

Elswyth's gaze darted over his face, much as her tongue flicked across her lips. "How?"

Cerdic congratulated himself. He had her as surely

as a rabbit in a snare. "Sit, and let us discuss *our*—" He emphasized the word. "—future."

"*Our* future?" She eased down on a stool opposite him.

"You must swear not to mention my presence to a soul."

"Not even your precious wife?" she sneered.

He adopted a casual mien, brushing crumbs from his green tunic. "I fear I may have been overrough with dear Roscelyn on our wedding night," he lied. "I doubt that she will be kindly disposed toward me."

"Truth tell?" Elswyth's blue-green eyes gleamed with satisfaction, then her look grew sharp. "What has that to do with *our* future?"

"How many Normans occupy Cyning?"

She frowned. "A dozen, plus one boy."

'Twas not so many after all, Cerdic reflected. But then few enough would be required once the trench and wall were complete. Yet to attack before the Danes were ready would give the rebellion away.

"You are in a position to know what goes on at the manor?" he asked.

"Who is not?" she huffed. "The new Norman lord has ordered the entire village to dig ditches and await his pleasure. Even I have been forced into service."

"How dreadful for you." He feigned a look of horror.

Her eyes narrowed and her tone grew indignant. "You speak of *our* future, then mock me. Not only must I serve the new lord, I know not how much longer I will be able to elude his unwelcome advances."

Cerdic mustered a jealous response. "The man dares to force his attentions on you?"

"He does," she sniffed with the hauteur of a queen.

Sweet Blessed Virgin, but dealing with Elswyth was a tedious chore. That she sought to convince him of such a tale was a mark of her stupidity. Considering Elswyth's greed, he could well imagine who was casting unwelcome advances upon whom.

But until he could gain Roscelyn's cooperation . . .

His thoughts warmed. Wulfwyn would be the key to Roscelyn's goodwill. He must somehow take the child hostage that his wife would comply with his demands.

"Fear not, sweetling." He returned his attention to Elswyth. "The Norman pig will not trouble you much longer."

"So you say, Cerdic. Yet you tell me naught of how this miracle will be wrought or when. Meanwhile, it seems as if *our* future will benefit you alone."

His lips fair twitched with amusement. The woman deliberately provoked him and the ploy was obvious. But if it were her desire to raise his ire, he would do his best to accommodate her.

Without warning, he clamped his hand over hers and rose, jerking the upper half of her body across the table. Ignoring her gasp, he circled around behind her, twisting her arm up between her shoulder blades.

Excitement surged through his loins as his gaze traveled to her hips, and he stared down at her backside. She'd turned her head to rest one cheek on the table and her teeth were bared against the pain of his hold.

"Think you I would share secrets of rebellion with a woman?"

She groaned and squeezed her eyes shut.

"Obey me, and you will be rewarded with riches beyond compare." He ran a finger over her rump, then flipped her chainse over her hips.

"Nay, Cerdic," she begged.

He smiled. Her entreaty would have more effect were it not filled with anticipation. The moist heat between her legs gave lie to her plea as well. Never had he met a woman who enjoyed such rough handling.

"Disobey me—" He raised his tunic and loosed his braies. "—and there will not be enough of you left to bury."

"How I have missed you," she sighed moments later. "There is nothing I would not do for you."

SIX

VARIN PUT HIS BACK into digging despite his aching forearm where the lady's sister had stabbed him. The scrape of shovels and thump of axes tore at the earth around him while men and boys grunted and called to one another.

Throttling Lady Roscelyn for her rude comments yestermorn at the well yet held great appeal, and God knew he needed to spend some of his anger before he spoke to her.

He tossed a load of dirt over his shoulder and grimaced.

Meanwhile, the memory of her sweet little body did naught to cool his blood. He'd spent no little time speculating on her breasts and wondering if they would prove as delightful as the rest of her.

"Pff." 'Twas time he should have spent considering fortifications and methods of defense.

"Mi'lord?"

Varin's heartbeat quickened to find Simon standing before him in the early morning fog. Had the man caught Lady Roscelyn at some treachery?

"What is it?"

The liegeman inclined his head and Varin followed his dark gaze where it shifted to both sides of him.

Bloodygore. In his eagerness to hear Simon, he'd forgotten the villagers who toiled beside him. "A moment," he bade the young man.

He clapped the sturdy back of the villager nearest him. "Ulric, is it?"

The thick-necked man straightened. Despite the chilling fog, he swiped sweat from his fair-skinned brow. "'Tis Ulric," he allowed, his tone uncertain.

"If you'll excuse me, Ulric, I shall soon return."

The man's brows lowered and his greenish eyes blinked, as if he were confused.

"I have a matter to attend," Varin explained. "You and . . . Hogarth, is it?"

The wiry man who worked on his other side glanced up and slowly nodded, worry etching his lined features.

"Please continue with your good work." Varin sought to ease the wiry man's discomfort with praise. "I shall return with all due haste."

Planting his shovel in the ground, he climbed from the trench, then halted, squinting.

Whatever was Arnulf about?

Holding the handles of a small cart where a single ox would normally be yoked, the giant challenged a group of young village boys. "More, more. 'Tis still light as a feather."

Children scrambled hither and yon among the mounds of dirt piled beside the trench. Grabbing all the rocks they could find, they tossed them into the cart.

A one-eyed, fire-breathing, baby-eating ogre. Varin snorted. Arnulf would not frighten a mouse. How the giant tolerated the shrieking ebullience of so many small children, he knew not.

Still, he was grateful. The young boys were performing an invaluable task. With so few rocks, none could be allowed to go to waste. They would be needed to line the ascending side of the trench to keep it from washing out.

Beckoning Simon, he headed toward a stream that wound from behind the manor toward the River Ouse.

The fog was more dense here, its heaviness pouring from the stream in thick swirling strands until he could scarce see the men who labored on the trench.

"What is it?"

"'Tis naught, mi'lord. The lady and her sister have returned from the village and are busy in the sheep pens. Considering the work that needs doing, I thought you might use me elsewhere for the moment."

Varin shook his head. 'Twas not at all what he'd expected to hear. "The sheep pens?"

Simon nodded.

"What do they there?"

The young liegeman shrugged. "They are tying red strings around the sheep."

Varin closed his eyes and rubbed at his face. Why ever would anyone tie red strings around sheep?

Opening his eyes, he exhaled. "Very well. You may take my place in the trench. I will see to the lady."

Bowing, the liegeman took himself off and Varin ambled closer to the stream.

He'd pointedly ignored Lady Roscelyn when she'd sat beside him during yestereve's meal. To have opened his mouth would have been to release the venom he'd felt at her know-all comments during his presentation at the well. 'Twould certainly have destroyed any chance of wheedling information from her.

Indeed, the sting of her waspish tongue had carried through the night, souring his dreams. Her disappearance from the hall before breakfast this morn had done naught but increase his ire to the point that he'd given himself to digging trenches, and that in spite of the throbbing that had immediately assailed him from the hole in his arm.

He caught himself. "Patience," he ground.

Patience.

He could not allow the woman to argue with his commands before the entire village. To do so would encourage dissent among the peasants.

Patience.

He would let her know that her contrary manner would not be tolerated, though he would do so with careful eloquence. If he'd learned aught yestermorn, 'twas that the lady was more clever than he'd imagined.

He studied the mist that swirled from the stream's surface. Not that she'd fooled him with her arguments on behalf of the villagers. Fields and orchards and animals.

The lady had objected to his defensive works only because they would make it difficult for her husband and his Danish allies to reclaim Cyning.

The idea rekindled the anger he'd worked so hard to tame and he gritted his teeth.

Patience, his toenails.

Did the woman think him so dull of wit that she could trick him with such thinly veiled arguments? Did she think he would lie down and quietly listen while she gainsaid his commands?

Without warning, two paws hit his shoulder blades, near carrying him into the stream.

"Christ's bones," he snapped, bunching his shoulders against the slimy tongue that licked his neck.

He shrugged the overgrown dog from his back and turned to scowl at the animal. "Get your flea-ridden hide from my presence ere I kick you."

Unimpressed with the threat, the dog's tail wagged furiously and its brown eyes regarded him with what appeared to be merriment. Indeed, the way the dog's tongue hung from its open jaws gave the impression that the animal was smiling.

'Twas the same look he'd oft seen on Lack's face.

"Pff. Mangy cur," Varin grumbled, discounting the overwhelming sense that the animal was indeed Lack. 'Twas not possible. He'd buried the animal himself.

Still, he eyed the dog's back, looking for evidence of the sword slash that had killed Lack. Unable to see aught for the animal's thick fur, he refused the temptation of a closer inspection.

Instead he narrowed an eye at the dog. "Do you not know that 'tis improper for males to go about kissing one another? Though what else could one expect from a Poppit? 'Tis no good name for a—"

"There ye be, boy."

Varin stiffened. The witchwife.

Was there no place where he could escape that the crone would not find him?

"Brung ye a fresh poultice."

He cast her a sour look. "I can think of many words to describe your poultices, but *fresh* is not one of them."

Regardless of his surly sentiments, he'd given up trying to discourage the old woman's insistence on seeing to his wound. Jerking his sleeve up, he held out his arm for her inspection.

"Wot have ye been doing that yer all swole up?"

"I have been . . ."

Words failed him as he noticed the tall, gangly woman who stood a short distance behind the witchwife. Or mayhap 'twas a girl.

Whatever she was, her eyes were different colors, one green, the other black.

Varin stared. If the hag scared Arnulf, the giant would fall dead in his tracks upon spying this . . . this . . . With her black hair and spindly arms, she reminded him of a spider.

As if the creature could hear his thoughts, she raised a black brow and her lip curled.

In the same instant, the witchwife slapped the poultice on his arm with far more force than necessary.

"Christ's bloody—"

"Wotch yer tongue, boy. I'll not be havin' me great-granddaughter exposed to yer swearin'."

He clamped his jaw shut. Why he tolerated the hag was beyond him.

Except that her poultices, for all their foul smell, did indeed relieve the ache in his arm.

"Best to cease wotever 'tis that yer doing. All that swellin' won't help ye to heal."

With that, the crone turned and headed for the manor, her spidery great-granddaughter following.

Varin watched them go, then returned his attention to the dog, who yet sat at his side.

A useless cur, an ogre whom none feared, a mean-tempered hag with a spider for kin, a demon child who would doubtless take great pleasure in carving his heart from his chest, and a tart-tongued young woman who stood on roofs and tied strings around sheep.

He raised his face heavenward. On his honor, he could not recall the atrocious sin he must have committed to deserve such punishment.

ROSCELYN RUBBED her back where it ached from wrestling with sheep. Angry as she was with Lufu, she'd had to beg the elderly woman's help this morn.

Indeed, she should have done so yesterday afternoon when she'd first noticed that some of the sheep were ailing.

But nay. She'd allowed her temper to get the best of her and had refused to speak to Lufu after the witchwife had denied her third request yesterday for a sleeping potion.

She puckered her lips. 'Twould be her fault if the sheep died. Though she'd left well before breakfast to fetch the witchwife, it might prove too late for the sick animals.

She started at a particularly loud bang from across the manor where a half-dozen men worked on piecing together several stout timbers—for what, she knew not. Nor did it matter. If scab did not kill the sheep, the incessant racket would.

" 'Od rot, but all this noise wears on me ears."

The witchwife's irritated voice sounded behind Roscelyn and she turned to see Lufu and Golde approaching the sheep pen.

Wulfwyn hurried to open the gate.

"I sees ye marked the ones wot's sick," Lufu commented, stepping inside the gate.

Roscelyn nodded, eyeing the number of animals with red strings around their necks. "There are so many, I wonder if mayhap we should treat the entire fold."

"I'm thinkin' yer right." The witchwife moved to inspect the sheep. "Have ye diff'rent colored string?"

Roscelyn inclined her head at a section of fence where several lengths of blue string hung. "We could cut that."

Lufu nodded. "Then lets us start with the blue."

Once Wulfwyn had cut the string, the witchwife turned to her great-granddaughter. "Let me have me tonic."

With that, the work began.

Wulfwyn draped a lead rope over the nearest ewe,

then clutched it with all her might when the sheep balked.

Taking a deep breath, Roscelyn grasped the animal's fleecy gray ears and straddled it. The ewe bleated and her woolly companions trotted about the enclosure as a single bawling mass, anxious to escape whatever torture had distressed the ewe.

Roscelyn wrinkled her nose as the scents of dung and urine wafted upward.

"Tilt her head more," Lufu commanded.

She moved her hand 'neath the sheep's scruffy neck and forced the ewe's head upward. 'Twas no easy task, considering the animal weighed at least half as much as she.

"How much of the tonic shall I give this one?" Lufu directed her question to Golde.

Roscelyn winced. " 'Tis no time for lessons, Lufu."

"Shh. How much?"

Golde surveyed the animal. "One spoonful."

Lufu poured a spoonful of brown, syrupy tonic in the sheep's mouth, then nodded. Golde removed the red string from around the animal's neck, replacing it with a blue.

Wulfwyn loosed the lead rope and Roscelyn leapt aside as the sheep trotted off.

Thus it went until it appeared all the sheep wore blue strings.

"Is that all?" Wulfwyn asked.

"Nay," Golde answered. "I have one more blue string."

Roscelyn wiped her hands on the folds of her brown tunic and swung her braid over her shoulder from where it had fallen forward. Squinting, she looked about for the one sheep without a blue string.

"I see it!" Wulfwyn shouted and dashed into the middle of the flock.

"What mix ye together for the tonic?" Lufu questioned Golde while Roscelyn watched Wulfwyn wrestle the rope over the last sheep's head.

"Lupine . . ." Golde's deep voice paused, then continued. "Wolf's comb, fennel—"

"Nay!" Lufu screeched, distracting Roscelyn. "That is the tonic for sudden mortality. Can ye remembers naught?"

"Do not fuss so," Golde replied, unruffled. "I was but testing your wits. I have heard said that elderly folk lose their thoughts easily."

"Thankless brat," Lufu huffed. "Think ye I have nothin' better to do than listen to yer callow prattle?"

Golde easily evaded the smack Lufu intended for her arm, and Roscelyn smiled in spite of her sore back. No other would dare taunt the crotchety witchwife thus.

"Settle yourself, Mimskin," Golde soothed. "I know the makings for the brew."

"Then let us hear," Lufu challenged.

"For pocks and scab in sheep," Golde spoke rapidly, stringing the words of her recital together, "lupine, the lower part of boar fern, the upper part of spearwort, and large beans ground up."

"And then," Lufu prodded.

"Pound them all together and mix with honey and holy water. Dose the ailing sheep according to size and sickness once each day for a week."

"Ye are indeed blood of mine," Lufu groused, "though where ye comes by yer stinging wit, I know not."

"It could not be a result of your dizzying intellect," Golde responded, then evaded another of Lufu's swats. "But, Mimskin, someone must stir your thoughts on occasion else your wits will wither. You should be grateful for my aid."

"Ros," Wulfwyn grunted, having captured the last sheep.

Raising her skirts, Roscelyn hurried to straddle the animal.

Then it struck her. Golde! Why had she not thought of it sooner? The witchwife's great-granddaughter would know the secret ingredients for a sleeping potion, just as she knew the makings for the sheep tonic.

Wulfwyn loosed the rope and Roscelyn's leg was mid-swing over the ewe's back when another cracking bang split the air. The animal bolted, catching her off balance.

For a whisker of a moment, she teetered, arms wheeling. Then she plopped on her backside.

"Are you all right?" Golde asked.

Roscelyn looked up at the tall young woman. It mattered not that Golde's lips twitched to contain her merriment. It mattered not that Wulfwyn was doubled over with laughter. It mattered not that she sat in filth.

Golde was the answer to her dilemma.

She fumbled to rise without placing her hands in the slime that covered the ground. Finally Golde clasped her forearm and pulled her erect.

"My thanks." She bobbed her head at the young

woman, then nodded at Lufu. "And thanks to you as well for your labors."

Holding the back of her skirts away from her legs, she hurried for the gate. "Wulfwyn, take the red strings to the stables for safekeeping. Then kindly fetch a fresh tunic and chainse for me and bring it to the kitchens."

A quick bath, a change of clothing, and she would seek Golde's . . .

Her steps slowed. To ask Golde's aid would be to ask Golde to deceive her great-grandmother. Glancing over her shoulder, she watched as Lufu and Golde strode across the manor grounds.

Her shoulders slumped. Nay. She could not do such a thing. Not only would it be reprehensible, 'twould place Golde in great danger should the Normans—

"Oof." Air whooshed from her as she plowed into de Brionne.

She stumbled backward and he caught her elbow to keep her from falling. Faith, it felt as if she'd walked into a stone wall.

"Your pardon, mi'lord. I did not see you."

He raised a sardonic brow and shook his head. "I would have a word with you."

"Later," she responded, thinking only of reaching the tub.

His hold on her elbow tightened. "Now."

Great toads. She blinked at the unyielding set of his jaw, at the anger in his blue eyes. She'd not meant to raise his temper.

"Your forgiveness." She affected her humblest tone. "I have—"

"You will shut your mouth until I give you leave to speak," he snapped, pulling her toward the hall.

She dug her heels in the ground. "But, mi'lord—"

Her breath caught as he spun her in front of him. "Quiet!" he roared in her face, his blue eyes molten.

All noise from the manor grounds ceased and she glanced about to see everyone in the vicinity staring at them.

Rage snapped her spine taut and she clamped her teeth together. When he steered her forward, she made no objection. Her head was too busy conjuring thoughts of his demise.

Indeed, had she a sword to hand, she would plunge it through his arrogant, black heart.

By the time he ushered her inside the hall, her jaw was so rigid she doubted if she were capable of speech. When he seated her on a bench, she folded her fists in her lap and stared straight ahead.

Varin planted his hands on his hips where he stood before her, eyeing the rosy color that stained her cheeks, the stubborn thrust of her little jaw, the near feral gleam in her golden eyes.

Her anger only served to feed his ire.

"My patience is flown with you, wench," he snarled. "You gainsay my every word, and I will not tolerate it. Henceforth, when I command your presence, you will not tell me later. You will attend me that instant, and you will do so without argument."

She shifted on the bench, her gaze focused somewhere beyond him.

"In future, you will keep your opinions regarding food and crops and horses to yourself. You will not raise objections to my orders, nor will you stir discontent amongst the villagers."

He scowled. Where she'd shifted on the bench before, she now fair wiggled about until he wondered if a word he'd said had penetrated her ears.

"You will give me your full attention when I speak to you," he snapped.

If she heard him, she gave no indication.

He cupped her chin and forced her head up. "Cease squirming!"

"Ooo!" she cried.

Leaping to her feet, she ducked past him.

"Get them off!" she fair shrieked, shaking her skirts.

"What off? Your clothes?" he thundered. 'Twas not to be believed.

"Ooo! Ooo!" She spun about, clawing at her tunic. "Muckworms! Get them off!"

Faith, she looked like a cat chasing its own tail.

Varin grabbed her shoulders, thinking to hold her immobile. "Muckworms?"

She shuddered, her weight shifting from foot to foot. "I fell in the sheep pen. They're crawling all over . . . Ooo!" She swiped frantically at her backside.

Varin spun her around and eyed the wriggling white grubs that clung to her tunic. "Christ's bloody bones. Hold still."

He brushed at her skirts, wrinkling his nose at the odor that rose from the brown material. "Why did you not say something?" he demanded.

"I tried." Her voice quavered. "You would not listen."

He shook his head. *Bloodygore*. She would not make

him feel guilty. "What were you doing in the sheep pen anyway?"

"Treating the sheep for scab."

"Do you not have a shepherd for such tasks?"

"Aye," she huffed.

"Then why does such work fall to you?"

"My shepherd is digging your trench, as you have ordered."

"If you did not gainsay my every word, I would have listened," he muttered, distracted by the squirming movement of her bottom.

Despite the worms, despite the smell, despite the roil of his inwit that he refused to acknowledge, he could not help but recall the appealing sight of her derriere in the witchwife's hut, the silken feel of her firm, round flesh.

His *coillons* tightened at the memory. Her sleek legs, the way her bottom had pressed against his groin when she'd come through the roof . . .

Plague take him for a Sodomite. He must do something to ease his celibate state.

"Ros?"

He glanced to see her sister standing in the doorway and his hand halted mid-swipe.

"Did you wish me to fetch you a clean tunic and chainse?" the girl asked, her tone uncertain.

He straightened. "Fetch them and be quick. The lady is on her way to bathe."

The child darted for the curtained section of hall where she and Lady Roscelyn slept.

"We shall speak later," he grumbled at the lady, "when you are less inclined to wiggle and squirm."

SEVEN

V ARIN ROLLED a wooden chalice between his hands where he sat at a trestle table in the empty hall the following afternoon.

He must be cursed. Aye. There was no other explanation for the misfortune that plagued him. His steward would be engaged in accounting William's English *demesne* for the foreseeable future. A king's messenger had delivered the baneful news just after the morning meal.

He raised the chalice and drank half its contents, grimacing at the bitter ale.

No steward. No one to account his fief. No one to tell him how many virgates he held, how much forest land, how much the peasants owed in rents and week-work. And that was but the beginning.

Lady Roscelyn's words about stores, food, vetch, an-imals—all hung over his head like an executioner's axe.

Though he could scarce count, he was not blind. He'd seen what provender the manor held when he'd first arrived. Once the messenger had left, he'd again visited the granaries, anxious to gain some sense of sup-plies. The difference was obvious. He'd wager that one of every dozen sacks of flour and grain was gone.

At such a rate, the barns would be bare within a fortnight. Nor did he know how much he might expect to buy with his money.

Self-derision curled his thoughts and he swallowed the remainder of the ale. Though it galled, there was but one person who could help. Lady Roscelyn had demonstrated her abilities in village affairs during his speech at the well and he'd already sent Arnulf to col-lect her.

He scowled. He would now have to beg and scrape for the lady's favor. Otherwise, he could not hope to succeed as lord of Cyning. With no knowledge of his po-sition, he may as well charge off unarmed and unpro-tected to fight a battle on a field with no location. He shoved the despairing thoughts aside ere they drained him of all strength.

"Pff." He shook his head. Would that he'd not pledged a daily meal to all who labored at the manor.

He rolled his eyes. Would that he'd not referred to the lady as Lady Honking Goose.

He grimaced and tried to avoid the thought that followed even as it bloomed afresh in his memory.

Would to God that he'd displayed the courtesy of listening to Lady Roscelyn yestermorn ere he so *eloquently* chastised her. That she'd had to sit with worms crawling about her clothing while he vented his spleen did not set well with *him*. He could scarce imagine the lady's outrage.

"More ale, mi'lord?"

Thinking Roscelyn had arrived, Varin straightened and started to rise. But 'twas only the brunette who'd so valiantly offered her service the other morn at the well. The same promiscuous brunette whom he'd mistaken for Lady Roscelyn.

"Mi'lord?" Pitcher to hand, the brunette awaited his command.

He resettled himself on the bench and held out his cup. "My thanks, Edith."

"Elswyth," she corrected.

"Yes, well . . ." He cleared his throat. "Leave the pitcher and fetch another chalice. Lady Roscelyn will be joining me."

"Oh?" The woman's blue-green eyes glittered with speculation. "I trust all is well."

"Aye," he answered, distracted.

Considering his mean treatment of her, he would first ask for Lady Roscelyn's forgiveness. 'Twas the least he could do. But should she refuse—

"Mi'lord?" The brunette interrupted his thoughts.

"What is it?"

"I asked how your arm fared."

"'Tis on the mend," he allowed, glancing about suspiciously.

Was the old witch about to appear from nowhere to

slap another of her foul-smelling poultices on his wound?

"Would you like for me to look?"

"Look?" Something moved in the corner beyond the hearth fire and he narrowed his eyes.

"At your arm."

'Twas naught but the shadow of a support beam wavering in the light from the fire. He and the brunette were alone. "My thanks for your concern, Elspen—"

"Elswyth."

Elswyth, Elswyth, Elswyth. He committed her name to memory, then waved her off. "I but require another chalice."

"As you wish, mi'lord."

The brunette leaned to place the pitcher on the table just as the door at the hall's entrance opened.

Lady Roscelyn.

Varin rose to welcome her, only to knock the pitcher from the brunette's hand.

"Your pardon, Elspen." He clutched her forearm as she teetered back on her heels, the ale having doused her front.

"Elswyth," she corrected in a breathless voice, clutching his tunic for balance. "'Tis my fault. I should have paid more attention."

She released his tunic and patted his chest. "At least I did not spill ale on you. But good lack, look at me."

Tsking, she rubbed the damp material, her hands gliding over her breasts.

The brunette's game grew clear. He eyed her bright blue tunic. Too small by half, he'd wager. Judging from the way her nipples protruded against the material, she wore no chainse.

In spite of himself, he smiled. The day was indeed black when he did not notice a woman's intent to seduce him. Truth be known, had Lady Roscelyn not arrived, had he not risen to welcome her and spilled the ale, he would yet be unaware of Eldred's ploy.

"Have someone else deliver a fresh pitcher and another chalice," he directed. "Then go and see to yourself."

The brunette cast him a whimsical smile and headed for the side door, hips rolling.

Shaking his head, he turned his attention to . . .

Lady Roscelyn, who stood just inside the door with her arms crossed over her chest, her lips puckered, and her little nose thrust skyward.

He fought the urge to duck his head. The lady was indeed outraged over his treatment of her yesterday.

"Is aught amiss, mi'lady?" he ventured, hoping his solicitous tone might mollify her temper.

"You did command my presence, did you not?" she demanded.

"I *requested*—" He emphasized the word. "—your presence."

"You were expecting me," she challenged, as if he might deny it.

He shrugged and shook his head to convey his lack of comprehension.

"You were not expecting me?"

He was floundering and he knew not what to say. "Of course I was expecting you. But I fail to see—"

"I may be a lowly Saxon wench to your thinking—"

She glared at him. "—but I am not in the habit of waiting attendance while a man and woman dally with one another."

"Dally?"

"Seek you to fool me with your bewildered looks? 'Tis obvious you and . . . clearly you were busy with . . . You were pursuing your own pleasure."

"You think that Eldreth and I—"

"Elswyth," she snapped.

He gritted his teeth and prayed for patience. Her accusing manner was all the more irritating for being unfounded.

"Faith, mi'lady, you sound like a jealous wife." The words were beyond his teeth before he could stop them.

The lady's eyes rounded, her lips parted, and her chest rose as she took a deep breath.

His annoyance vanished, replaced by amusement. 'Twas a most charming indignant look, full of golden and rosy hues, warm enough to thaw the chill of cold bones on a frosty night.

"I am jealous!" The words finally whooshed from her.

"So you admit it."

The flush on her face deepened and she dropped her arms to her sides. "Wha . . . You . . . I admit no such thing."

He covered his mouth and coughed to hide a grin. Faith, but the woman rattled easily. 'Twas the most fun he'd had since his arrival at Cyning.

And 'twould likely be the only fun he experienced, he thought, sobering. He could no longer delay the task at hand.

"My apologies, mi'lady. I did but jest. Truth tell, Eldreth—"

"Elswyth," she hissed.

"Eldred, Elspen, Edith, what matter? The wench brought a pitcher of ale. I directed her to bring another chalice for you. And there is the end to it. Now if you would, kindly come and join me." He gestured at the bench opposite the table from him. "There is an important matter I would discuss with you."

Roscelyn inclined her head and strode toward the table with what she hoped would appear great dignity. 'Twas no easy task when she longed to turn and stalk away—to avoid the man's disturbing presence that left her feeling angry, frightened, and weak all at once.

The giant underlord had not shared the reason for de Brionne's summons. She'd fretted all the way to the hall, wondering if someone had overheard her pleading with Lufu for a sleeping potion, or worse, if someone had discovered the scroll. Indeed, she worried that mayhap something untoward had occurred to Gunderic.

To arrive and find the lecherous lord and Elswyth at play had heated her edgy senses to boiling.

She stepped around a bench and seated herself, watching as de Brionne did the same. He swiped ale from the table with the sleeve of his undertunic and she puckered her lips, awaiting his leisure.

"I, er." He paused to clear his throat, his gaze focused on the table. "I suppose I should begin by apologizing."

Apologize?

"'Twas unkind of me to refer to you as Lady Honking Goose the other morn."

She blinked. "Your pardon?"

At last his gaze rose to settle on her. "'Tis important that my authority not be questioned by the village folk. They will hardly serve a man they do not respect. In future, I would that you address your concerns in private with me."

That was it? He wished to apologize?

"Your forgiveness, mi'lord. Henceforth I shall save my arguments for your ears alone. If that is all?" She half-rose.

He raised a hand. "There is one other matter."

Now what? She sank back onto the bench.

For a moment, de Brionne's regard was hesitant. Then he smiled and she could feel no more warmth were she standing before the sun on a hot summer day. "You are to be commended on your knowledge of village affairs. How did you come to be so well versed in such matters?"

Apologies followed by compliments? The lazy warmth his smile wrought vanished, replaced by dark clouds of wariness. She leaned back from the table as if the tiny bit of distance might improve her chance of escaping whatever deception was at hand.

"I learned estate matters from my mother. When she died, I assumed her duties."

He rubbed the table with a forefinger. "'Tis uncommon for a woman to possess such skills."

She puckered her lips while considering the comment. "Are you saying I do not speak the truth?"

His gaze snapped back to her face. "Nay. That is not at all what I said. 'Tis just that men usually handle affairs of the land."

"You do not think women possess the wits to perform such duties?"

He slapped the palm of his hand on the table and his blue eyes hardened. "I do not seek to discredit you in any manner, yet you take insult at every word I speak."

"What am I to think when a Norman suddenly rains apologies and compliments on my head?"

"I begin to wonder why I bother asking aught of you," he ground. "'Twould be simpler to command you do my bidding on penalty of your housecarl's life."

Fear spurted through her belly. Though she had no clue to what he referred, clearly she'd placed Gunderic in jeopardy. She opened her mouth to apologize, to soothe his temper, but the bang of the side door prevented her.

"Here ye be." Afled, the dairymaid, bustled in carrying a pitcher and a cup, her round cheeks flushed. "Sorry fer the delay, but ever'one's busy with the cookin'."

De Brionne cast her a surly look. "You are more timely than you can know."

Afled set the pitcher and cup on the table and darted Roscelyn a worried glance. "Is there aught else ye be needin' fer now?"

De Brionne shook his head.

The dairymaid cast one last look at Roscelyn. "Then I'll be back to me duties."

Roscelyn watched her go, wishing the matronly young woman could stay, wishing she did not have to sit alone with de Brionne.

"Ale?"

Reluctantly she returned her attention to the Norman and nodded.

He poured her a cup and slid it across the table, then downed two cups of his own in quick succession.

"Where were we?" he asked while pouring himself a third. "Ah, yes. I believe we were trading insults."

She moistened her lips. "Your forgive—"

"The fault is mine," he interrupted. "Through my own ignorance, I must beg your favor, and the thought . . ."

He paused and searched her face, then took a deep breath. "I need your aid."

Her lips parted. Apologies, compliments, threats— and now the man would admit that he needed her help?

Confused, she studied his countenance, looking for any hint of deception. His regard was steady, not shifting. Tiny grooves radiated from the corners of his eyes, white in contrast to his tanned complexion. His firm, clean-shaven jaw did not twitch to betray any lie.

"My steward will not be available to me for some time," he said at last. "I was hoping you might agree to help me with your knowledge of the estate."

She clamped her teeth together to keep her jaw from falling to the table. He wanted her help with the estate?

Though his tone was sincere, she could not banish the doubt that seized her. Did he seek to trick her in some way?

"Exactly what sort of help do you need?" she hedged.

"I am a warrior. The only fields I have overseen are battlefields. My direction of peasants thus far in life has consisted of ordering more meat or wine for myself from table servants. The only animal with which I am familiar is my horse."

"What of your family? Surely they—"

"I am an orphan." His words grew clipped and invited no questions. "I was raised at court."

"I see," she murmured, though she did not.

Whatever was his idiot king thinking to appoint such an inexperienced man to govern an estate as vast as Cyning? De Brionne could not possibly succeed.

She folded her hands on the table and lowered her gaze against the stab of inexplicable sympathy she felt for him.

Mayhap 'twas his willingness to admit his ignorance, to reveal his vulnerability. He could not know that he was giving her the very thing she wanted most in all the world—to see to Cyning's welfare.

Whatever the reason, compassion for the man rose in her chest, then twisted painfully when she fought it down.

She could afford to feel nothing but hatred for de Brionne. 'Twas no fault of hers that his king had placed him in such an untenable position. With luck, his dull-witted king had placed men of de Brionne's incompetence at every manor in England.

Nor would she feel regret at taking advantage of him.

She looked up. "Free my housecarl."

Her demand caught him mid-sip from his cup and he choked. Coughing, he slammed the chalice on the table and swiped his sleeve across his mouth. "Free your housecarl!"

He cleared his throat repeatedly, glaring at her all the while. At last he caught his wind. "Think me stupid at your own risk, mi'lady. I may not know the workings of estates, but I have dealt with brazen women far more clever than you, and I have yet to lose."

"Brazen . . . more clever—" It took all her will to curb her temper. "What you have done with women is a concern for your wife and priests. If you want me to—"

"I have no wife—"

"Verily can I see the reason—"

"—and my regard for priests is about as great as yours."

She inhaled sharply. "What is your meaning?"

"I heard your pretty words to the priest the other day. To try to trick him into blessing a witch's den exposes the low value you place on holy men."

"Oh?" She raised a brow. "You would have allowed him to burn Lufu's place?"

"Without demur."

"But then who would have fixed the poultices for your arm?"

"I would not have need of poultices were it not for your sister."

"Very well," she allowed. "Who would have prepared the potion to ease the miller's fever that he could grind your grain? Who would have prepared the poultice for the toolmaker's gout that he could supply shovels and axes for your trench digging? Who would mix the tonic for your sheep that will provide food for your table?"

At his sullen regard, she knew she'd convinced him of Lufu's value. Satisfaction swelled in her breast. Now if she could gain Gunderic's release, the housecarl and Wulfwyn could slip away in the night without anyone the wiser. "If 'tis your wish that I manage your affairs for you, then you will free my housecarl."

"I do not wish *you* to manage aught. You will instruct me that I can manage matters on my own."

The toad-eating thickwit.

She tried a different approach. "Would you free Gunderic if I gave my word that nothing untoward would occur?"

"Pff. Your perception of what is untoward is doubtless very different from mine, as is the meaning of what constitutes your word."

She felt like banging her head on the table, or better yet, his. "You trust me to teach you the workings of an estate, yet you doubt my word?"

His lips curved in a grim smile. "You may as well rest your facile tongue, mi'lady. 'Twill have no effect on me. I trust you so long as I hold your housecarl prisoner. You will teach me, and teach me well, or your man will forfeit his life."

As her chance to free Gunderic slipped away, so did her control. "'Tis a measure of your baseborn cowardice that you would stoop to such a low means of coercion."

"I will use any means necessary to protect *my* lands and the people who tend them." His voice rasped with intensity. "In that, I suspect we are much alike, mi'lady."

She looked away that he would not see the rage in her eyes. Let him think her defeated, that she would meekly accept his orders. She would get Gunderic free if she had to—

"Do your lips always pucker thus?" de Brionne inquired. "Or is it your wish for a kiss?"

Her gaze snapped back to his face. "You are a pig."

"A lowly, muck-eating Norman pig," he expanded on the insult, "but a pig you will serve."

"If that is all, your pigship," she sneered, "I have wallowed in your company enough for one day."

She started to rise when his big hand clapped over her forearm.

"Have a care, mi'lady. While I understand your anger and will overlook it at present, do not think I shall remain so complacent in future."

The material of her sleeve provided no protection from his touch. Warmth radiated up her arm, feeding on her strength, demanding . . .

Demanding what, she knew not. 'Twas even more absurd that she should feel a sudden compulsion to give something of herself to him.

She scowled.

He deserved nothing, and contrary to his thinking, they were nothing alike. She would never display the mercenary disregard for life and dignity that de Brionne . . .

Memories of her wedding feast stole through her head to taunt her.

Would she not have committed a mortal sin—would she not have murdered Cerdic—rather than embroil her land and her people in war?

She eyed de Brionne's hand where it covered her arm. Would she not sell her soul to see that Wulfwyn and the scroll reached the abbey?

Disturbing as the realization proved, it nevertheless sowed the seeds of an idea.

She raised her gaze and stared hard into de Brionne's eyes. "Do as you will with my housecarl," she bluffed. "Kill him if it pleases you. He is but a means to an end that will never bear fruit so long as he remains prisoner. Unless I am able to attain that end, I will not lift a finger on your behalf."

Where he'd held her arm before, his thumb now traced slow circles over the material of her sleeve. An acute awareness of him seized her, both a tantalizing sample and a warning of his prowess.

"What end would that be, mi'lady?" he inquired, his voice quiet as the sneaking advance of a cat about to pounce on a bird.

'Twas chilling that he made no comment on her lack of concern for her housecarl's life. Was the man so accustomed to the brutal act of killing defenseless people? Would her words provoke him to carry out his threats against Gunderic?

"The end you seek, mi'lady?" he coaxed.

She blinked and swallowed the fear that had risen to clog her throat. "My sister is promised as a bride of Christ," she said, gathering the seeds of her idea.

Abruptly his fingers stilled. "Your pardon?" He frowned and cocked an ear toward her as if he'd misunderstood her words.

"My sister is promised to an abbey—"

"The demon?" His features and his tone were incredulous. "A bride of Christ? Surely you jest."

"I do not jest," she snapped, jerking her arm from

his grasp. "Gunderic was to have provided her escort to Saint Dunstan Abbey. I only awaited Gunderic's injuries to heal before sending him and Wulfwyn to the abbey."

He snorted. "The roof would collapse at her very approach. Walls would crumble. . . . Sit. I did not give you leave."

Her body quivered with rage while she rose from the bench. "I'll not sit and listen while you insult my sister."

With that, she headed for the entrance doors. Insufferable man. She would prepare a sleeping potion herself. Though she could not recall exactly how much of what to mix, she remembered well enough what Lufu had used to prepare the concoction that Cerdic had drank.

"A moment, mi'lady," de Brionne hailed.

When she did not break stride, his tone grew coaxing. "Mayhap we can strike a bargain."

Though she longed with all her angry heart to ignore him, his offer gave her pause.

She turned to face him and inclined her head. "A bargain?"

He leaned back and crossed his arms over his chest. "If you will agree to teach me all I require, I will consider your request."

She turned back for the door.

"Very well," he groused. "I will see that your sister reaches the abbey."

"When?" she asked, not deigning to face him again.

"Within the fortnight."

She stiffened. "Now."

"Nexxtt weeek." He ground the words, drawing them out.

Her back yet turned to him, she made certain no trace of the triumphant smile that curved her lips was reflected in her voice. "Tomorrow."

"Done," he snarled, the sound of his hand slamming on the table ringing sweet in her ears.

EIGHT

FIVE DAYS LATER, Roscelyn arose from her pallet,
her every bone protesting the movement. Weary and
sore after the journey to the abbey, she would be allowed no respite. De Brionne had made it clear yestereve that he expected her to begin his instruction this
morn.

She called for hot water and pulled clean garments
from her storage chest. The early morning grunts and
snorts of men-at-arms, along with the clap of trestle tables being erected, easily penetrated the curtained section of hall that served as her bedchamber. A lonely
bedchamber now that Wulfwyn was gone.

Melancholy drifted aimlessly through her senses as

she pondered which tunic to wear. The green or the brown? Black would best suit her mood, but she owned nothing of that dismal color. Selecting the brown, she took up soap and washing linens once the hot water was delivered.

'Od rot. Rather than moping about, she should be congratulating herself. True to his word, de Brionne had ordered Arnulf and two of his liegemen to escort Wulfwyn to Saint Dunstan. He'd even allowed Rosce-lyn to accompany the group when she'd insisted that 'twas improper for Wulfwyn to ride alone with three men.

Her sore muscles aside, the journey had been pleas-ant enough, the weather overcast but not foul. Indeed, what had begun as a sour-voiced contention on Wulfwyn's part—that Saxon housecarls were far superior to Norman men-at-arms—had ended with Arnulf and Wulfwyn cackling like two old crones as each strove to relate a story more bloodthirsty than the other's.

Roscelyn paused in washing her face to smile. The giant was truly possessed of a good nature where chil-dren were concerned. 'Twas the first time since . . .

Her smile faded and she clutched the sides of the wash stand against a sudden rush of anguish.

'Twas the first time since her brothers' deaths that she'd grown ill over gory tales of war. 'Twas the first time since her wedding that Wulfwyn had behaved like her old self.

Wincing, she slapped a washing cloth in the water and bent over the washstand to scrub her face. She would not allow such thinking to cloud her accomplish-ments.

Wulfwyn was safe. Gunderic had come to no harm in her absence. By now the scroll was on its way to the pope, and the Normans . . .

Her scrubbing slackened to a halt.

Sweet Blessed Virgin. She squeezed her eyes shut and shook her head. Could her thoughts spare her no quarter?

Opening her eyes, she stared at the steaming wash water. Nay. The pestering truth would not leave go. In her haste to protect Wulfwyn and save England, she'd not fully considered the consequences of her actions.

Stupid, dull-witted fool that she was, she could scarce imagine that de Brionne would peacefully quit Cyning.

Nay.

De Brionne would be much more likely to stand and fight . . . and die. And the good-natured Arnulf would die with him.

As if her thoughts summoned de Brionne forth, she heard the door to her father's bedchamber open, followed by the sound of his footsteps as he strode past the curtained section of hall.

Sick to her very soul, she quickly finished washing. Once dressed, she grabbed her gray cloak and made her way to the trestle tables where de Brionne insisted she sit beside him.

"How fare you this morn, mi'lady?" he inquired.

"I suspect she is tired," Arnulf remarked, seating himself across from them.

She lowered her gaze before de Brionne's scrutiny. "I am well enough."

"Pff. You appear droopy as the jowls on yon hound."

He gestured at Poppit where the dog lay beside the hearth fire.

"He misses Wulfwyn," she grumbled, "and I am not droopy."

"And sour," he added as a servant delivered a loaf of fresh, steaming bread. "Does she not look droopy and sour to you, Arnulf?"

"Not in the least," the giant responded, tearing a chunk of bread from the loaf. "She looks like a lady about to inflict a mortal wound to an overlarge magpie."

De Brionne snorted. "You are one to talk of overlarge."

Roscelyn's spirits plummeted as their cheerful banter continued. The realization that she might well be responsible for their deaths sat like lead in her belly and 'twas a struggle to eat.

Yet she could hardly entrust the lives of her people to a man who knew nothing of estates. Nor would de Brionne allow her to manage affairs. He only wanted her instruction so he could manage things on his own.

What would become of her once his instruction was complete, she knew not.

She forced herself to swallow a bite of bread.

Nay, 'twas for the best that she'd sent the scroll. Surely de Brionne would surrender Cyning once it grew clear he could not hold it.

When de Brionne at last stood and gestured for her to rise, she was only too glad to leave the table. Fastening her cloak, she pulled the hood over her head as they stepped outside to gray skies and drizzle.

"Where would you like to begin?" she asked.

"In the granaries, if you please."

She strode toward the barn that held wheat grain, nodding at several peasants as they passed. Once inside, she moved to light an oil lamp, then turned . . .

Her lips parted and her heart dropped to her belly as she stared past de Brionne. Fully half the grain sacks had disappeared in the week since she'd last counted the stores.

'Twas not possible.

"Your expression does little to comfort me," de Brionne remarked.

Her hands shook as she set the lamp on a shelf and snatched her tally sticks from a bin. Just as quickly, she returned the tally sticks to the bin and again picked up the lamp.

"Come, mi'lord." Ere he could object, she grabbed his hand and pulled him outside.

"Where do we go?"

"To check the flour." She led him into the neighboring barn.

She drew up short upon crossing the threshold. In spite of the daily meals the peasants received, there should be more sacks of flour. Many more.

"Mice?" De Brionne's tone brimmed with sarcastic sweetness.

Dear God, was it possible that the village folk had stooped to thievery? Surely not. They had never done so before. And yet . . .

"I await your instruction, mi'lady steward."

De Brionne's caustic tone did naught but stir her temper. Doubtless, he thought her an incompetent fool.

"What do you advise, mi'lady?" he goaded, as if he were challenging her ability to reason.

She glared at him before the lamplight. "Lesson one, mi'lord. Never attempt to bribe goodwill from the village folk."

He scowled. "Bribe?"

"That day at the well, mi'lord. You implied the peasants would lack for naught because of your great wealth. You then yielded to their every demand without demur. The ease with which you were fooled into believing their tales of woe has done naught but encourage their disdain and emboldened them to steal from you."

A muscle knotted in his dark, begrizzled jaw and his countenance grew hard and cold as a blue wasteland. "My thanks for the lesson. If you will excuse me, I shall endeavor to remedy the peasants' low regard for me."

She winced as he stalked off. A pox on her waspish tongue. 'Twas like to get her people killed.

"A moment, mi'lord," she called at his retreating back.

Though she knew he heard her, he continued on, his stride stiff and deliberate.

"Faith, but you do not take instruction well," she quipped.

His steps slowed, but he did not turn to face her.

"Do you not wish to recover the stolen grain?" she fair shouted.

He halted and glanced over his shoulder. "I need no assistance from you to recover aught. I will choose one of every two peasants and gut them until someone confesses to the crime."

"But then you will have no one to dig your trenches or build your walls," she pointed out. Falling to her knees and begging his mercy would be her last resort.

"Fewer people will require less food."

"True," she acquiesced, "but what if you could have all? Your trench, your wall, your food, and the villagers' respect?"

At last, he turned to face her. "I would have to wonder what part you played in this affair that you could so easily recover what has been stolen."

She refused to rise to the insult. "On my honor, mi'lord, I had no idea . . ." She paused.

Had she kept up her duties, she would have realized the moment a sack of grain went missing. But nay. Even as she'd busied herself with the scroll to provide for her people's future, she'd neglected to care for their current needs.

She'd not tallied the stores in a week and now a terrible shortage was imminent.

She took a deep breath and stared de Brionne in the eye. "Truth tell, mi'lord, 'tis I who am responsible for the theft."

For a moment he held her gaze, then his eyes rolled heavenward. "Aye. I can see from your great size that you have gorged yourself on stolen wheat and flour."

" 'Tis no jest, mi'lord. I could have—"

"Why must you shoulder the blame for that over which you have no control?" he demanded. " 'Tis irritating."

"I could have prevented the theft. And I pray I can recover much of what is gone."

He shook his head at her, his look surly. "I suppose you would have me gut you instead of the peasants."

"If 'tis your pleasure to carve on someone, I promise

to make it worth your while. I will scream and cry and moan and groan, and beg your mercy to my final whimpering breath."

His gaze darted down her person from the top of her head to the tips of her toes, then slowed as it traced a return path to her face, lingering on certain places. Abruptly his eyes narrowed with speculation and his countenance reflected the cunning of a predator, a clever but lazy wolf that sought to coax a rabbit into its jaws rather than waste the strength to run it to ground.

'Twas difficult to stand on the spot before such a look, not to turn and flee. Yet perversely 'twas a look that appealed to her senses like nothing she'd ever known.

At last he raised a brow. "Pff. You are too puny to make the task of gutting you worth the effort."

"As you will, mi'lord." She relaxed, feeling as if she'd just escaped being eaten. "Shall we see to the missing grain or no?"

"Very well. Where do you suggest we begin?"

"Lesson number two, mi'lord. When grain is missing, one should first look to the mill."

❧❧❦❧❧

WITHIN THE QUARTER hour, Varin steered his mount along the village lane, cursing the fact that Lady Roscelyn perched sideways behind him.

Bloodygore. He should have made her walk.

He had more important things to consider than the manner in which her small arms clung to his waist.

Weighty matters far more significant than the rub of her breasts against his back. Needs far more pressing than his straining shaft.

Yet even as he fought to concentrate on the fact that he'd been robbed, that heads should currently be rolling with his displeasure . . .

He grimaced as Rok's hoof hit a hole and the animal dipped, bringing the lady's thigh to bear against his hip.

Why must she be so smart, so stubborn, so willing to defend her people at her own expense? 'Twas worse than irritating. 'Twas damn near saintly.

Most annoying of all was her ability to manipulate him into doing her bidding. A bride of Christ, his eye. He would have sworn her sister's delivery to the abbey somehow involved a rendezvous with her husband. 'Twas the reason he'd sent an additional two men to follow Arnulf and the two liegemen who'd accompanied the underlord. Varin had fully expected trouble and the additional men would provide support.

But nothing had occurred. No ambushes. No Saxons or Danes. No attempts by Roscelyn or her sister to escape.

"To the right, mi'lord. The mill is yon."

The way she pointed brought her breasts up hard against his back, sending fresh lightninglike spikes of desire down his spine, straight to his *coillons*.

The sensation near crossed his eyes and he could not have been more glad to see the shores of Normandy than he was to see the mill situated upriver from the village. He urged Rok to a faster pace to reach the building.

Gut her, indeed.

To have the lady in his bed, to watch desire burn her golden eyes liquid, to hear her pant with wanton abandon, to bury his shaft deep inside her . . . that was the form of punishment he preferred. Let her scream and moan and groan and whimper for his touch.

She leapt to the ground the moment he drew rein, then stood aside, waiting for him to dismount.

Swollen and aching, he gritted his teeth while tethering Rok to a willow that stood beside the millpond. 'Twas a miracle he could stand erect, but at least he was again capable of thought.

Not so Roscelyn. Flustered, she was glad to be off the horse and away from such close contact with de Brionne. Leading the way to the mill's entrance, she flapped the neck of her cloak, hoping to ease the heat that consumed her. Would that she could blame such on the sun, but the drizzle of rain was hardly warm.

Nay. Loath though she was to admit it, 'twas de Brionne who caused her to swelter thus. Another moment holding his waist, another brush of her breasts against his solid back, another sway of the horse beneath her hips and she would have died from want.

Want of a paltry Norman, she thought, recalling her response to Lufu's suggestion that she concentrate her efforts on the new Norman lord. Why she should feel aught but hatred for the man was a mystery.

Except she could not deny his consideration of the village folk. Regardless of his self-seeking motives, his kindness to the peasants was unprecedented, as was his kindness in seeing that Wulfwyn reached the abbey. Indeed, though de Brionne had imprisoned Gunderic, he made certain the housecarl was properly fed and even allowed Lufu to check Gunderic's wounds.

Under the circumstances, it seemed grotesquely unfair that de Brionne had unknowingly delivered the means for his own ruin.

"'Twould be nice if we reached the mill before dusk," de Brionne prodded from behind her.

Realizing her steps had slowed to a crawl, she sped up, her sympathy for the man vanishing.

He deliberately raised her ire with his baiting. Lady Honking Goose, indeed. Stealing her composure, leading her to feel like an unfledged nestling—What was she thinking to feel any compassion for the man?

Caught up in her angry musings, she was unprepared for what her eyes beheld upon entering the mill.

She drew up short.

The place was empty. The giant millstones sat silent, no sacks littered the floor, no dust filled the air. The miller shouted no commands to his minions, for they were digging trenches and building walls at the manor.

"Well?" De Brionne planted his hands on his hips. "I see naught of any missing grain."

She shivered, the breath leaking from her mouth in damp, smoky tendrils. Even were the miller present at the mill and working day and night, he could not possibly have ground all the grain that was missing. There should be sacks everywhere.

Ere she could gather her thoughts, de Brionne clasped her elbow and pulled her back outside.

"A moment, mi'lord. Something is very wrong."

"You have the right of that," he snapped, heading for his horse.

She struggled to comprehend the lack of grain bags. Mayhap the miller had moved them to a safer place. 'Twould be foolish to leave so much lying about with no one at the mill to guard against theft. But the only place big enough to hold such great amounts was the wheatary at the manor.

She watched as de Brionne unwound the reins from the willow, then mounted his horse and held out his hand.

Recalling her inability to reason when in such close company with the man, she shook her head. She needed time to think. "If 'tis all the same to you, I will walk back to the manor."

"'Tis not all the same to me. I am in a hurry."

"Then take yourself off."

"What, and leave you to hide every morsel of food in the village? Nay, mi'lady. Give me your hand."

"I tell you, there is more here than meets the eye."

"Do not make me dismount and come fetch you."

Overbearing lout. Slapping her hand in his, she clambered up behind him, kicking his shin in the process. His sharply indrawn breath filled her with satisfaction.

"Well, let us be off. You did say you were in a hurry."

"Aye," he ground. "Best to hold tight. I would not wish you to fall on your tender little derriere."

With that, he spurred the horse forward at such a pace that she indeed had to hold close to remain seated. Her pique quickly ebbed and fear overrode any desire she might have experienced at his nearness. "Mi'lord, please, allow me to question my people ere you go . . ." She swallowed hard. "Ere you go slitting gullets."

At his lack of response, she continued. "As I mentioned, dead peasants will hardly be able to serve you."

Still he said nothing.

She frowned. Could he not hear for the thunder of the horse's hooves?

She clutched his muscled belly and molded herself to his back that she might get her mouth closer to his ear. "Please, mi'lord. If anyone deserves to die, 'tis me. Had I kept to my counting, this would not have happened."

"None will die," he finally spoke, his raised voice lending a harshness to his tone. "My men will search out each hovel and confiscate all until there is not a piece of grain or a measure of flour left in the village."

She winced. "If I may say, the village folk will be equally hard pressed to serve you if you starve them."

"They will not starve. They will come to the manor that their food may be allotted to them and records kept."

Relief as vast and deep as the ocean flooded her.

She rested her cheek against his shoulder blade and closed her eyes. 'Twas an excellent plan, one she would personally ensure met with success, even if she had to work day and night.

"I have but to consider your punishment."

Her eyes flew open and she drew back from his shoulder. "My punishment?"

"You did offer to serve as the scapegoat for your people. I intend to keep you to your word."

NINE

"TOAD-EATING THICKWIT," Roscelyn muttered the following morn where she stood outside her father's bedchamber door awaiting de Brionne's permission to enter.

While he'd spent yesterday afternoon questioning the miller, the baker, and a number of other villagers—to no avail, for the theft remained a puzzle—she'd worked her fingers to the quick counting the confiscated stores, a chore that would take at least a week to complete. And this was her thanks?

A public flogging was near preferable to the task that lay before her. At least 'twould be over quickly, unlike this scourge. Indeed, she'd thought de Brionne to be joking yestereve when he'd pronounced her punishment.

You will present yourself to my chambers and pay me a different compliment each morn.

When she'd balked, he'd added to the sentence.

You will wish me sweet dreams each night ere I retire.

When she'd opened her mouth to protest, he'd threatened to make her kiss his forehead morn and night and his feet as well should she continue to gainsay him.

She started at a loud crash. Shooting a look over her shoulder, she saw the village swill-head, Ricberht, scrambling to right a trestle table. Two other peasants scurried to help him, all the servants appearing anxious and edgy in the wake of de Brionne's actions yesterday.

Roscelyn returned her attention to the bedchamber door. Crossing her arms over her chest, she tapped a foot beneath the hem of her green tunic. She had more important matters to attend than inflating a man's opinion of himself.

The moment she was free this morn, she intended to question several people herself. Though she was nowhere near finished counting, she'd seen enough to know that the missing grain and flour would not be found among the stores confiscated from the village. The realization had struck terror into her heart, and she prayed de Brionne had wealth aplenty.

Not that she'd yet mentioned aught of the matter to him. Until she could present him with a few answers, she feared he might make good his threat on gutting the peasants.

She glared at the door impatiently. Contriving a compliment to pay him under such circumstance was nigh impossible.

Your hair is most attractively arranged this morn.

She rolled her eyes.

Your tunic sets off your eyes to exquisite perfection.

Her lips puckered.

My, *what a lovely red pair of horns on your head, and such a fetching pointed tail.*

She smiled grimly. 'Twas a compliment nearer the truth.

Abruptly the door swung open and a dark-haired man whisked past her ere she could blink.

"His lordship bids you enter." The squire bowed in the man's wake.

She schooled her features. She would not allow such an absurd punishment to rattle her.

Stepping into the windowless chamber, she found de Brionne standing fully clothed and smiling before a candle. A fat rat about to be served a full wheel of cheese, she thought peevishly.

"You may take your leave, Adam."

Once the youth had departed, he turned his attention to her. "Good morning, mi'lady."

Her gaze darted to survey him quicky from head to toe. His hair *was* neatly groomed, she noted, and his blue tunic did indeed set off the color of his eyes.

'Twas all she could do to keep from wincing. Why must he be so handsome?

"Do you not have something to say to me this morn?" He raised his brows expectantly.

"Your mood is very cheerful for a man who's been robbed," she groused. "'Tis absurd that you play at games when you have a thief to catch."

Rather than putting a tuck in his tail, her words only seemed to amuse him. "Is it your desire then to kiss my—"

She held up a hand to halt his words. Opening her mouth, she meant to praise his hair or even his choice of tunics. But at the challenging glint in his eyes, the devil took her tongue.

"The sight of your face is as lovely as a daffodil after an unexpected frost."

His countenance reflected disappointment. "Can you think of nothing more manly than a flower for comparison?"

Shaking his head, he strode past her toward the door. "I suppose 'twill have to do."

She turned her head that he would not see the smile on her lips. If only he realized how black and slimy daffodils appeared several days after a frost.

Without warning, his hand clamped over her shoulder.

Ere she could protest, he spun her about and kissed her.

He released her just as quickly and she stumbled backward.

"To help you think of more manly compliments in future," he explained.

She raised her fingers to her lips and stared at him.

"Come along." He beckoned her out into the hall.

"As you pointed out, we have a thief to capture and time is wasting."

Reeling from the shock of his stolen kiss, she made her way to the table, heat fanning her face.

She should be outraged. She should have slapped him for his effrontery. At the very least, she should have rebuked him.

Instead, she sat at the table beside him and ate what was served without tasting a bite, her gaze lowered. To look at him would only add to her chagrin, for deny it all she would, she'd found pleasure in his kiss.

The instant the meal was over, she rose from the bench.

"A moment, mi'lady." De Brionne halted her. "I would accompany you to the granaries to see the results of yesterday's efforts."

"I have scarce begun to tally everything," she remarked, hoping to dissuade him. She could not hope to go about questioning people with him underfoot. "Do you not have other matters to attend?"

His look grew sharp. "You take exception to my presence?"

"Aye," she huffed. "I have had my fill of daffodils for one morn."

"Daffodils?" Arnulf inquired, rising from the bench opposite them as servants began clearing away the breakfast remains.

De Brionne snorted. "The lady claims my face is as lovely as the daffodil after an unexpected frost."

The giant frowned a moment, then blinked. He pursed his lips and glanced at Roscelyn, the barest hint of merriment sparkling in his hazel eyes. Shaking his head, he cleared his throat. "A daffodil after the frost, eh?"

"Pff." De Brionne waved the question aside and stood. "I would have you take the carpenter and as many men as you require to the forest today. We need more timber for the wall. Once I am finished in the granaries, I will join you."

Arnulf nodded and took himself off, whistling a merry tune.

De Brionne ushered her toward the door. "I have a question or two regarding the miller and the baker."

Roscelyn squinted against the rising sun upon stepping outside. The morn was uncommonly warm and she wished she had time to enjoy it.

"What is it you wish to know about the miller and the baker?" she asked as they made their way to the wheat barn.

They both nodded at the dairymaid and her assistant as they passed, each woman carrying two pails of milk. Then the butcher's boy ran past, near colliding with the soapmaker.

De Brionne shook his head. "I would wait to speak until we gain the privacy of the wheatary."

Within moments they entered the dark musty barn and Roscelyn lit a lamp. "What is it you wish to know?"

De Brionne ignored the question, his gaze traveling over the sacks that filled the barn from floor to ceiling. "'Twould appear all has been recovered," he remarked smugly.

"Indeed, 'twould appear thus," she conceded, "to the untrained eye of a man who knows nothing about estates."

De Brionne's gaze swung to bear on her. "What mean you?"

Abruptly she puckered her lips. The words had flown past her teeth ere she'd thought.

"Are you saying that all has not been recovered?"

Plague take her spiteful tongue, though mayhap 'twas for the best. The sooner de Brionne knew the worst, the sooner they could plan how best to proceed.

Ere they could do aught, she would need to know how much wealth he possessed in order to determine what they could buy.

She strode to a small bin and pulled out a bundle of tally sticks. "You can count?"

"God, no."

She paused at his horrified expression, then dismissed it. "'Tis time and past you learned."

"Nay, mi'lady. Counting is for—".

She raised her brows when he said no more. "Counting is for what?" she prodded at last.

"'Tis not for a seasoned warrior," he snapped.

"Nonsense." She could hardly convince him of the perilous state of affairs if he could not count. "I'll not have you arguing with my every word because you don't understand simple numbers."

He crossed his arms over his chest. "I will not learn to count."

She frowned as a thought struck. Was he afraid he would be too dull-witted to learn the workings of numbers?

"You are an intelligent man, mi'lord," she soothed, unaccountably charmed by his apprehension. "Numbers are not difficult to master. You will see."

"I will not see."

"Come and try," she coaxed. "By week's end, you will be almost as proficient at counting as me."

His look grew surly. "You will do the counting and report your findings to me."

For a moment she puckered her lips. Faith, but he behaved no better than a child.

"Very well," she huffed, her patience at an end. "You do not have enough wheat to carry you through the winter. You wish for proof?"

She marched to the bin and slammed the lid back.

"This is what the manor had after the harvest." She held up a half-dozen bundles of sticks. Tossing one bundle on the ground, she held out the remaining five. "This is what was left after our men departed for battle."

She threw two more bundles on the ground. "That is what has been used since the battle, and this!—" She shook another bundle at him, then dropped it. "—is what was stolen."

She held out two remaining bundles. "This is what is left to feed your men and the entire village. 'Twill scarce see us a fortnight past the new year."

His gaze darted from the bundles in her hand to the bundles on the ground and his jaw knotted. "You exaggerate."

"Indeed, I do. This will be the amount left provided the wheat is measured out in half shares. To use as much as is normal, we would not make Christmas."

He scowled. "Matters cannot be that dire. There is too much here."

"As you will," she said in a conversational tone. "Shall I pass out the wheat in full measures?"

"Nay." He frowned. "I suppose I shall have to trust your word."

"I suppose you shall since you refuse to learn to count."

"Counting is for Sodomites," he snarled.

She blinked and drew back. Had she heard aright? "Sodomites?"

His lip curled in answer.

"Is this a belief that all Normans hold—" She forced a reasonable tone. "—or is it a belief peculiar to you alone?"

"It is a fact obvious to any person with eyes," he huffed. "One need only look at the men who count. 'Tis clear they enjoy the company of other men and animals and I'll have no part of it."

Though heat crawled up her throat and over her face at the frank discussion, she could not resist pointing out the error of his thinking. "But I am no Sodomite."

"Nay, but you are the daughter of a Saxon, are you not?"

Her lips parted and rage stole her breath. Unable to bear the sight of him, she bent and scooped the bundles from the ground.

"Your forgiveness, mi'lady. I did not mean . . ."

She rose and returned the bundles to the bin. If she did not get away from him, she knew not what she might do.

"'Twas a cruel thing to say and I did not mean it."

Closing the lid on the bin, she turned to walk past him.

"Please, mi'lady." He clutched her arm, stalling her.

"I apologize from the depth of my soul. On my honor, I would not deliberately hurt you."

It took all her strength to affect a dispassionate look, not to give in to the warmth of his touch, to ignore his apology. "You have taken everything from me that was dear. My father, my brothers, my land. There is nothing you could say or do that could hurt me at this point."

"Cease," he hissed, pulling her against him.

Her pulse leapt as he wrapped an arm about her waist, holding her close.

"For once you will allow the blame to fall where it should, and that is with me."

He tilted her face up and kissed her, his lips gentle. "Forgive me for my nasty insult," he murmured against her mouth.

She shook her head against the weakness and longing that crept over her.

He ran his tongue over her lips, coaxing and tender. "Please, *mignonne*. Say you forgive me."

She placed her hands on his chest, intending to push him away, but the beat of his heart waylaid her.

Strong and sure, it pulsed through her hands and up her arms, raising her blood, rippling outward through her body.

Drawing on every bit of strength she possessed, she turned her head. "I forgive you."

She held her breath as he stilled. Though he clung to her waist a moment longer, he made no attempt to kiss her again.

"Pff," he groused at last. "You forgave me far too easily."

He dropped his hand from her waist and she stepped away, embarrassment burning her face.

"I shall endeavor to do more damage with my insults in future."

She glanced up to see a teasing glint in his eyes.

"Of all the insufferable . . . If that is all," she snapped, "I have more important things than your odious company to attend."

He cast her a crooked smile. "You enjoyed my kiss?"

She gaped. "Enjoyed your kiss!"

"I thought as much, though you could stand a little instruction at such."

The man was not to be believed. "Is your audacity always so boundless?"

"Aye, 'tis. I believe I shall avail myself of your knowledge and learn to count after all. Though you will not mention such to another soul. I would not wish to cut your tongue from your head. 'Twould ruin you for kissing."

"If 'twill keep you from pawing me, I will cut my own tongue from my head."

"Silly woman. I did not paw you." He raised a brow and cast her a devilish look. "Though if you wish to know how a good pawing feels, I would be delighted to show you."

His words sent a perverse chill of excitement to tingle her nape. Not that she would admit such. Instead she rolled her eyes. "Do you wish to learn to count or no?"

"I will try my hand at it. But if I feel the slightest interest in man or beast—"

"Good lack! Either you will cease your disgusting prattle or I will leave."

He made an exaggerated show of closing his mouth and pursing his lips.

"That is better," she remarked. Returning to the bin, she withdrew one bundle of tallies and moved closer to the door where the light was best. "Come and see."

"A bunch of little red sticks," he grumbled.

"Pay attention," she ordered. "Each notch on a stick indicates a sack of wheat."

"Why are they red?"

"To distinguish them from other tallies."

"Other tallies?"

"Green for barley, blue for rye, brown for oats, white for flour. There are many other things that must be accounted besides wheat."

His gaze darted between the tallies she held and the bags of wheat. "You do all of this counting yourself?"

" 'Tis not difficult, mi'lord."

"Varin."

"Varin?"

"Considering that you have been intimate with me, I think you may safely call me by my first name."

"Intimate with you!"

"Is that not what I said?" he inquired solicitously.

She crossed her arms over her chest and glared at him.

"You are most appealing when you pout thus."

She would not encourage his impertinence by responding, though 'twas difficult to maintain an imposing façade when his compliment caused her to blush. Nor was she pouting.

He chuckled and held up a hand. "Mercy, mi'lady. I promise to behave."

She narrowed an eye and inclined her head.

"On my honor, I will do my best."

"Very well," she huffed. "As I said. 'Tis not difficult to tally the stores."

"Pff. 'Twould take me fully a week just to notch the sticks for the wheat."

"There are tricks to make it more simple. For example, each tally signifies four rings."

"Rings?"

"Rings are comprised of four sacks."

He squinted at the tallies, then shook his head. "I do not see—"

"Here, mi'lord."

"Varin."

"As you will." She knelt on the ground near his feet and crooked her finger for him to join her.

Reluctantly he squatted beside her. "We will now play in the dirt?"

She pointed at four notches and scratched four lines in the earth. "Four sacks of wheat." She circled them and scratched one line beneath the circle. "One ring."

He nodded and gestured for her to continue.

She drew three more circles of four with lines beneath them. "Four rings, one tally stick."

He frowned. "Why do you count them like that instead of in dozens?"

"You catch on quickly, mi'lord. Indeed, the counting does in a way match a dozen."

"I see no dozen."

"It takes a tally's worth of wheat a week to feed a dozen people."

He pulled a face. "That much?"

"You must consider that a full grain sack yields only half a sack of flour after milling, and the miller receives multure—"

"Multure?"

"Multure is the miller's payment for grinding the grain. For every two dozen sacks of grain he grinds, he receives one."

He crossed his eyes, then dragged his hands over his face. "I begin to see why those who count are Sod . . . er, men of peculiar habits. They are driven to madness by such complex reasoning."

She rose and brushed the dirt from her knees. " 'Tis not easy to grasp all at once, but you will soon understand."

He rose to stand beside her, surveying the sacks of grain. "How many people must this serve?"

"Near a hundred."

"How many dozens is that?"

"About eight."

He glanced at her scratchings in the dirt. "So I will lose eight sticks of wheat a week?"

"Nay. You will lose four."

His brow furrowed and he jammed one fist on his hip, the index finger on his other hand jabbing at the lines she'd drawn.

Finally he scowled. "According to what you just told me, I will lose eight."

He was indeed sharp. The realization left her feeling a ridiculous sense of pride in him. "Eight it would be, except as I said, the wheat will have to be given in half measures for it to last beyond the new year."

"Pff. Eights, sticks, dozens, halves, rings. Call it what you will. Why is there so little?"

"If you will recall, mi'lord—" She measured her words. "—there was a great battle recently. I believe you were in attendance."

"So?"

"Half the fields were harvested early to provide food for our men. As a result, we lost fully a third of the normal yield."

"Cease with your numbers. They make no sense to me."

"Wheat requires reaping at a certain time in order to produce its greatest yield," she explained patiently. "Had the fields reached maturity before they were harvested, our men would not have required nearly as much of the total crop."

"How do you intend to make up for this great loss?"

The note of accusation in his tone stirred her temper. As if she had any control over the timing of battles. "I would not need to make up for this great loss if I did not have to feed you and your pack of hungry wolves."

His features hardened. "You'd have had to feed your Saxon men had they returned from battle."

"They'd have returned with enough gold to buy what we lack." She would not tell him of the occasions when they'd returned from war empty handed. "And why, of a sudden, is this *my* loss? As lord of Cyning, 'tis your loss as well."

His look grew surly. "As your lord, I command you

to repair the loss since 'tis you who are responsible for it."

"Mi'lord—"

"Varin."

"Varin! I do not think you understand the enormity of your situation. 'Tis not just the wheat. Along with the peasants, you and your men will have to make do with half measures of everything from ale to cheese. Your horses will have to get by on half their normal fodder. The manor's livestock will have to be slaughtered not only for meat, but so the vetch that the animals consume can be eaten by people."

"Of all the . . . you dare to . . ." He drew himself up, an indignant look on his face. "My men and I will not do with half measures," he snapped. "We most certainly will not eat vetch. 'Tis to us that the defense of Cyning falls and we must keep up our strength. As for our horses . . ."

He scowled. "Know you the value of such animals? Even did they cost nothing, there are only so many bred each year. They cannot be replaced, and you are daft indeed if you think I will leave them to go without nourishment."

"Fine! Take the food from babes' mouths and feed it to your mighty steeds," she hissed. "Gorge yourselves while the village folk starve."

Red stained his tanned complexion. "I would not deny the peasants if the situation warranted."

"If the situation warranted? Think you I speak false?"

"I think you overstate matters."

"Overstate?" She stared hard at him. "As scarce as is

provender at present, 'tis bountiful compared to what you will have come spring. For wont of your trench and your wall, your winter crops will not be sown. Where the spring harvest would save us, we will have nothing. While you promise that none who serve you will starve, I have yet to see this wealth aplenty that you claim to possess."

Abruptly his nostrils flared. "You may trust in my wealth as greatly as I may trust in your ability to count."

The blue of his eyes deepened, then solidified to ice. "'Tis my king's command that I fortify Cyning against attack. Whether through blood and sweat, or by cunning and deceit, I will see my king's will done."

He advanced on her, crowding her backward with his big body.

"You will not dissuade me from my purpose with your claims of imminent starvation. I will not lose the only land I've ever owned because I neglected the building of defensive works."

Her back came up against the wall and she shifted sideways.

He slammed a hand on the wall beside her head to halt her movement. "I will kill any who seek to wrest Cyning from me."

She edged in the other direction, anxious to escape his rage.

His other hand came up and slammed the wall to her other side. "I will never again be a landless beggar. I will marry one of William's nieces and increase my holdings, and no Saxon army, no Danish fleet, and certainly not you will stop me."

TEN

ROSCELYN WAS ONLY too happy to rise from her pallet after a restless night. 'Twas well and good she'd sent Wulfwyn and the scroll to the abbey. De Brionne was a greed-ridden bastard. The only thing he cared for more than land was his king's commands.

"Through blood and sweat, or by cunning and deceit," she muttered. And she was supposed to trust in his wealth?

At the thought, her heartbeat picked up its pace. What if he possessed no wealth?

What if he'd lied in order to gain the peasants' cooperation?

Not bothering to fetch warm water, she washed

quickly with cold water. 'Twas no more chilling than the idea that de Brionne had lied.

If he *had* spoken false of his wealth, only the scroll and the riches it would provide could save Cyning now.

She pulled on a fresh chainse. Regardless, de Brionne would never marry his king's niece. Once the scroll reached the pope, he would not own so much as a plow strip of land with which to support the woman.

Her lips puckered. How she longed to tell the peasants of her suspicions concerning his wealth. 'Twould be a pleasure to see the village folk refuse to dig his trench or build his wall. Let him explain that to his king.

But nay.

Such was apt to get someone killed, for de Brionne was fierce in his determination to complete his defensive works.

Prithee God, let the Normans be gone from England ere we run out of food.

She crossed herself and refused to consider that de Brionne would likely die before England was free.

Cyning would be well rid of the cold-blooded lout, as would she.

"He is vanished." Adam's alarmed voice cut into her thoughts. "The bed linens are untouched from yestermorn."

"Is his sword there?" Arnulf asked, his voice and his footsteps approaching then retreating as he passed the curtain in the direction of the bedchamber.

Roscelyn quickly donned a dark-gray tunic and grabbed her gray cloak. Stepping from the curtain, she near collided with the giant as he returned from the bedchamber.

Upon spying her, he halted. "Have you seen his lordship?"

She shook her head. After wishing him sweet dreams last eve, she'd sought her bed.

Arnulf's worried gaze moved past her to survey the hall.

"Has he disappeared like this before?" she inquired.

"Never."

'Twas absurd that she should feel anxious for him. Like as not, he was out with Elswyth or some other such woman.

Regardless . . .

"He has not slept in his bed?" she asked.

"It appears he may have sat on it, but it is still made."

"When did you last see him?" She could not prevent the rising timbre of her voice.

The giant frowned. "We both sought our beds at the same time yestereve."

"Come." She took the giant's arm. "Let us check with everyone else."

But none had seen or heard Varin after he'd gone to bed. As servants arrived to set up tables for the morning meal, all were questioned, but none claimed any knowledge of his whereabouts.

Meanwhile, her fear increased. There were all manner of accidents that could befall a person. Bludgeoned while trying to break up a brawl amongst drunken peasants. A slip while walking alongside the River Ouse.

Could he swim?

Mayhap he'd gone out riding and been thrown by his great horse.

"Gilbert, Hugh, check out back of the hall," Arnulf ordered. "Roger, John, begin in the kitchens and comb the area to the front of the manor."

The giant strode for the entrance doors.

Roscelyn hurried to keep pace, finding an odd comfort in the big man's presence. "Where do you go?"

"To check with the guards at the gate."

"Let us see if his horse remains in the stables as well," she suggested.

Arnulf nodded and an icy rain pelted them as they struck off.

She pulled her hood over her head, scarce able to see. If the sun had risen, there was little evidence of it and the torches that usually illuminated the manor grounds were gutted before the wet wind.

Mud squished beneath her boots as they made their way along. But ere they reached the stables or the guards at the gate, Roscelyn clutched Arnulf's sleeve and pulled him to a halt.

Light spilled through a crack in the door of the wheatary.

"What is it?" the giant asked.

"There should be no light coming from yon barn." She raised her voice to be heard above the torrent of rain and pointed. "Nor should the door be ajar."

"Wait here." The giant drew his sword and edged forward.

Roscelyn held her breath as his silhouette neared the barn. She blinked against the rain to watch him ease the door open with the tip of his weapon.

Abruptly he sheathed his blade, then motioned for her to join him.

Ushered inside the barn ahead of him, she knew not whether to laugh or cry at the sight that greeted her.

Curled together atop several sacks of grain lay de Brionne and Poppit, Varin's black cloak causing the dog's gray fur to appear silver. Clearly the man had spent the night counting, for her red tallies were scattered on the floor.

The giant moved to shake him. "Wake up."

Varin's eyes were scarce open before he scrambled to stand, stumbling over Poppit.

"What!" Even as he fell to one knee he was drawing his sword.

Poppit barked and bounded to leap on his back, near toppling him.

"Down, dog," he thundered, only to receive a great lick to his face.

"Pff." Arnulf cast them a disgusted look. "The two of you are not worth the spit of a goose."

Roscelyn puckered her lips. What Poppit saw in the man, she knew not.

Except that Varin had sat up all night counting whereas no other lord, not even her father or brothers, would have bothered.

She shook off the sweet feelings his efforts engendered. Now that she knew he was safe, she wanted nothing more than to take herself off. Turning, she started out the door when de Brionne called to her.

"I would that you remain, mi'lady." His tone was conciliatory. "There are a few issues we need to discuss."

Gathering her courage, she fisted her hands in the folds of her cloak and continued out the door. He would

never again command her senses with but a sweet word
or a kind gesture. Not after he'd bared the blackness of
his heart to her.

She'd taken no more than a dozen steps when
Varin's arm wrapped around her waist from behind, lifting her off her feet. The cloak fell from her head and
cold rain drizzled down her nape as he carried her back
inside the barn.

To kick and struggle seemed somehow demeaning
and she refused to lower herself thus. Instead she held
her body rigid and unyielding. "Release me," she gritted
from between clenched teeth.

Though he set her feet on the ground, he maintained his hold on her waist, his front pressed against
her back.

"By your leave, mi'lord." The giant appeared at
once aggravated and flustered. "I shall go call off the
search that has been instigated by your mysterious disappearance."

Without waiting for a response, the big man strode
away, leaving her alone to maintain her anger, which
was fast fading before the warmth of Varin's hold.

Well, not completely alone, she reflected. Poppit
remained, his tongue hanging from his mouth where
he'd dropped to sit on the floor.

"Leave go," she ordered, not daring to glance over
her shoulder.

"Nay. You will hear me out ere I release you."

His warm breath whispered over the top of her head
and she fought the weakness that drifted like an indo-
lent summer breeze over her senses.

"I would say I am sorry for my cruel words yesterday, but 'tis your own fault. Have you any idea of the passions you stir in me?"

She winced at his ragged tone and the wistful feelings it inspired.

"You pit me against myself until I scarce know what I am saying. 'Twas not my intent to bully you. 'Tis just . . ."

She felt his chest expand against her back as he took a deep breath. Then he drew her closer and his chin brushed the top her head.

She held her breath against the tumultuous whirlwind that threatened to carry her away.

"I am sorry for the losses you have suffered." He gave her waist a gentle squeeze, lending credence to his words. "I truly regret the misery you have endured. But I cannot deny that I am profoundly glad that Cyning has fallen to me. Believe what you will, but de Brionne was once a revered name in Normandy. I seek only that which I have lost, just as you would seek to recover the family you have lost if 'twere possible."

By all that was holy, she would feel no sympathy for the man. "'Twould seem you would better recover whatever 'tis that you've lost in the place where you lost it."

His chest again expanded against her back with his breath. "Would that such were possible."

Was it her imagination or did bitterness tinge his tone? "Why is it not possible?" she asked quietly, unaccountably troubled.

"It is no longer there."

"You speak in riddles, mi'lord."

"'Tis no secret, mi'lady." Though the bitterness left

his tone, she could feel the tension that coiled through his body. "My father betrayed William to the French king when I was a babe. My mother took her own life rather than bear the shame. Chances are you will hear of it sooner or later when lords and ladies come calling at Cyning."

"But you were raised at court," she puzzled. "Why did William not return your holdings once you were of age?"

His tone grew self-deprecating. "I was held hostage at court until it became clear that my father would not ransom me."

"Your father lived?"

"He may still live, for all I know. He didn't just betray William. He deserted my mother and me for the promise of great rewards at the French court."

"But William kept you," she persisted, anxious to hear that his entire life had not been miserable.

"He kept me as a slave."

Roscelyn scowled. "How can you serve a man who treated you thus?"

"Had William not treated me thus, I would not be the man I am today, and for that I am thankful."

"Thankful?" She could not prevent the rage she felt against his king from staining her voice. "He stole your land and—"

"He did not steal my land, *mignonne*. He gave the lands of a traitor to one of his half sister's husbands."

Roscelyn pursed her lips. "Is it one of their daughters that you will marry?" she asked at last.

"Aye."

Her spirits plummeted so low that even the torchlight appeared dimmer. Varin would indeed need an estate as vast as Cyning's to provide for a niece of royalty.

She frowned as another thought occurred. "Has this king's niece any brothers?"

"Nay. She has only two other sisters."

"I see." Roscelyn stared at the rainwater seeping beneath the barn door. Clearly Varin would one day inherit his family estate through marriage. 'Twas no more than she would do were their positions reversed.

If only she could banish the emptiness that the knowledge wrought.

She changed the subject. "So how is it that you managed to gain William's favor?"

"That was easy. I broke Arnulf's nose in a wrestling match."

She twisted in his embrace to stare at him. "You broke Arnulf's nose?"

He grinned. "Aye. And I had to cheat like the devil to do it."

"You cheated your friend?"

"We were not friends at the time. Arnulf was William's champion and 'twas an opportunity to bring myself to William's attention." He rubbed her waist playfully. "Arnulf had got the best of me until I managed to grab a small rock and hide it in my fist. Clever, eh?"

"Clever!"

"I thought you'd agree."

She scowled at him. "I do not agree. I cannot believe Arnulf has aught to do with you."

"Pff. The overgrown oaf would have smothered me

had I not done something. Meanwhile, I broke three knuckles in the bargain. Have you no sympathy for me?"

His deep voice combined with the warmth of his body and the hold of his powerful arms around her waist until she could fight her senses no more.

Would that she could remain in his embrace forever, that she could take the security and comfort he offered and store it deep inside her for all time.

When he turned her in his arms and kissed her, she welcomed the gentle touch of his lips. Closed her eyes and rested her palms against his chest. Never had a man held her with such tenderness.

His fingers stroked the back of her hand while his thumb massaged her palm, then slid up her throat to cup her chin, tilting her face that her mouth would be more accessible to his assault.

He prodded her lips open with his tongue and slipped past her teeth, light and teasing, encouraging her to respond, as if she could resist. 'Twas like she'd drank some potion that inspired her senses and emboldened her to explore, and the more she discovered, the more she sought.

His breathing deepened, the kiss no longer gentle, but demanding. Cocksure. An unspoken promise that he was capable of fulfilling her every want, would see to her every need. And lest she doubt, his hand moved from her chin to massage her breast, drawing her nipple to stiff erection, proving his mastery over her.

The hand about her waist pulled her closer, as if he could bury his body within hers.

She drank of his mouth that he might quench her

hot thirst. She rubbed her breasts against his hand and chest that he might assuage the ache that throbbed in her nipples. She ground her hips against his that he might provide surcease from the moist, squirmy feeling that assailed her.

Dropping his hand from her breast to join the other at her waist, he swayed to and fro, turning ever so slightly. 'Twas like some ancient, pagan dance, a ritual that celebrated a feast of the flesh. Her feet moved without effort, her hips undulating to the slow rhythm he set.

Abruptly realization struck and her eyes flew open. The rhythm, the movement—'twas no pagan dance. The man was ever so slowly maneuvering toward the grain sacks where he'd been sleeping.

Terror swooped over her like a great black shroud. Shaken to her very soul, she did the first thing that came to her head.

In keeping with his next step, she ground the heel of her boot squarely on his toes.

Her release was instant, his howl eliciting a similar response from Poppit.

It required no effort to affect a look of horror, and she covered her mouth. "Are you all right?" She spoke through her hand.

"Bloodygore! Quiet, dog!" Clutching his foot, he hopped the remainder of the distance to the grain sacks and plopped on one.

"I am so sorry for my clumsy feet."

He shook his head and removed his boot to examine his toes. "Nay." His patient tone was clearly forced. "'Tis not your fault. 'Twas but an accident."

"Look, mi'lord. The rain has ceased. Let us go to the hall that we may break our fast."

At her suggestion, he jerked his head up to stare at her. "You did it apurpose," he snarled.

She mustered an indignant gasp. "I most certainly did not."

He eyed her with suspicion, then wrinkled his nose. "Where is my compliment this morn?"

Her lips puckered. A compliment. Poppit licked her hand and she scratched his ears while searching for something to say.

Abruptly she glanced down at the dog and 'twas all she could do to keep from cackling like an evil old crone. She would give him a compliment. Had he not feared he would develop an interest in animals once he learned to count? And here he'd slept with Poppit.

"You possess all the attributes of a great counter. Now might we go that I may get some dry clothing and eat?"

He jammed his foot back in his boot and rose. "There is something about your compliments that bespeak falseness."

He hobbled forward and gestured for her to precede him, staying well clear of her feet.

ELEVEN

VARIN EYED Roscelyn where she sat beside him at the table. She'd stepped on his toes apurpose. He would swear to it.

You possess all the attributes of a great counter.

There was an insult in her compliment as well. He was sure of it.

Not that he could blame her. Whatever had possessed him to try to tumble her atop a host of grain sacks in a barn? Especially when he'd sought only to apologize for his appalling behavior yestermorn.

He'd had no right to treat her with such meanness, and the fact had sat like sour wine in his gut all the while he'd counted last night.

Roscelyn had been nothing but honest and forth-right since his arrival at Cyning. Yet each time something out of the ordinary occurred, whether a demand to escort a child to an abbey or the theft of grain and flour, he immediately grew suspicious of her.

Not that he shouldn't be vigilant where she was concerned. To ignore the threat her husband represented would be foolhardy. But to leap to conclusions at her every word was not only a waste of his energy, 'twas detrimental to his goals.

Two boys delivered honey and steaming loaves of bread and he tore a chunk from the tray that was set before him.

If he were to succeed as lord of Cyning, he needed Roscelyn's help until his steward arrived. Indeed, judging from what little he'd learned thus far about the manor's affairs, he was as dependent on her as a babe newly birthed.

Frowning, he chewed with slow deliberation.

Mayhap that was what caused him to so mistrust her. 'Twas most uncomfortable to place oneself in the hands of another for safekeeping, especially when those little hands belonged to a Saxon.

Still, 'twas no excuse for his treatment of her yestermorn. To think he'd implied she was the daughter of a Sodomite.

He tore another chunk of bread from the loaf. Worse, he'd truly believed her to be exaggerating the horrendous lack of provender.

Like an idiot, he'd made jokes and teased her while she'd tried to explain the bleakness of the situation. And when his thick head had finally managed to grasp the truth of the matter, he'd immediately sought to place the blame for the stolen stores on her.

Meanwhile, he'd poisoned himself with mistaken conclusions at her implied suggestion that he should be planting crops instead of building fortifications.

She was the enemy.

She was conspiring against him.

She hoped to convince him to quit his defensive works that the manor would be left vulnerable to a Saxon attack.

A wedge of cheese was set before him and he carved a slice. 'Twas unsettling that he'd thus allowed rage to rule his reason. In future he must better control himself around Roscelyn.

But, bloodygore, he'd never met another woman like her. He slid a glance at her where she sat drizzling honey over her bread.

If he were honest with himself, he would admit that he no longer desired merely to charm information from her. Indeed, the idea was somewhat repulsive and he'd deliberately avoided asking aught of her husband.

Nay, he wanted more. He wanted Roscelyn for the simple pleasure of having her.

"I say, Varin?"

He glanced up to find Arnulf regarding him with raised brows.

"Aye?"

"I asked if we should cut more timber this morn, considering the rain."

He realized the servants were carting away the trays and serving boards. The meal was through and he could scarce recall eating.

"Nay." He returned his attention to Arnulf. "Let us

do the cutting and hauling when the weather is dry. For the moment we had best continue lining the trench with rocks. Mayhap this afternoon we can continue with the digging."

The giant nodded and rose.

"A moment." Varin halted him. "I would that you send Ulric and Hogarth to me straightaway."

"As you will." Arnulf nodded. Beckoning the other liegemen, he set off.

"Mi'lord," Roscelyn began once they were alone.

"Varin."

"Varin." She bowed her head. " 'Twas noble of you to practice your counting."

"Now there is a compliment. Noble, you say?"

She smiled. "I thought you might like it."

Plague take his pestering inwit for insisting he did not deserve the praise. Truth tell he'd practiced the counting only because he'd hoped to prove her wrong. A splendid waste of his time, not that he would admit as much to Roscelyn.

In fact, now that he thought on it, his counting *had* served one purpose. It had convinced him to consider the need to sow the winter crops.

"Might I inquire why you wish to speak with Ulric and Hogarth?" Though the lady yet smiled, there was hesitation in her eyes.

"You may not. You may . . . Sit," he ordered as she rose. "I did not give you leave."

"Your pardon," she huffed, plopping back on the bench. "I thought you wished me gone while you spoke to Hogarth and Ulric."

"If I want you gone, I will say so."

She crossed her arms over her chest, and he eyed her rigid jaw, her puckered lips, the tilt of her little nose. This was the wench he wanted for the simple pleasure of having her?

He shook his head at his own obvious lack of sanity. Aye, she was beautiful, but he'd known many beautiful women. Why he should find this woman in particular so appealing was a mystery he could scarce wait to solve.

Indeed, her courage, her stubbornness, her sharp wits and quick tongue—the very fact that she was Saxon and he Norman—all should dispel any interest he might find in the woman. Yet 'twas most exciting to think of her between his sheets.

The arrival of Hogarth and Ulric interrupted his pleasant musings.

"Ye wished to see us, Sir Varin?" Hogarth inquired, his lined face curious but not fearful as it had been that first day they'd worked side by side in the trench.

Varin gestured at the place Arnulf had vacated. "Kindly join us a moment. I would hear from you both what you know of winter planting."

A frown claimed Ulric's ruddy complexion. "Yer pardon, Sir Varin, but Lady Ros knows more 'bouts such than us."

"Be that as it may—" He waved Ulric's comment aside. "—I would hear from each of you what your usual toils would consist of were you not busy with the trench and the wall."

Hogarth scratched his thinning pate. "We'd of been done with the plowin' and sowin' by now, eh, Ulric?"

"Aye, 'cept fer this year we might still be sowin', wot with the great battle and all."

Varin frowned. "Normally you would be finished with the sowing?"

Both men nodded, and Ulric added, "Give or take a week. 'Tis Lufu wot tells us when to plant."

"The witchwife?"

"Her charts of the heavens determine the best time for planting," Roscelyn interjected.

"Is there any village affair in which the crone does not have a hand?" he demanded sourly, though in truth he was angry with himself.

Plague take his toenails, but 'twould appear Roscelyn had done well to tell him about the winter crops. He would have to see to the matter before he continued pursuing the mystery of the missing grain and flour.

But once the sowing was complete . . .

"'Twould seem that once your sowing was done you would have naught to do until spring."

The seams on Hogarth's face deepened and he lowered his gaze. Meanwhile, Ulric's thick jaw hardened.

Now what? Clearly both men had taken exception to his question.

"Take no offense," Roscelyn soothed. "His lordship is unused to the daily affairs of living. He has a steward who usually sees to such duties."

"I meant no insult," he added. "'Tis just that I . . . I have spent most of my life on the battlefield. Please, tell me what you do after sowing the crops."

Ulric cleared his throat. "'Tis the time when we sees to repairs."

"Repairs?"

"Aye." Hogarth nodded. "We patches our roofs and walls. We tends to the combin' of wool and the weavin' of cloth."

Ulric leaned forward, resting his elbows on the table. "We fixes the fences wot pens the animals and the hedgerows wot keeps the animals from the fields. And then there's the repairs to the manor."

Hogarth rolled his eyes. "The dovecote's 'bouts to fall over. 'Twon't be no easy task to shore it up."

"Likely have to tear it down and start all over," Ulric agreed.

"Don't forget the cow byre," Lady Roscelyn added.

"You have the right of that." Hogarth shook his head. "Don't knows wot will collapse first."

Varin listened, appalled by his own stupidity. He should have realized there was no rest for the peasants.

As the three discussed the work that needed doing, he noted their easy manner with one another. They smiled, they winced, they shook their heads and chuckled, they gestured and argued points, and . . .

His soul twisted and he knotted his fists in his lap beneath the table.

How could he have questioned Roscelyn's authority on the state of affairs? The evidence was everywhere. The dilapidated barns, the tattered clothing that Ulric and Hogarth wore, the fact that a lady of the manor was reduced to mucking about in a sheep pen.

How could he be so dull-witted?

"Your pardon," he interrupted the conversation, and nodded at the men. "My thanks for sharing your knowledge. I would like to speak with you further at the first opportunity. For now, the lady and I must inspect the fields."

❧❧❧

THOUGH THE RAIN had stopped, the sky remained gray as Roscelyn rode behind Varin toward the fields. She should feel naught but anger that he'd sought to tumble her in the wheat barn.

She grimaced. Truth tell, she'd enjoyed his advances. She'd certainly not asked him to stop.

The fact that he'd sat up all night trying to tally the wheat beat bittersweet in her heart. That he'd called upon Ulric and Hogarth for their knowledge on sowing the fields was a mark of his respect for the two men. 'Twas more than she hoped that he would at least consider planting the fields.

"Are you going to direct me on where to ride?" Varin pulled her from her reverie. "Or shall I guess?"

Realizing they'd reached the end of the village lane, she pointed left, then winced as her breasts pressed against his back.

"That—" She cleared her throat. "That way."

They took the droveway that ran through the middle of the fields, halting midway along the furrowed rows.

"Hold." De Brionne turned in the saddle and pressed a hand against her belly as she made to dismount, sending darts of squirminess to enflame her senses.

"If 'tis all the same to you, I'd prefer to remain in the saddle that I may better see."

"Very well. Bodewell furlong runs from there . . ." She leaned back to prevent her chest from touching his back and pointed at a strip of furrows. " . . . to the meadow, yon."

She swept her hand right, then gritted her teeth as her breasts yet again made contact with him.

Great toads! "Would you object if I dismounted?"

He glanced over his shoulder at her. "Yes, I *would* object."

"What is it to you?" she groused. "While you sit comfortably, I can scarce move without . . . without . . ."

Turning slightly in the saddle, he raised a brow. "Without what?"

"I can scarce move. That is all."

"You mean you can scarce move without your breasts rubbing my back. . . . Here, easy. You'll unsettle Rok with all your thrashing."

She could not get from the horse fast enough. The moment her feet hit the ground, she turned to glare at him. "With luck, the brute will throw you and trample the brains from your odious head."

"You cannot mean it. The sight of so much blood would make you sick for days."

"I'm sure your blood would prove the exception."

He raised a brow and shook his head. "Never have I met a woman with such . . . delicate sensibilities. Forgive me. I await your instruction."

She halted. "Delicate sensibilities, my eye. You will promise to behave or I shall return to the manor forthwith."

His shoulders slumped and his nose wrinkled. "I promise," he grumbled.

"Dismount. I'll not break my neck looking up at you all morn."

He did her bidding and she leveled a threatening look on him when he adjusted the crutch of his chausses.

"I cannot help it," he defended himself.

Keeping her distance, she again pointed at the fields. "Bodewell furlong runs from there, yon."

De Brionne, frowned, eyeing the area she indicated. "That is all?"

"That is all?" she repeated.

He threaded his horse's reins through his fingers. "I cannot see how that small patch of land will support me and my men."

She should no longer he astounded by his ignorance, she told herself. "Mi'lord—"

"Varin," he corrected.

"Varin. Along with Bodewell furlong, you also hold Littleholly—" She pointed out another furrowed patch of land."—and the Willows, which runs to the river over there."

His brow remained drawn as he surveyed the fields. "Come. Let us walk to the river. I can scarce see the field for the slope of the land, and Rok can have a drink as well."

She nodded and he led the horse forward.

"Is it too late to plow and sow the winter crops?" he asked as they walked along.

"I cannot imagine that 'tis too late, though the yield may be much less than normal. Lufu would know more on the subject."

"Pff. I know not why the village folk have need of

you, or me, or anyone. It seems the old crone rules the roost."

She shook her head and smiled at the thought. "Lufu's disposition does not lend itself well to arbitrary matters."

"That is a vast understatement."

"Have a care, mi'lord. Lufu is not a good enemy to make."

He cast her a sour look. "You do not exhibit any fear of the woman."

"Ha." She returned his look with amusement. "'Tis Lufu who fears me, or rather the lack of me. If I were not about, she might be forced to listen to the peasants' complaints, and I do believe she would rather swallow poison."

They reached the river and Varin led the horse to the water while she stood on the bank.

Faith, but the two were a handsome pair, a mighty god and his steed come to carry the sun across the sky. Indeed, considering the warmth he engendered in her body, the longing she felt for his strength, the thirst that wilted her will at his touch, Varin could be the sun's earthly brother.

She lowered her gaze as he led the horse from the river and tethered its reins around a willow.

Surveying the fields they'd traversed, he crossed his arms over his chest. "I suppose 'twould be sufficient to feed the manor."

"Nay, mi'lord—"

"Varin."

"As you will, Varin," she acquiesced. "These fields

will not nearly provide for the manor's needs. Two-thirds of a furlong scarce feeds a family of six."

Scowling, he turned to face her. "If two-thirds feeds a family of six, then 'twould seem I have a full furlong more than I need."

She sighed patiently. 'Twas like trying to hold a small child still at Sunday mass. "Indeed, 'twould seem thus."

At the glint of satisfaction in his eyes, she wagged a finger at him. "One of your fields will always lie fallow to repair the soil."

His gaze scanned two fields. "I still have more than I need."

Though it disturbed her to raise the subject, she did so anyway. "Presumably you will have a family to feed."

"I have told you I am not married."

"And I suppose you are far too pious to produce heirs with your king's niece." She snorted. "Judging from the looks the peasant girls cast your way, Cyning will be overrun with your illegitimate offspring nine months hence."

His features brightened even as he clucked his tongue. "'Tis unbecoming for a lady to speak of such. You sound like a jealous fishwife."

"Jealous! Of you?"

"Even you will admit I am most handsome." He cast her a winsome smile and stepped closer to her.

She rolled her eyes. 'Twas her own fault for introducing the matter, but good lack, the man had not a shred of decency.

"Come, mi'lady. Say you find me handsome."

She ignored his ridiculous banter. "Your men will have families. On harvest boon days, you will have to feed the entire village. Meanwhile, you also have animals to feed."

His shoulders slumped. "The villagers have animals," he groused. "Yet they survive on two-thirds a furlong."

"Aye. They own a few chickens, a goat, mayhap a few pigs and sheep."

"A few chickens? There are so many that I wonder how anyone can complain of hunger."

"Chickens are necessary for eggs and henhouses are robbed by all manner of wild animals. Nor do the villagers possess such stock by the scores as do you. Have you any idea how much your Norman horses eat?"

"I am a lord of the realm," he snapped peevishly. " 'Tis not my duty know such."

" 'Twas not a challenge, mi'lord."

"Varin," he growled.

"Varin!" She planted her hands on her hips. "Lord or no, you had best learn to count, and while you're at it, you'd best learn to write as well. Otherwise you will not know how much to accord for whom or what. Nor will you know if your steward is stealing from you."

De Brionne's nostrils flared and the sinew in his jaw knotted.

"If 'tis your wish for my instruction, then cease your huffing and puffing."

He narrowed an eye at her. Then abruptly a lazy grin claimed his lips and he sidled toward her. "You are very cute."

Warmth rode across her face and she held up a hand. "Your words are overly familiar and you stand too close."

"I do not believe my nearness is half as familiar as your discussion regarding my illegitimate offspring."

"'Twas not meant as a personal . . . I mean . . ."

The lowly worm fair beamed at her inability to deny his statement. 'Twas no easy task to unclamp her teeth that she could speak. "My intent was to point out that you would someday have a family, which you would presumably feed."

"'Twas quite a compliment, all the same. Is it all the peasant girls who lust after me or only a few?"

"Can you think of nothing else?" she demanded.

"Is the number so great that I might use them to learn to count?"

"Another word and I shall take leave."

"Oh, my. I see I have again distressed your prudish, er, delicate sensibilities. My apologies."

She drew herself up. "You care not one whit if you distress me."

"Admit it, mi'lady. You enjoy my company."

"I will admit no such thing."

"Shall I prove it to you?"

He took a step closer and her heart pitter-pattered like a silly young girl's. Excitement refused her to give ground. "Prove what?"

"How much you enjoy my company."

Her gaze darted from the deep blue of his eyes to his lips, her pulse racing at the memory of their earlier encounter.

He reached out to take her arm in a gentle grasp and tugged her toward him. Then he lowered his lips to hers.

When she turned her head, he nibbled at her cheek and ear. Then his tongue traced a soft, moist path to her throat.

She opened her mouth to deny him, but God help her. With one beat of her heart, her body was on fire. 'Twas as if he were the only water in hell's searing inferno, her only hope for relief from her blistering senses.

How sweet to feel his lips on her. How enticing.

He released her arm to enfold her in his embrace and she mirrored his actions, wrapping her arms around his waist. Her hands slid upward to knead the sinew that strapped his back, as if she could absorb his power.

When his lips returned to hers, she took his tongue in her mouth without hesitation. Ragged breathing blew hard in her ears, though she was not sure whether 'twas his or hers.

Then he captured her tongue with his teeth and coaxed her inside his mouth, tasting her, drawing on her, inviting her deeper.

He leaned into her, forcing her back to arch, and she moaned as her breasts were crushed against his chest. His hands bunched the clothing at her waist and she felt his hard shaft press against her.

She ground her hips against him while his hands moved to hold her there, forcing her to match the stroke of his rhythm. She adjusted her stance, spreading her trembling legs, uncertain what drove her to do so, only that she needed to be much closer.

A groan tore from his chest and he fumbled with

her skirts. She felt his hand move between her thighs and struggled to make herself more available to him, though how she could do so, she knew not.

Suddenly he withdrew his hand. When he pulled his mouth away, she felt like shrieking with frustration. Quivering and expectant, she awaited his next move.

When he did nothing, she opened her eyes to slits.

At the look on his face, her eyes opened wide and her breath caught.

The lowly bastard was regarding her like a fat tom-cat who'd just feasted on a field of mice.

"There, you see? You enjoy my company."

"Ohhh," she huffed. "Release me."

He raised a brow. "You first."

She blinked, then snatched her arms from around his waist and swatted at his hands. "Lecherous brute."

"And you are Lady Demure?"

He moved one hand to trace her lips with a finger—a finger yet damp with the evidence of her desire. He clucked his tongue. "'Tis quite an example of your un-willingness."

She tore from his grasp. "You are the most vile, loathsome, despicable . . ."

Her words faltered at his wicked grin. "I would never have guessed that such a sanctimonious little despot possessed such a passionate nature."

Without another word, she spun and half walked, half ran toward the village. Though his deep chuckle burned her ears, 'twas nothing compared to the secret heat that smoldered between her thighs.

Yet even as she raced from his embrace, two questions matched her stride for stride.

What had become of her hatred?

When had she begun to enjoy the challenge of the man?

"Come, mi'lady." Varin caught up with her just as she reached the village lane and held out his hand.

Pointedly ignoring him, she marched on.

He brought his horse up to ride beside her. "We have much more to do ere the day is through."

She clamped her teeth together, refusing to respond.

"I thought we might put our heads together," he cajoled, "and try to determine what became of the missing grain and flour."

"I believe our heads have been together enough for one day," she snapped.

"I was hoping, as well, that you might agree to consider where best I might commit my wealth."

She halted so abruptly that his mount was several paces past her before he could rein the horse to a halt.

"'Twould be my pleasure to tell you where you might *commit*—" She emphasized the word. "—your wealth. I'm certain 'tis a place with which you are quite familiar since 'tis the same place from whence your foul mouth takes inspiration."

De Brionne's lips twitched with amusement even as he attempted to foist an insulted look upon her, a fact that only added to her annoyance.

When a full-blown gale of laughter issued from him, she rolled her eyes. Odious man. She stomped off down the village lane.

"Ah, mi'lady," he called to her retreating back. "You are are more rich than the sweetest of cream."

TWELVE

C ERDIC APPROACHED Elswyth's not long after sunset. Though they were scheduled to meet at their place in the forest two days hence, he was anxious to put his plans into motion.

Mud sucked at the soles of his boots where he carefully cut across the droveway, the same droveway where he'd spied his wife and her Norman lover earlier. He was just returning from the abbey and had paused to watch them traverse the fields. 'Twas quite a display he'd witnessed from the concealment of the forest.

Not that it mattered. He had Wulfwyn. And while it had required no little amount of cleverness and deceit on his part, he'd managed to secure the secret scroll from the abbess. Or rather half of the scroll.

'Twas the reason he was anxious to put his plans into motion. Roscelyn held the other half of the scroll and he intended to have it from her as quickly as possible.

Meanwhile, he knew not how long he could tolerate Wulfwyn's presence. The girl continually babbled, speaking to the dead and all manner of demons.

He shivered. Did he not need her to force Roscelyn to his will, he would have killed her ere now. As it was, he did his best to stay well clear of the girl.

Without warning, torchlight appeared ahead of him, outlining several cottages. He dropped to a crouch, though he should be safe enough at this distance.

'Twas the old witchwife. He watched her walk down the lane in the direction of her cottage, the torch scattering shadows and flickering light as she went. He rose from his crouch as she reached a bend in the lane.

In the next instant, he again crouched when she paused and turned in his direction. For a moment she stood there, a crone from the depths of hell carrying the fire of Satan. Then she turned and continued on around the bend.

Cerdic swiped the back of his prickling neck and rose. God be damned, but Wulfwyn had him spooked.

Striding forward, he reached Elswyth's without further incident, glad to find her yet awake.

"Cerdic!" She started at the sight of him. "What do you here?"

"I have just arrived from the abbey."

"You risk much in coming so early," she chided. "Were you able to fetch Wulfwyn?"

"Aye." He smiled, a sudden confidence filling him. "Has all gone well in my absence?"

"It has not," she huffed. "The Normans have discovered your theft and have confiscated all the grain and flour in the village. By Roscelyn's command this very eve, we must all abide on half measures of food. Meanwhile, she feeds the Normans to their content."

"Fear not, mi'lady," he soothed. "Your reward is near at hand."

She raised a skeptical brow. "Oh?"

He stroked his beard and his gaze ran the length of her. "Do you think you might deliver this to Roscelyn for me—" He pulled a lock of red hair from a pouch at his waist. "—along with a message?"

A long, weary sigh escaped her mouth. " 'Tis e'er my pleasure to serve you, mi'lord."

'Twas yet early when he left Elswyth's, and he was most grateful that he would not much longer have to suffer her whining complaints. Once he met with Roscelyn, he would rid himself of Elswyth once and for all.

Abruptly a door opened to his right and light spilled out into the lane. He squinted into the surprised eyes of an old cottar woman. Turning his head, he hurried down the lane.

A pox on the old bitch. Had she recognized him?

VARIN LAY on his back in bed and stared into the darkness, unable to sleep. After much coaxing and scraping and begging, he'd finally succeeded in gaining Roscelyn's cooperation. Together they'd questioned a number of people about the missing stores, including several of his own men.

'Twas Roscelyn who'd managed to figure out how the theft had been carried out.

He ran a hand over his grizzled jaw.

On two occasions the baker had spoken to a man loading a cart at the granaries. The man claimed to be one of Varin's liegemen charged by Varin to deliver grain to the mill. The baker, not acquainted with all the Normans at Cyning, had assumed the man spoke the truth.

'Twas a story Varin's man Hugh had confirmed, though with a different twist. On a number of occasions while standing guard at the manor's gates, Hugh had seen the same man with the cart. Except the man claimed to be a peasant sent by Roscelyn to fetch grain for milling.

Varin scowled into the darkness. Knowing how the grain and flour had disappeared had only raised more disturbing issues.

The man in the cart clearly knew Cyning. He'd known where to fetch the grain and flour, he'd devised different stories to cover his tracks, and he had known Roscelyn's name. Yet a description of the man provided no clues to his identity. Roscelyn could not place him, nor could anyone else.

His thoughts skipped forward to the evening he'd spent with Roscelyn counting his money.

Taking a deep breath, he held it before he exhaled.

She'd not had to say aught. He'd known by the crestfallen look on her face that his wealth was not as plentiful as he'd imagined.

Not that they would starve, praise the saints. Rather, they would have to manage on half measures of food for the foreseeable future.

He would definitely have to plant—

"To arms! To arms!"

His hackles rose and he bolted to sit up. 'Twas his burly liegemen Gilbert's voice.

He leapt from the bed and threw open the door to find the man racing in his direction, a torch to hand.

"The village, mi'lord. We are under attack."

Adam followed on Gilbert's heels and within moments Varin was dressed and armored. "Go assist any who need help with their byrnies," he ordered the squire, belting his sword at his hip.

Coming from the bedchamber, he noted Lady Roscelyn's distressed features where she peeped through the curtain. "You will stay here," he commanded.

After shouting orders for half his men to remain guarding the manor and the Saxon housecarl, he headed outside to the stables where Rok stood saddled and waiting. "Well done," he commended the stable master, swinging up into the saddle.

'Twas then he noticed the big dog. Illuminated by the glow of a torch, the animal's eyes watched him with burning intensity.

"Fetch a rope," Varin ordered the stable master. "Bind that cur as you will, but make certain he does not follow me."

The man quickly did his bidding, and Varin turned his attention to his men. "Move, move!" he exhorted as the liegemen hurried for their mounts.

Not waiting any longer, he dug his spurs in Rok's sides and the destrier leapt forward.

Flames lit the night sky as he thundered toward the village. Upon gaining the lane, he was forced to slow his pace to avoid trampling peasants.

Screams, cries, and shouts rent the smoke-choked air and people rushed to and from the well with buckets of water.

He halted and surveyed the people while the flames roared. If the village were yet under attack, he could not tell.

"Save us!" A woman clutched his leg and Rok shuffled.

"Where are the attackers?" he demanded.

The woman's eyes fair rolled in her head and she gripped his leg more tightly.

"Calm yourself. You are safe. Is the village still under attack?"

"I don't knows," she wailed.

Bloodygore. 'Twas complete chaos.

"Sir Varin!" Ulric's voice reached his ears and he looked to see the bull-necked man fighting the crowd to reach him.

"Are we yet under attack?" Varin bellowed.

The man gestured at a flaming hut, then began clearing a path through the knot of people. "Move aside! Aside, I says. Let his lordship through."

Varin pried at the peasant woman's hand where she yet clutched his leg. "Move, or you will be trampled."

Arnulf arrived to rein in beside him.

"Look. The giant!" a child's voice shrilled above the clamor. "The giant is come."

A small girl, perhaps seven or eight, ran to the underlord's side. "Sir Arnulf. Can ye blows the fire out?"

"Will ye kills the lowly muckers wot did it?" A boy joined the girl.

Walther and Roger arrived and Varin was finally able to nudge Rok forward along the path Ulric had created.

"Mi'lord Varin!"

He squinted, trying to determine the identity of the man who ran toward him. "Hogarth?"

Faith, he scarce recognized the fuller for his blackened face.

"You are uninjured?" he asked.

The man nodded, gulping air. "Near a dozen men. Looted a good dozen huts." He clutched his chest and panted. "Gone. To the forest."

Without warning, the man dropped to his knees. He swayed once, then collapsed.

"Christ's bloody bones." Varin fair leapt from Rok and tossed his reins to Roger. "Arnulf. Let us get him to the witchwife's."

The giant scooped the unconscious man from the ground and Varin hurried forward. The old woman was standing outside her door and motioned them inside the moment she spied them.

Arnulf had to fair bend double upon entering the cottage, but once Hogarth was laid on a pallet, the witchwife quickly located three sword wounds.

Leaving the man in the woman's capable hands, Varin and Arnulf returned outside and remounted.

"Roger, Walther," Varin called. "To the forest."

'Twas all for naught, he reflected an hour later. The night made it impossible to follow any sign of the attackers' direction. What the darkness did not hide, the forest shielded.

Returning to the village, he and his men helped extinguish the fires, an arduous task that took almost the remainder of the night.

The danger over, Varin began gathering information from the villagers and making plans for capturing the thieves once dawn broke.

Not just thieves, he reflected, taking a short respite for a drink from the well. They were murderers as well. An elderly man and his wife had perished in the flames.

"Yer lordship?"

He turned to find a ragged boy of perhaps twelve years standing behind him.

"Could we speaks fer a moment?"

"Not now, boy. My eyes burn, my head aches, and I am weary to the bone."

"It bes of great matter."

Varin studied his resolute countenance, the rigid set of his thin shoulders. "What is it?"

The youth glanced about. "I don't thinks I should be speakin' fer anybody to hear but ye."

"Very well." Foreboding settled over him. "Let us step over yon."

He motioned the boy to follow and strode to one side of the lane. "What is it you wish to say?"

"Them wot attacked us . . ." His voice shook. "One of them wot attacked us were Lord Cerdic."

"Lord Cerdic?"

"Lady Ros's husband."

Varin stared. "How do you know? Everyone says the men wore hoods."

"'Twere him, all right. Know'd his belt and the sword he wore. Used to clean it fer him."

"Come to the manor on the morrow—" Varin gestured. "—and I will reward you with coin."

The youth shook his head. "Don't want no coin. 'Twere me grandparents wot was killed."

"If it means aught to you, he will die. You have my solemn oath."

"If it bes all the same to ye, I'd be in yer debt if ye'd not say 'twas me wot told ye."

Varin nodded. "You have my word."

THE FIRST GRAY LIGHT OF DAWN found Roscelyn in the village. Though de Brionne and his men had been armed, mounted, and thundering from the manor grounds with the swiftness of a descending whirlwind, the attackers had vanished into the forest by the time they'd reached the village.

She surveyed the smoldering ruins of cottages, blinking against the thick smoke that suffused the fog. The acrid stench of charred huts was stirred by the comings and goings of Norman men-at-arms, who sought the raiding party with renewed vigor now that there was light.

She turned her gaze away from the rubble that was left of cottar Sibert's place. The elderly man and his wife had perished in the flames. With only two young grandchildren to see to their remains, the bodies had been taken to Lufu's where the witchwife had offered to prepare them for burial.

Meanwhile, the tanner's hut had been completely obliterated, along with the homes of the carpenter and the toolmaker. Apparently food was the motive for the raid. Only by the grace of God were there not more dead.

She pursed her lips. Fuller Hogarth might soon be listed among the dead.

"Mi'lady, a word." Varin's hoarse voice sounded behind her.

She turned and her breath caught.

His face and hair were black with soot from the fires he'd helped extinguish. In sharp contrast were the whites of his eyes, along with the blue. The impression was that of a demon just ridden in on hell's fury.

He glanced about. "Let us get out of this smoke."

With that, he held out his hand, also black, and pulled her up behind him. Urging the destrier forward, he cut upwind of the smoke and rode to the river, where they dismounted.

Striding to the water, he knelt to scrub his face.

"I fear you are in need of soap, mi'lord," she remarked, hoping to lighten the strain she sensed in his rigid stance.

Shaking his hands, he rose, the whites of his eyes more red in appearance now that the black soot had been washed to gray. "I need more than soap."

A sudden urge struck her to ease his exhaustion, to clean him up and put him to bed with a plateful of food.

"You wished to speak with me?"

For a moment a muscle in his jaw twitched. Then he exhaled. "That twaddling village priest has already approached me. He wants coin to say Mass for the villagers who died. I know not how much to offer."

Her lips puckered. The priest's greed was appalling, and 'twas hardly Varin's place to pay him. "I shall speak to Thuri Priest."

"You will not. 'Twas under the auspices of my protection that these people died. 'Twill be by my coin that Mass is said for their souls."

She bowed her head before his fierce gaze. "Three silver coins will be enough to pay for Mass and the gravedigger's fee."

"If you'll excuse me, I have a search to continue."

She glanced up to see him mount his horse. "A moment, mi'lord."

His gaze snapped to her face, his look both wary and expectant. 'Twas a look made all the more intense by the soot.

She pursed her lips. "Considering your generosity, I am sorry to ask, but those whose homes were burned have no place to go. I would have them stay at the hall until they can rebuild."

His intense gaze cooled. "Of course."

He nodded curtly, then spurred his horse forward, leaving her with a grateful though heavy heart.

THIRTEEN

❧❦

OIL LAMP TO HAND, Roscelyn quietly left the crowded hall well before dawn. She would not wish to disturb the village children who now resided at the hall, or their parents or anyone else for that matter. She but needed to see Lufu ere the day's work began.

Two days had passed since the attack on the village, two days of mornings spent in the fields, followed by afternoons of labor on the defensive works.

She winced. Two days of bleak imaginings, of wistful longing, of doubts, regrets, and hopeless musings that had served to tie her in such knots that she must beg Lufu's counsel.

The smell of fresh-hewn wood filled the air as she approached the drawbridge that had been laid late yesterday afternoon to span the completed trench.

"'Tis early for you to be up and about," a voice sounded ahead of her.

Raising the lamp, she spotted Walther, who guarded the entrance to the manor.

"I need to see Lufu ere the sowing today."

The freckled liegeman surveyed the darkness that surrounded her. "You go alone?"

She nodded, though Walther's question gave her pause. Since the attack, 'twas well and good to be cautious. The thieves had never been captured. "There is a guard in the village, is there not?"

"Two," Walther responded.

"Then I shall be safe." She bobbed her head and started forward, only to halt at the sudden sense of gratitude that struck her.

"Walther?"

"Aye?"

"Does Var—er, his lordship—does he ever thank you?"

The man's fair brow furrowed. "Thank me?"

"It cannot be easy to stand attendance all night while everyone sleeps."

"'Tis my duty to serve my lord." He shook his head and shrugged, as if he did not understand her concern.

"For what it is worth, you have my thanks."

With that, she strode forward, her heels clomping on the drawbridge. 'Twas an odd sensation to walk across the mighty tree trunks that had been lashed together with great bands of leather and driven through with iron rods. She could scarce wait for Wulfwyn to see the marvel.

Her spirits flagged at the thought. How she missed her sister. By now the scroll should be well on its way to the pope, and Wulfwyn would be anxiously awaiting a reply.

Anxiously waiting to come home.

Her thoughts circled to the dilemma that had plagued her for two days. If she did not do something, Varin would be gone, possibly dead, by the time Wulfwyn returned from the abbey.

She shuddered against the soul-wasting fear that trickled through her blood like poison at the thought.

Varin . . . The man whose determination had seen the drawbridge built that all at the manor could sleep without the worry of attack. The man who'd paid for a Mass to be said on behalf of two lowly cottars. A lord who would lower himself to work side by side with peasants.

Not that she hadn't loved her menfolk with all her heart. But her father and brothers believed 'twas God's will that the village folk were born to provide for them, not the other way 'round.

They would never dream of paying for the burial of cottars. They would never work alongside the villagers to fortify Cyning, for they would consider such tasks beneath them.

They certainly would not have allowed those whose homes had been destroyed or damaged from fire to abide at the hall, as had Varin.

He'd even given Timric, the grandson of the cottars

who'd been killed, over to Arnulf for training as a squire. Despite Varin's initial reaction to the contrary, he and his men were making do with half measures of food and without complaint.

Power and strength he possessed in abundance. Will and self-determination ruled him. Arrogance and pride were bred in his bones. Yet he maintained a compassion for others.

All in all, Varin was an incomparable boon to Cyning, and 'twould be by her hand that Cyning would lose him.

The idea yawed before her like a vast black ocean of pitching desolation.

Despite the fact that the Norman bastard-duke William had illegally laid claim to England, despite the fact that there were yet Saxons in the field preparing for battle, despite the fact that her father would likely roll in his grave, 'twas Varin she wanted to rule by her side at Cyning.

'Twas unthinkable that she would never again experience the challenge of his incorrigible behavior, the warm sense of security he engendered.

The maddening desire for his touch would remain unfulfilled.

She staunched the venomous flow of thick-comings that threatened at the thought of his death.

Sick and afraid, 'twas all she could do to stumble the remaining distance to Lufu's cottage, where her reception was anything but warm.

"Ye'd best be near death to be wakin' me," the witchwife snapped.

Roscelyn blinked against the stinging sensation in

her eyes, then did her best to swallow the cursed lump that suddenly clogged her throat. She took two deep breaths and exhaled slowly.

"How fares Hogarth?" she asked, unable to think of a way to present the true trouble that plagued her.

"Is that wot ye come 'round here fer?"

Roscelyn nodded, then shook her head. The lump swelled in her throat and she took two more deep breaths.

It did no good. The third breath near strangled her, then gusted outward on a sob.

"Hogarth is fine," Lufu shrilled. "Ye will cease that racket this instant. Ye sounds worse than a host of howlin' cats and I'll not be hearin' it."

Gulping and choking, Roscelyn clutched her stomach and wailed.

"Cease, I says, or I'll throw ye out the door."

Her chest heaved and she gasped for air, then sobbed anew.

"'Od rot. Come an' sits afore ye collapses." Lufu steered her to a stool. "Wakin' me in the middle of the night so's I can listens to ye bawl like a babe. Wot's wrong with ye?"

Roscelyn shook her head, unable to speak.

"It's the boy, ar'nt it?"

She nodded.

"Did I not tell ye he was yer destiny? But nay. Ye insists on doin' all in yer power to avoid the inevitable. And now look at ye. A greater mess I never see'd."

Roscelyn sniffled and swiped at her nose. "'Tis not the simple matter you make it seem. I doubt Varin realizes he's my destiny, and if he knew . . ."

Fresh tears gathered in her eyes. "If he knew what I'd done, he would hate me."

The witchwife narrowed her eyes. "Wot have ye done now?"

A ragged sigh tore from Roscelyn's chest and she bowed her head. "I have a sent a scroll to the pope that will destroy the Normans' claims to England."

"Wot?"

She need not worry over Varin's reaction, she thought, as she relayed the story of the scroll. Lufu would kill her long before Varin discovered what she'd done.

Without a word, the witchwife shuffled to fetch her shawl from a peg. Drawing it around the gray chainse she wore, she picked up a candle.

She lit the candle from the oil lamp and set it in a holder on the table. Then she leveled a stern look on Roscelyn.

"Ye must never let the boy know of the matter."

Roscelyn frowned. "That is all? You are not going to berate me? Rail at me for my stupidity? Heap curses on my head?"

"Bah." Lufu waved her questions aside. " 'Twould be a waste of me breath. Ye never listens to aught I says."

Roscelyn straightened on the stool. "I always hear what you say."

"Then cease yer whinin' and hear this, girl. Ye have but one chance to save yerself, and that is to marry the boy."

"Marry him!" She searched Lufu's wizened face. "He intends to take one of his king's nieces to wife. 'Twould take more magic than even you possess to inspire him to troth himself to me."

The witchwife snorted. "Ye yerself are the magic. The boy already blows hot fer ye. He but needs a bit of coaxin'."

"Coaxing?"

Lufu rolled her eyes. "Aye. Like a bone before a hungry dog."

Roscelyn shook her head. "I am no good at such winsome trickery."

"Ye do as much ever'day to gain the village folks' cooperation."

"That is different. I do not have to compete with a king's niece for the villagers' cooperation."

"Think, girl!" Lufu looked as if she might take a swat at her head. "The boy will marry ye if ye carries his babe."

Roscelyn gaped. "Are you suggesting I get myself with child?"

"I ar'nt suggestin'. I'm tellin' ye wot needs doin'. A man with a wife who carries his babe don't so much bother with who sits on a throne so long's his family and lands is secure."

"I would never resort to such a thing," she hissed. "'Tis . . . 'tis despicable. Nor is there any guarantee that such would ensure a trothplight from the man."

"Ye do wot ye will. Make yerself as miser'ble as ye wants fer now. In the end, the boy is yer destiny."

Unable to listen anymore, but not wishing to insult the elderly woman, Roscelyn rose from the stool. "I must return to the hall and fetch the seed for sowing to-day. Meanwhile, I will think on it."

"Ye'd best think hard, girl. One way or t'other, the boy will take a wife. It may as well be ye."

Golde came through the door just as Roscelyn made to leave. The sight of the young woman did naught but remind her of Wulfwyn and she struggled anew with tears at the loneliness she felt.

"Whatever is wrong, Ros?"

She sniffled and shook her head.

"Mimskin?"

"Praise the saints I'll never be goin' through such nonsense with ye," Lufu quipped.

"There, Ros." Golde patted her back. "What nonsense?"

Lufu snorted. "Boy troubles."

"Oh." Golde's features reflected the barest hint of sadness.

"Pay me no heed, Golde." Roscelyn did her best to smile. "The sight of you reminds me how much I miss Wulfwyn."

"Then I shall have to come visit you more often."

Nodding, Roscelyn made it out the door before tears could again claim her.

SCOWLING, VARIN MARCHED from the noisy hall and headed for the drawbridge. Roscelyn had never arrived to pay him a compliment this morn. Nor had he been able to ask her to estimate the amount of lumber he'd need for the wall as he'd planned.

Instead, for the first time since his arrival at Cyning, Lady Roscelyn had given Simon the slip.

Not that he could blame his liegeman.

Bloodygore. 'Twas his own fault if she'd sneaked

away to meet her husband. He should have confronted her about the man after the attack. Yet Arnulf had counseled patience and . . . and . . .

The devil take his soul. Truth tell, such a discussion would have destroyed the tenuous bond that he'd developed with her.

Loath though he was to admit it, he looked forward to her instruction, enjoyed making her blush with his lewd remarks, took great pleasure in her intelligence, in the way she puckered her lips when she was angry.

Nor could he imagine she would aid a husband who'd murdered two of her people. A clumsy, stubborn bundle of unshakable integrity and determination where Cyning and her people were concerned, she would more likely kill the lowly cur.

The thought set fire to his tail. Bloodygore. If Roscelyn *knew* her husband was responsible for the village raid, 'twould be just like her to try to serve justice on the man.

"Good day, mi'lord." Walther greeted him where he stood at the entrance to the manor grounds.

He drew to a halt before the liegemen. "Have you seen Lady Roscelyn?"

"Aye. She has just returned from the village."

"Just returned?"

Walther nodded. "She left earlier to visit the witch-wife."

Varin raised a brow. "But she is here?"

The liegeman again nodded.

Varin planted his hands on his hips and looked back across the manor grounds. "Where?"

"She headed in the direction of the hall." A worried

look crossed the liegeman's freckled features. "Is all well?"

Varin waved off Walther's question. "If you see her again, tell her I am looking for her."

With that, he strode back across the manor grounds, stopping to peek in each barn he came upon.

He snorted. What was the wench thinking to wander about alone in the dark?

A stupid question, he chided himself. Roscelyn never did aught without reason. Rather, her reasoning seldom took into consideration her own welfare.

'Twas always someone else who commanded her concern. Her sister, her housecarl, the witchwife.

"Pff." Though she was yet young, 'twas a miracle she'd survived thus far.

And where was she?

He slammed the door on the oat barn and strode for the hall. If he found her seated comfortably within, he would flay the ears from her head with his anger.

But she was not in the hall, nor had any of the servants who bustled about the kitchens seen her.

Christ's bloody bones. Where could she be?

As the sky grew pink, he started down the path that wound behind the hall. Simon had followed the woman to the graveyard on several occasions. If Varin did not find her there, he would pay a visit to the witchwife.

ROSCELYN EYED THE PEBBLES beneath the surface of the clear stream that ran behind the manor. Though she'd meant to visit the seed barn to prepare for the day's sowing, Lufu's advice would allow her no respite.

Thus had her feet carried her to the graveyard, and finding no ease there, she'd sought the comfort of the brook.

I would that you marry me, mi'lord, so kindly see to the arrangements. She mouthed the words, then rolled her eyes. She could well imagine Varin's response to such an order.

She tried again. *Mi'lord, I wish to marry you if you will have me.*

She wrinkled her nose. Nay, nay. Varin would do naught but laugh at such.

Mi'lord, I love you with all my heart and will surely perish if you do not marry me.

"Hmph." She may as well ask him to run her through with his sword. 'Twould be preferable to expose her innards to his gaze than to reveal her true feelings for him.

Great toads, if only she could make Varin love her. If only . . .

She imagined him speaking to her, the gruff timbre of his voice, the deep purr of his tone. *I long for you body and soul. You are everything that is dear to me. Marry me that our union shall be sanctified by the Church and in the eyes of God.*

Would that she could elicit such a trothplight from him, but he was more apt to choke to death ere he would say such to her.

She puckered her lips. What Lufu thought she could accomplish with ease was not possible.

The boy blows hot fer ye.

Heat suffused her face as she recalled the witch-wife's words. Blow hot for her, he might. Such did not a trothplight make. By his own admission, he'd known many women. He would hardly commit himself to her on the basis of a desire that could be satisfied by women more beautiful and experienced than she.

But marriage to Varin was the only opportunity for her to save him. That it served her deepest most secret desire only made her feel guilty.

"What are you about?"

She spun at the angry sound of Varin's voice.

"You will not again leave the manor without informing someone of your whereabouts." He halted before her, his black cloak blending with the dark trees that surrounded him.

"Your forgiveness." She ducked her head at the muscle that twitched in his jaw. "I knew you wished to begin sowing today and had several questions for Lufu. I only meant to—"

"You have been crying?" he demanded, his tone yet angry.

She lowered her gaze and shook her head.

He reached out and tilted her face up. "You have been crying," he stated.

She tried to remove his hand from under her chin. She needed to think, which was near impossible in his presence. "What is it you wish?"

"I wish to know why you cry," he snapped.

She stared into his eyes, unable to imagine life without him. " 'Tis just . . ."

Faith, she would not start weeping again. " 'Tis just that I am missing my sister."

He released her chin to trace her jaw line with a knuckle. " 'Tis your own fault for sending her away." His harsh tone gave way to gruffness.

In spite of herself, her eyes watered. "I miss my father and brothers as well. 'Tis sometimes difficult to accept that I will never see them again."

His gaze darted over her face. "What of your husband, mi'lady? Do you miss him as well?"

Though the question struck her as odd, she supposed 'twas the natural thing to ask. "I scarce knew my husband. We were married less than a day ere he left for battle."

"You had only just met?"

"Nay. My family and his have known one another for years, and Cerdic was an occasional guest."

He frowned. "Then how is it that you scarce knew him?"

"His time was spent with my father and brothers, not in my company." She shrugged. "What difference does it make? He is gone."

"You will remarry?"

She blinked at the question. Why would he ask such a thing, unless 'twas his wish . . .

Nay. 'Twas only her foolish longing that made her think he might wish to marry her.

Still, she could not completely banish the delirious hope that his question aroused.

"Remarry?" She hedged. "I know not from one day to the next whether or not I'll have a home."

He scowled. "I would never make you leave Cyning."

"Nay?" She pressed, anxious to know the reason for

his question, "What use will you have for me once your steward arrives? And what will happen when you marry your king's niece? Do you think your wife will allow me to abide in the manor?"

"My wife will do as I say."

Her hope vanished and her temper stirred. "How you will treat your wife is none of my concern. But you will not order me around as you wish. I shall take sanctuary with Wulfwyn once your steward arrives."

"You will not."

"Why would I stay? Cyning is no longer mine. 'Tis yours. And 'twill someday belong to your children."

Ere she realized his intention, he pulled her against him. "You will stay because I want you."

"Nay."

"And because you want me."

He crushed his lips on hers and she shuddered at the instant torrent of desire that near turned her bones to slush.

Want him? Nay. 'Twas far worse than any want.

'Twas a need unmatched by aught she'd ever experienced. A hunger that could never be assuaged, a fever that would never find surcease. And knowing that his blood boiled hot for her did naught but excite her sweltering senses.

She clutched at his back and opened her mouth in surrender, welcoming his tongue and his breath, straining against his solid body.

"Say you want me," he whispered against her lips.

She nodded.

"Say it."

She quivered from head to toe. "I want you."

"Mi'lord?" came Elswyth's voice. "Oh, your pardon. I did not mean to intrude."

Heat flashed across Roscelyn's face and she tried to pull away.

"Bloodygore," Varin muttered, though he made no move to release her.

"What is it?" he ground over his shoulder.

Elswyth's tone grew breathless. "Your underlord bid me to find you that you would know the morning meal awaits. I shall tell him you are . . . occupied."

"Leave go." Roscelyn pushed against his chest as the brunette turned and walked away.

"Lowly bitch," he ground, releasing his hold.

Air hissed at her sharp intake of breath.

"Not you," he amended. "Elspen. I know not how you tolerate her odious presence in the hall."

Refusing to acknowledge the satisfaction that curled through her at his dislike of Elswyth, she inclined her head. "You had best learn to be impartial where the villagers are concerned. Otherwise you will create dissension among your people."

He shook his head. "How you manage to remain so artless in a world filled with such deceit is beyond me. I can scarce imagine what would have become of you had I not arrived."

FOURTEEN

The FRAGRANT SCENT of Lufu's herb-spiced soap did nothing to ease Roscelyn's qualms as she bathed in the dairy the following day. 'Twas quiet for the moment, ominously so, like the stillness that crowded the air before an approaching storm. That the noonday sun shone brightly outside served only to unbalance her senses.

Sinking lower in the barrel tub, she wished the hot water might do something to melt the frost of her apprehension.

She'd vacillated all night over the merits of Lufu's advice. A night in which she'd despaired over her lack of knowledge on charming men, the fear that Varin would not have her, the anxious excitement that coursed through her body at the idea of sharing his bed.

In the end, it had been her terror at the thought of his death that had driven her to act. She would begin her wooing of Varin at the evening meal and hope that she could compete against his wish for marrying into royalty.

She grabbed a pitcher of water and doused her hair. Though she'd heard naught from Wulfwyn, the scroll was undoubtedly on its way to the pope. 'Twas only a matter of time ere the Normans would be forced to fight for England, and 'twas a battle they could not win.

For those who survived, there was Normandy. But for Varin . . .

She shivered despite the hot water.

Varin would doubtless defend Cyning to the death and she'd be a fool to discount the possibility.

She ran the soap through her hair and scrubbed at her scalp.

There was but one way to prevent such. She must somehow wring a trothplight from him, though she disagreed with the witchwife on the method for going about such.

To her thinking, 'twould be best to tease Varin while holding herself just beyond his reach. She must make him lust for her to the point he would sell his soul to have her.

Meanwhile, she would use the scroll to ensure that no Saxon or Danish force attacked Cyning, and she would use her marriage and hopefully Varin's child to keep him at Cyning after his Norman brethren were driven from English soil.

Grabbing a pitcher of clean water, she rinsed her hair.

Above all, he must never know what she'd done. Regardless of the fact that her plans were meant to save his life, he would hate her for it.

Rising from the barrel, she dried herself quickly and dressed in her finest tunic of a rich purple color. Her father had claimed it suited her to perfection.

She winced at the thought.

Her father. Would he truly approve of her marriage to Varin as Lufu claimed? Or would he wish her to deny her love for Varin and wait for a Saxon husband?

Her hand rose to cover her mouth and she shook her head against the thought. She could search heaven and earth and not find another man more suited to rule Cyning.

The door opened and Afled bustled inside with her two young assistants. All three carried pails of milk.

Roscelyn frowned at the dairymaid. "Where are your children?"

"They's over with Dunne at the laundry. 'Tis such a fine day, I wanted fer them to gets some fresh air."

Roscelyn forced a smile and nodded. " 'Tis indeed a fine day."

Gathering her soiled clothing, she headed for the empty hall where she fetched her comb and sat beside the hearth fire to dry her hair.

Marriage.

Her thoughts again drifted to Varin. Without question, she could not hope to find a husband as handsome. Faith, his looks could charm the worms from apples, the warts from toads.

Marriage. The word tugged at her senses, wrapping her in comfortable warmth and lifting her spirits.

She combed her hair with slow deliberation. What would it be like to take him inside her, to feel his seed ripen in her belly?

She lowered her head and blushed at her own thoughts. If she could make Varin desire her the way she desired him, she would be married tomorrow.

At the thought, she sobered. She could hardly accomplish such in one night. 'Twould take some bit of time to elicit a pledge from him.

If he would have her at all.

The thought stole her confidence. Though she was not ugly, there were many women more beautiful than she. Nor was her blood derived from royalty. She was Saxon, not Norman.

Varin had no need of her land. To his thinking, 'twas already his. She could offer him no wealth without telling him of the scroll. Regardless, he was not the type to betray his loyalty for gold.

Whatever made her think she could lure him into a proposal?

Yet she must, she thought desperately. She could not allow doubts to dissuade her. 'Twould cost her Varin.

Rising from the hearth fire, she hurried from the hall.

Ale. She would fetch a cup to bolster her courage.

But one cup did nothing to ease her misgivings. Nor did two.

By the time peasants and men-at-arms began arriving for the evening meal, her apprehension had reached desperate proportions. Despite three cups of ale, she could find no comfort.

Taking her seat at the table, she anxiously awaited Varin's arrival.

When Afled came through the side door bearing pitchers of ale, she called for another cup.

"Are ye certain, mi'lady?" the dairymaid inquired.

Roscelyn nodded and forced a smile at the look of concern in the dairymaid's brown eyes. "I am fully grown, Afled. Do not worry."

"As ye will." The woman filled her cup, shaking her head. "Just ye have a care. Yer not used to so much ale."

The dairymaid moved down the tables and Roscelyn sipped at the brew as the hall filled with more liegemen and peasants.

Conversation rose to the rafters and children raced about the great room, shrieking and fighting while their parents scolded and soothed wounded feelings.

She'd just called for another cup of ale when Varin arrived, Poppit following in his wake.

She winced at his weary countenance. The dark shadow of his grizzled jaw emphasized the hollows of his cheeks and she realized with dismay that he was losing weight. Without question, 'twas a result of the half measures of food.

"If I could have a moment of your time after the meal," he said as he passed behind her, "I would . . ."

His words trailed away as he took his seat beside her at the head of the table. He licked his lips and stared.

"Is there some special occasion?" he inquired.

Her heart skipped a beat at his perusal. "Special occasion?"

He inclined his head, his gaze darting over her features. "Your hair is unbound."

"Oh." Her hand went to her nape as if to confirm his statement. Faith, she'd forgotten to braid her hair. "I . . . I washed it and was waiting for it to dry."

He inhaled, then straightened in his seat. "'Tis a most intriguing scent. Where did you come by such?"

"'Tis only soap." She shrugged and shook her head.

His gaze shifted to her tunic, then returned to her face. "'Tis a most fetching color you wear. Why have I not seen it before?"

"My . . . my other tunics need cleaning." She swallowed dryly.

Arnulf arrived to seat himself on the bench opposite her. "Whew. I am . . ."

His eyes rounded. "Faith, mi'lady, but you are balm to my tired eyes."

Warmth stole across her face and she lowered her gaze. "I have not had a chance to braid my hair."

"Would that you never had the time for such," Varin commented.

At his raspy tone, she glanced up to find him regarding her with no little amount of interest. Indeed, where he'd looked weary but moments past, his eyes now surveyed her with a decidedly predatory cast.

The mixed odors of steaming bread and barley gruel carried inside the hall to distract her. How she would eat when her belly flip-flopped, she knew not.

She dipped her fingers in the wash bowl in the same instant as Varin and their hands connected, jolting her senses.

Her immediate instinct was to withdraw, but she

quickly recalled herself. Her scheme for getting him to the altar would never work if she avoided the most casual of contact with the man.

A pox on her timid sensibilities. With sure strokes, she set to washing Varin's hands for him. "I can scarce credit all you have accomplished on your defensive works in so short a time," she remarked casually, her fingers gentling as she traced a cut that scored one large, callused palm. "I saw wood stacked behind the hall this morn. Do you intend to build something there?"

When he did not answer, she glanced up.

Her movements slowed, then halted at the heat in his eyes. "You are angry?"

"Hardly." He raised a brow. "I find I am famished."

She ceased her ministrations and dipped her head. "My apologies for the half-measures of food."

It required no effort to sound sincere. How could she be so stupid? The man had labored all day and was doubtless starving.

He clasped her hands before she could pull them from the bowl. "'Tis not food for which I hunger."

Her head snapped up at the low curl of his voice. His teasing mien did not conceal the serious undertone of his meaning. She saw it like a wisp of smoke in the shadowed blue reaches of his eyes, scented it in the simmering air that seemed to emanate from him, felt its hotness caress her flesh when he massaged her sensitive fingers.

The spell was broken as a serving boy came between them to place a tray of bread on the table. Then bowls of barley were served.

Shaken, she suddenly longed to escape the table.

She'd had enough of seduction for one eve and longed for nothing more than her bed.

"You are not eating." Varin cut into her thoughts. "Here."

Dipping a piece of bread in his gruel, he held it out to her. Resigning herself to eat, she reached to take the morsel from him.

He snatched it from her reach and raised a brow. Opening his mouth, he indicated she should do likewise.

She vacillated between bold assertiveness and shy withdrawal. At last she snapped the bite he offered, then jerked her head away from his hand.

His eyes sparkled with mischief and he flashed her a wolfish smile. "Have you a taste for flesh this eve?"

A blush warmed her cheeks.

His voice lowered to a raspy whisper. "While I prefer that my fingers remain whole, there are other parts of my body upon which you may feast to your content."

She choked and grabbed her cup, only to find it empty.

"Here." Varin passed her his cup.

Eyes watering, she gulped the brew.

Dizziness assailed her and she took several deep breaths before the world righted itself.

"Here, sweeting."

She turned to find Varin holding another morsel for her. Leaning forward, she wrapped her lips about the tips of his forefinger and thumb, taking the food into her mouth.

She smiled, though her lips suddenly felt numb. Not that it mattered.

The only thing that mattered was the interest Varin displayed in her person.

"I was thinking." Though his tone was light, it contained a note of tension. "I am indeed fortunate to have such a beautiful, mysterious lady for company."

"Mysterious?"

"Aye. Each time I think I begin to know you, I am dazzled with yet another intriguing element of your nature. Tonight, for example, you are most . . . beguiling."

She stiffened with alarm. Was he accusing her of being deceitful? "What mean you by beguiling?"

"Why, charming, of course," he answered smoothly, as if there were no other meaning for the word. "I dare say I have never met a woman more so."

Suddenly confident, she called for more ale. Nibbling at the bits of bread he offered, she licked his fingers clean with her tongue. At his raised brow, she smiled. She would charm her unsuspecting quarry all the way to the altar.

Her fortitude stood her in good stead a half hour later when Varin rose from the table.

'Twas a shame. Just when she had him where she wanted him, she must now seek her bed. Sighing, she rose, then clutched the table when her body swayed.

Varin took hold of her arm. "My apologies, but as I mentioned earlier I need a word in private with you."

Though she could not recall for certain if he'd mentioned such earlier, concern crowded her stomach at his troubled expression. "Is all well?"

" 'Tis not something I wish to discuss where everyone can hear. It concerns the stores. If you would attend me in the bedchamber a moment, I have need of your knowledge."

"Of course," she agreed, and allowed him to lead her forward.

"Would it bother you overmuch if we closed the door?" he asked once they'd gained the bedchamber and he'd lit a candle. "I would not wish anyone to overhear."

She hesitated but a moment, then nodded.

Closing the door, he motioned her nearer.

Leaning forward to hear what he would say, she was caught unprepared for his kiss. 'Twas a leisurely, gentle kiss, one that presented no threat. One that she could not resist. After all, he did not so much as touch her with his hands.

Sweet languor spread through her limbs, even as a more dangerous yearning developed at her core. Yet Varin seemed to take great pains to hold himself from her. After several moments, she grew impatient with the lack of physical contact.

Spreading her hands at his waist, she stepped closer, hoping to encourage him. Still he made no move to hold her, did nothing to comfort her longing for the solid feel of his body molded to hers. And as he denied her, so did her desire grow.

At last, she opened her mouth and touched her tongue to his lips.

Though he continued to withhold his body, a groan rumbled low in his chest. The sound vibrated through her senses, teasing her nipples erect, playing against her woman's flesh until the area fairly twitched.

Desperation handily won over any shame she might

feel. She stepped full into his body and wrapped her arms around his waist, rubbing her front against his.

Ere she could blink, an animal growl erupted against her lips. Abruptly he snatched her against him and fed greedily upon her mouth, nipping and sucking on her lips and tongue, robbing her of all will and self-possession.

She clutched at his tunic as his hands massaged her shoulders, her back, her waist. His thick shaft ground into her belly and he rucked up her skirts to plant a leg between hers.

Lost to all but the flames that licked at her nipples and seared her core, she writhed against the hard muscle of his thigh. She sucked on his tongue as if that would quench the fire that consumed her.

His lips never left hers as he pressed her back against the wall beside the door. And then he was wrestling with her underdrawers, pulling at the draw-string, moving his leg long enough to shove them to her knees.

She bucked against his hand where it lingered between her thighs, felt the wet heat that slathered his fingers where they brushed her skin.

She whimpered into his mouth when his hand left her, then moaned with satisfaction in the next breath when his thigh returned to jam between her legs.

Held about the waist by one of his hands, she grew aware of his other where it moved against his stomach. The vague realization that he was working the strings of his braies and chausses stirred in her consciousness, but then he drew so deeply on her mouth that thought failed her. She could do naught but ride the sea of lust he inspired.

When her underdrawers fell to the floor, she could only pray for surcease from the burning torment that wracked her body.

When his hands clutched her bottom and he raised her over his rod, she did not shy.

When she felt the tip of his arousal at the entrance to her core, she could scarce await the intrusion of his swollen shaft. Felt certain that his invasion would provide the release she sought. Wrapping her legs about his hips, she opened herself to his onslaught—

Pain!

So sharp it took her breath.

Gasping, she clenched her teeth. Sweet Blessed Virgin.

He captured her jaw when she tried to turn her head. His breath came hard and fast as he sunk himself to the hilt, and she gritted her teeth when he shuddered.

He buried his face against her neck in the stillness that followed, and as greatly as she'd longed for his touch mere moments ago, so now did she yearn to distance herself from him.

"Are you . . . finished?" she managed at last.

His chest expanded against hers as he drew a deep breath. Easing her feet to the ground, he stared at her. "Why did you not tell me you were a maid?" he asked quietly.

She shook her head against the self-loathing she felt. "I did not mean . . . I had not intended . . ." She closed her eyes against the shame she felt.

"Hush." He swung her up in his arms to cradle her

against his chest. "Had I any idea, I would have taken more care."

He carried her to the bed and sat, still holding her. "Forgive me. I misunderstood your playful mood during the meal."

His gentle kindness only served to make her feel worse.

"'Tis no fault of yours," she whispered raggedly against his chest.

"Of course 'tis my fault. I lured you to my bedchamber and took unfair advantage."

She could stand no more. "'Tis I who encouraged you. And I did it apurpose in the hope you would marry me."

For long moments he did not respond. Just sat and continued to hold her.

At last he drew a deep breath. "Why would you wish to marry me?"

She winced. "You are a good man. You are good to my people. You are intelligent and honest and kind."

"But what of your husband?"

Raising her head, she searched his shadowed countenance. "I keep telling you he is dead."

"Nay, mi'lady. He is alive and well."

She tried to rise but he tightened his hold, preventing her. "You lie," she spat. "If you have no wish to marry me, then say it and be done."

"You truly believe he is dead?"

His incredulous tone fed her anger. "Gunderic saw him fall to a Norman sword."

"Then your housecarl lied. Your husband's dealings with the Danes are well documented."

Her heart skipped, then hammered in her chest. "Gunderic would not lie to me about such."

"Then mayhap he was mistaken."

"You are certain he lives?" Her voice scarce cleared her dry throat.

"'Tis the reason I am here. 'Tis the reason I build defensive works. Your husband will return to take Cyning, and likely with a force of Danes for support."

She squeezed her eyes shut and panted. Cerdic was alive? He would return to Cyning? Her body shook at the thought.

"What has the lowly bastard done to you?"

Unable to speak, she shook her head.

"If I am to marry you, there will be no secrets between us."

"He did naught to me. 'Twas Wulfwyn . . ." She swallowed hard and took a deep, shaky breath. "On my wedding day, I found Cerdic forcing his attentions on Wulfwyn."

In great, gulping breaths, she told him how Lufu had mixed a sleeping potion that she'd slipped in Cerdic's ale, how he'd thought she'd tried to poison him, and of his final threat to her.

You shall suffer the remainder of your days.

The telling of the tale did naught to ease the terror that gripped her. Even the warmth of Varin's embrace provided her no comfort.

The memory of Cerdic's vow oozed through her head like venom, paralyzing her ability to feel aught but fear.

FIFTEEN

ROSCELYN AWOKE wrapped in Varin's embrace
the following morn. Snuggling her back closer to his
front, she enjoyed his warmth. The fear that had tor-
mented her last night had vanished like a cold gray mist
before the heat of a rising sun.

It had been the shock of learning Cerdic yet lived
that had so rattled her. Combined with the fact that
she'd drank too much ale—as well as having just lost
her maidenhead and the tension of the entire day she'd
spent worrying over how best to charm Varin—'twas
more than she could tolerate.

Varin's continued reassurances had finally convinced her she had nothing to fear. Guards had been

posted in the village and at the drawbridge. Ulric, along with a dozen other village men, had been given weapons and were being trained to use them. Each day that passed brought the moment nearer when the wall would be complete.

Nor could Cerdic know that Wulfwyn was at the abbey. Indeed, her sister was safer at Saint Dunstan than she would be at Cyning.

Smiling to herself, she hugged Varin's forearm.

She had Varin. In possessing the scroll, she possessed the means for protecting him. And while she was sorry that Gunderic remained a prisoner, she was also glad of it. Had Gunderic been free, Varin would have surely accused the housecarl of aiding Cerdic.

She wiggled deeper into the hollow of Varin's shoulder. Nay. She had no cause for alarm. As Varin had pointed out, 'twas Cerdic who should be fearful.

"For a petite person," Varin's sleepy voice rumbled close to her ear, "you require a great deal of bed space."

Roscelyn stilled. "My apologies."

When she tried to move away, his embrace tightened. "I suppose I may as well accustom myself to it now. I will have to endure many nights of crowding once we are married."

She pursed her lips. "You are certain, mi'lord?"

"I do not know that I will ever grow entirely accustomed to such a shortage of bed space, but I will do my best."

"Nay, Varin," she pressed. "Are you certain you wish to wed me?"

"What better wife could a man ask for?" He kissed the top of her head. "You do not eat nearly as much as my horse, you do not bite or kick as hard as Rok, and you are much prettier."

"What of your king's niece?"

"I have never seen her and know not how she would compare to Rok."

"Can you not be serious?" she pleaded. "What of your desire to again hold your family lands?"

"What's done is done, Roscelyn. You and I will wed, and there is the end of it."

He squeezed her waist, dropped another kiss atop her head, then rose to light a candle. "Unless 'tis your wish for Adam to find you abed and half dressed, I suggest you arise and clothe yourself. As well, we have matters to discuss."

She watched the sinew flex along his back as he bent to scoop her tunic off his storage chest where it rested against one wall. Though he'd worn his braies to sleep, they did little to hide the muscular length of his legs.

And there was the end to it, she thought.

No words of affection for her. Nothing to indicate he took any joy in the prospect of their marriage. Only an appreciation that she was not like his horse.

But what had she expected? A pledge of his undying love?

He tossed her tunic at her. "Well, mi'lady? 'Tis most difficult for a man to think when a pretty lady lies in his bed."

She scrambled from the bed, heedless of the fact that she wore naught but her chainse.

"Take your ease, Roscelyn," Varin soothed. "I shall do my best to not ravish you again until we are wed."

She flushed at his words even as the tingle of excitement coursed through her blood.

"Unless, of course, you cannot wait." Though his mien was teasing, there was a speculative edge to his tone.

She raised a brow. "I believe I will endure. Indeed, I believe 'twould be best if I remained in the curtained section of hall until after our marriage."

He shook his head. "Ungrateful wench. Just see if I will appease your lust when you come creeping 'round my bed at night."

She rolled her eyes. "That will never happen."

"Pff. You will lay on your lonely pallet dreaming of my body until your passion is so aroused, you will be unable to resist. And when such occurs and I deny you, 'twill be your own fault."

She shook her head. Great toads, but the man was full of himself.

Yet even as she thought it, there was a part of her that hungered for his touch at this very moment. A part that apparently showed on her face, for Varin's eyes suddenly darkened.

"Continue looking at me thus, and you will find yourself on your back without further delay," he threatened.

Embarrassed that he could read her so easily, she held up a hand. "Did you not have a few matters you wished to discuss?"

He sobered. "I shall have to approach my king for permission to wed you."

"Think you 'twill be a problem?"

He shook his head. "But I am not certain whether or not we will have to annul your current marriage."

She lowered her gaze as her spirits fell. She needed no reminders that Cerdic was alive.

Abruptly Varin pulled her into his arms. "He will never trouble you again. You have my word on it."

Closing her eyes, she relaxed in the comfort of his gentle embrace.

He cleared his throat and set her away from his body with great deliberation. "Your pardon, mi'lady. I can see that I am going to have great difficulty in escaping your constant desire for me."

"My desire?"

"Faith, can you not control yourself? Ere you attack me again, let us conclude our business."

Turning away from her, he fetched a leather bag. Moving to the bed, he opened it and several finely wrought pieces of jewelry tumbled forth.

"These belonged to my mother." He spread out two torques, one gold and one silver, and a brooch studded with diamonds, rubies, and sapphires. "How much food do you think these might purchase?"

All of a sudden, she felt like weeping. The jewelry had been meant for the king's niece, she felt certain. 'Twas the greatest of gestures that he would sell such valuables to feed the people of Cyning.

"Nay, mi'lord. I would not allow you to lose the only things of your mother's that you possess."

"Will they purchase enough that we can increase our current consumption of food? 'Tis difficult to pit half-full bellies against such rigorous labor as the defensive works require."

"I believe we could increase the allotments for the time being with the money you have." Would that she could tell him of the wealth they would soon share as a result of the scroll. Not that she dare.

"Allow me a couple of days to tally the stores to the smallest measure," she said instead. "Then I will know better."

"You are certain you do not wish to avail yourself of my body at present?"

The abrupt change of topic made her realize their arms were touching where they stood beside the bed.

She scooted away and hastened to open the chamber door. "By your leave, I shall eat, then see to my counting."

"Coward," he called at her back. "You will regret your decision this very night."

Shaking her head, she strode into the teeming hall where the trestle tables had already been erected.

Her steps slowed as the room quieted. Faith, but it seemed every person in the room surreptitiously regarded her approach.

And why would they not? Gossip spread quickly, and like as not the entire village was already wagering on when her first babe would be birthed.

"Mi'lady," Arnulf's voice trilled in the sudden quiet. "Come and sit that you may settle an argument between Ulric and me. The man boasts he can sling a stone from a hundred paces with the accuracy of an archer and I say 'tis not possible."

"He can, Sir Arnulf," came a boy's excited voice.

"We see'd him do it," said another.

"Bah." Old man Ansel scowled. "Ulric exaggerates. 'Tis more like fifty paces."

With that, demands rose to the rafters for a contest.

Roscelyn hurried to sit opposite the giant. "My thanks, Arnulf."

"For what?" he asked.

Varin strode to the table. "What is all this hue and cry for a contest?"

"I fear Arnulf has stirred contention amongst the ranks in order to save me from embarrassment," Roscelyn remarked.

Varin's features hardened. "Someone dares to bandy your good name about?"

Wincing, she shook her head. "Come and eat before the fare grows cold."

Instead he banged his fist on the table and bellowed for silence. "Whatever contest is at stake, let it be carried out in honor of my trothplight to the Lady Roscelyn."

"Hear, hear." Ulric was the first to raise his cup. "To Sir Varin and Lady Roscelyn."

Her face flushed, 'twas all Roscelyn could do to eat. "If there is nothing you require of me, mi'lord, I would see to the granaries. Mayhap we can afford a small feast for this contest of Ulric's."

At Varin's nod, she took herself off.

A heavy mist dampened the morn, leaving the world gray. She made her way across the manor grounds to the granary that held the oats and barley, her thoughts drifting to her sister.

What would Wulfwyn think of her marriage to Varin? Would that she could speak to her ere the deed was done, but 'twas not possible.

Not unless she traveled to the abbey. 'Twould be sheer madness to do so with Cerdic so near.

She stepped inside the barn and lit a rushlight.

Nor would it be safe at Cyning until the scroll had been delivered and the threat of war had subsided, she reminded herself.

Sighing, she took her tallies from the bin and had just began counting when Elswyth's voice sounded behind her.

"I hope you enjoyed spreading your legs for Varin."

Roscelyn turned, scarce able to believe her ears. "What?"

" 'Twas quite a sight to see the Norman feeding you at the table last eve. Everyone in the hall witnessed it. Even now the wagers run hot in the village as to when you will birth your first babe."

Roscelyn eyed the brunette. She was unkempt and it looked as if she had not slept in some time. Due, no doubt, to a night spent entertaining a man, perhaps several from the looks of her.

"Since you obviously weren't present in the hall at breakfast—" Roscelyn measured her words, "—you will be glad to know of my upcoming nuptials."

"So you will have two husbands? Does that not go against Church teachings?"

"Why do you say that?" Roscelyn asked, foreboding claiming her senses. None of the villagers knew that Cerdic lived.

"I have a message for you." The tilt of Elswyth's pointed chin and the manner in which she spoke were challenging.

Roscelyn refused to be baited. "Then say it and begone."

"Your husband commands your presence, tomorrow noon, at the forest's edge by the meadow."

Stunned, 'twas a moment before she could speak, and even then she barely managed a whisper. "Cerdic?"

"'Tis amazing you recall his name, considering your love of the Norman," Elswyth sneered. "You must indeed be talented to hold the interest of such a virile man. I wonder when he will tire of you?"

Gathering her wits, Roscelyn inclined her head. "'Tis difficult to feel ashamed before your blatant envy."

Her barb hit its mark, for Elswyth near shook with anger.

"And what is this nonsense of Cerdic?" Roscelyn continued before the woman could respond. "I have no time for your lies."

"'Tis no lie," the brunette snapped, and opened her hand with a flourish.

Roscelyn stared at the lock of red hair.

Wulfwyn's?

Nay. It could not be.

"At what game do you play?"

"'Tis no game. If you wish to ever see your sister again, you will meet Cerdic on the morrow."

"You are a fool if you think to convince me Cerdic would harm my sister," she blustered.

"Surely you are aware of Cerdic's . . . violent nature. 'Twas he who raided the village, and do you know why?"

Ere Roscelyn could say aught, Elswyth continued. "The old cottar woman saw him and he wished to conceal the fact that he'd slit her throat."

"Cease," Roscelyn hissed.

Elswyth shrugged. "I saw Wulfwyn myself this morn. Cerdic holds her that you will do his bidding."

Roscelyn could muster no response so thick was the fear that swept like plague through her body. Her muscles contracted and she shivered.

"You will meet me at the manor gates tomorrow and I will escort you to the proper place. And if you speak of this to a soul, your husband wishes you to know that Wulfwyn will suffer greatly before she dies. He says to remember your wedding day that you will have faith in him."

She smiled cunningly and was gone, leaving Roscelyn to wrestle with her terror.

What unspeakable acts had Cerdic already committed against Wulfwyn?

Nay! Elswyth lied. There were many people with red hair.

Unbidden, memories of her wedding day surfaced in her thoughts.

If Elswyth spoke the truth, if Cerdic indeed held Wulfwyn . . .

Panic shot through her limbs and she fair raced from the barn. She must find Varin.

There was no telling what horrors Wulfwyn was enduring. She'd scarce taken a dozen strides when it occurred to her.

If Elswyth saw her talking with Varin now, she would doubtless pass the information on to Cerdic.

Abruptly she stilled, glancing about.

Indecision gripped her. What was she to do?

She would kill Cerdic.

Tonight, once everyone was abed, she would fetch a

sharp-bladed knife from the kitchen. And tomorrow, when she met Cerdic, he would die.

But as terror overrode her, so did doubts assail her. Cerdic was no small person. Nor was he unseasoned in battle.

Nay. She could never hope to take him alone. She must enlist Varin's aid.

The sooner she rescued Wulfwyn, the quicker her suffering at Cerdic's hands would end.

Panic engulfed her as she imagined all manner of abuse being inflicted on her sister. Clutching her waist, she feared for a moment she might vomit.

Cease, she ordered her frantic imaginings. To allow terror to reduce her to a babbling idiot would hardly serve Wulfwyn. Better to think on Cerdic's defeat.

She smiled grimly. Varin would be pleased to capture Cerdic, if for no other purpose than to hand him over to King William for a reward. She frowned at the thought.

If Cerdic were the king's captive, she would be unable to kill the bastard, and she'd be boiled in oil before she'd allow him to live. Somehow, some way, she would kill the son of Belial.

Meanwhile, she would tell Varin what had transpired and have Wulfwyn home this time tomorrow.

She'd only started forward when she again drew to a standstill. Varin might be so thrilled with the notion of capturing Cerdic, he might have little regard for Wulfwyn's life.

A vision of Cerdic holding Wulfwyn at knife point, threatening to kill the child, seized her thoughts. What if Varin laughed and told him to proceed?

Nay. Varin would never endanger Wulfwyn for his own gain. He was not the type of man who would stoop to such.

Her eyes rounded and her heart seemed to freeze in her chest as another thought occurred.

Did Cerdic know of the scroll?

Was it possible that he'd learned of the document from her father? Mayhap Wulfwyn had hoped to save herself from Cerdic by telling him of it, not that Roscelyn would blame her.

Cerdic would not hesitate to tell Varin of the document if her husband thought it would save his wretched hide.

Nausea gripped her belly and she quickly returned to the barn where none would see her sickness.

Collapsing on a grain sack, she held her head in her hands.

She would go with Elswyth tomorrow and meet Cerdic. There were too many unanswered questions. She would discover for herself what she could, then decide whether or not to tell Varin.

SIXTEEN

I<small>T APPEARS YOU</small> have little regard for your sister's life," Elswyth snapped where she awaited Roscelyn at the entrance to the manor. "You are late."

"Know you Varin's whereabouts?" Roscelyn asked, trying to catch her breath. Though the day was clear, the sun was no match for air that was so cold it stung her lungs.

Elswyth cast her a disgusted look. "You go to meet your husband, yet you ask after your Norman lover? Cerdic was truly cursed the day he wed you."

"Shut your mouth. If Varin sees me, we are like to be waylaid. I would avoid him if possible."

Elswyth snatched Roscelyn's arm. "You had best

forget your Varin and concentrate on your husband. Cerdic will not be pleased with your tardiness."

Roscelyn glanced over her shoulder as Elswyth pulled her forward. Plague take the sense that she was being watched. Her gaze swept the teeming courtyard where men and boys labored to cut and strap timber, but she could see naught to confirm her suspicion.

'Twas likely no more than apprehension that caused her to feel such, she told herself. Still, she cast looks over her shoulder as they sped down the hill. The way was clogged with people coming to and going from the manor, and once they reached the village, matters more pressing captured her attention.

Varin was striding down the lane, conversing with Ulric. Praise the saints he had not seen her. She jerked Elswyth between two huts.

"What are you about?" the brunette demanded angrily.

"Lower your voice," Roscelyn hissed. "Varin approaches."

Together they skirted around the back of several tofts, weaving past a number of goats, chickens, and pigs. Finally Roscelyn approached the lane and cautiously peeped around the corner of a weather-beaten hovel.

Varin was well beyond them and heading for the manor. Nodding at Elswyth, she stepped out into the lane and continued toward the fields.

She again glanced over her shoulder as they cut across the freshly furrowed plow strips of ground. "There are few who cannot see the direction in which we travel," she worried, more to herself than to Elswyth.

"Surely your great wit can derive some explanation for your going to the forest," the brunette sneered.

Faith, but she'd had enough of Elswyth's bullish manner. "You had best pray it is so. If I am discovered, rest assured I shall make no effort to hide your duplicity."

They crossed the meadow where several boys tended sheep and entered the forest. Allowing Elswyth to take the lead, she silently counted her steps. Should she need to return to the place, she would know where she was going. So engrossed was she in committing each tree and bush to memory that she stumbled into Elswyth's back when the woman finally halted.

"'Od rot. Can you not watch your step?"

The brunette's words scarce registered as she looked beyond the woman's back.

Cerdic.

Her heart pounded with the sickening thump of the butcher's axe on the block. Standing beneath the falling branches of a dead oak, two scurrilous creatures of doubtful parentage had accompanied him.

"Come hither, wife," Cerdic ordered, his tone sharp as the crack of a whip.

Roscelyn commanded her feet to carry her forward until she stood before him. He was not as tall as she remembered, and his patched chausses and tunic resembled the garb of a peasant.

"Have you no greeting for your husband?"

She stared into his dark, unblinking eyes, eyes that were empty and unfeeling as a viper's. Gathering her courage, she decided against trying to curry his favor. 'Twould gain her naught.

"Elswyth claims you hold my sister," she challenged.

He jerked his head and his minions grabbed her arms. Despite the panic that threatened to overwhelm her, she did not struggle against her captors. Any fear on her part would likely serve to excite Cerdic's perverse nature.

His emotionless gaze never left her eyes as he ran his hands over her body and she was grateful she had no weapon on her person. He knelt and ran a finger inside both her boots, then slid his hands upward along the inside of her thighs.

A calculated smile curved one side of his lips as he rose. "'Twill be my pleasure to continue my examination of your person at the first opportunity. Unfortunately, I have not the time at present."

He nodded at his men, who released her. "Elswyth tells me you have taken a liking to your new Norman lord."

Roscelyn chose her words carefully and forced a measured tone. "Who would know better than you that things are not always as they appear? Since I do not see Wulfwyn, I assume she is not in your keeping. Therefore I see no reason to remain here and discuss the state of my affairs with you."

He clasped her arm with bruising strength before she could turn away. "Rest assured, I have Wulfwyn safely tucked away. She will suffer the torments of hell if you fail to do my bidding."

Though she almost winced at his painful grip, she managed to affect a doubtful look.

She took a deep breath.

She must not think of Wulfwyn alone and at his

mercy. She must appear strong and unmoved. Otherwise he would get the best of her.

She studied his face. He was more lean than the last time she'd seen him, and his features bore lines of struggle and deprivation.

"I would hear your demands—" She maintained a dispassionate tone. "—though do not think I will agree to aught unless I feel your scheme has merit."

"You will agree, regardless of your feelings, or Wulfwyn will perish."

She snorted. "You would have to prove you hold my sister before I would blindly obey your commands. Let us put aside the question for now. Mayhap your plot has something that would appeal to me."

She made certain Elswyth caught the glance she directed at her, then lowered her voice so only he could hear. "I assume your plan requires some intelligence else you would have Elswyth perform your commands."

His eyes shifted to regard the brunette. Doubtless, Elswyth would realize they were speaking about her. With luck, the stupid woman would feel threatened and become disruptive. A small accomplishment, but if it annoyed Cerdic even a little, Roscelyn would be satisfied.

Cerdic relaxed his grip on her arm. "I would have a moment alone with my wife," he announced to his henchmen. "Await me here."

He steered her away from the men, but before they could get far, Roscelyn felt her hair snatched from behind.

"Think you to twist Cerdic's thinking with your silver-tongued lies?"

"Release her hair and await me yon." Cerdic gestured for the brunette to join his men.

"What have you to say to her that I cannot be permitted to hear?" Elswyth demanded.

"We will speak later."

"We will speak now," the brunette persisted. "You would entrust her with your secrets, knowing she spread her legs for a Norman dog?"

Roscelyn saw hesitation cloud Cerdic's face. Now was not the time to lie. "Elswyth speaks the truth, mi'lord. I gave myself to the bastard that he would treat my person and the peasants with more kindness."

"Liar," the brunette sneered, then faced Cerdic. "She not only willingly went to his bed, they are so fond of one another that he has proposed marriage to her."

Plague take the woman. Roscelyn's gaze never left Cerdic's eyes as she responded. "You have done naught for me or my people. If I must defile myself to gain the Norman's goodwill, so be it, and if he commands I marry him, so much the better."

Her hatred for Cerdic served her well, for she allowed it to claim her features that it would lend credence to her lies. "The night will come when he will grow careless, and then I shall slit him from throat to groin."

Cerdic cast her a disbelieving look. "You could not kill a bug. Your aversion to blood is too great."

She shrugged. " 'Twould seem the blood of Normans would prove the exception. Indeed, 'twas my pleasure to stab the bastard his first night at Cyning."

"Do not listen to her, Cerdic. 'Twas Wulfwyn who stabbed the Norman."

Roscelyn raised a brow. "Come, Elswyth. Who do you seek to fool with such a tale? While you might be able to convince Cerdic of many things, he knows I would never allow Wulfwyn to endanger herself thus."

Her husband inclined his head. "You have changed much since we parted. I would not have thought you capable of such."

Elswyth snarled and lunged at her then, her fingers hooked like talons. Cerdic grabbed the woman before she could sink her nails in Roscelyn's face.

"She lies," Elswyth shrieked as Cerdic dragged her writhing body to his men. "You are stupid to believe her words."

Roscelyn winced at the dull thud of Cerdic's fist slamming into Elswyth's face. The loudmouthed shrew crumpled in a heap and Cerdic spoke to one of his men, though Roscelyn could not hear what he said.

Abruptly he turned back to her and she ordered her features to reflect dispassion. While she kept her eyes trained on him as he approached, from the edge of her vision she saw the two henchmen carry Elswyth off through the woods.

'Twas eerie how birds' songs echoed sweetly through dappled sunlight as if naught were wrong. A bright yellow, winged insect stroked its way across Cerdic's path and she swallowed the bile that rose in her throat. She desired nothing so much as to be gone from this place, never to see Cerdic again.

"You were right," Cerdic acknowledged, halting before her. "Elswyth has not the wit to assist me. I doubt you would willingly tell her where you have hidden your half of the scroll, much less trust her to deliver it to me."

She slanted him a questioning look. "Scroll?"

"Do not dare pretend ignorance with me." He raised his hand as if he would strike her.

" 'Twould not be an auspicious time for me to sport bruises, considering the Norman lord's great love of me," she remarked, unflinching.

"You had best watch your clever tongue when in my presence," he snarled, though he lowered his hand. "I can torture places on your body that will never be seen."

She wrapped her cloak more tightly around her shoulders to hide the shudder that wracked her. The idea that he was torturing such places on Wulfwyn's body near turned her insides to ice.

"Your father himself told me of the scroll," Cerdic continued smoothly. " 'Twas my good fortune to speak with the abbess at Saint Dunstan when I went to fetch my dear little sister-in-law. She was only too grateful for your sending the scroll to her and wished me to pass along the blessings that were being said in your name."

Roscelyn would betray no trace of her sunken spirits. The only thing worse than Cerdic's possession of the scroll was the fear that Varin would discover it.

"I suppose 'tis another thing you hold that I will not see," she commented in a disbelieving tone, despite the fact that it might cause Cerdic to make good on his threats to her person. "You must truly think me gullible to believe such tales."

His hand shot out to clutch the neck of her cloak. Spinning her around, he ran a hand beneath the folds of material.

"You will hand over your half of the scroll," he

hissed in her ear, massaging her belly. "When the Danes arrive, they will find a safe haven at Cyning. The Normans will be dead, for you will have poisoned the manor well with the same potion you used to poison me on our wedding night."

She fought the tremor of loathing that threatened and affected a reasonable tone. "You might wish to consider that along with the Normans, you will be killing valuable livestock as well. The animals' troughs are filled from the well."

His hand stilled and she continued. "Your pardon, mi'lord, but I could not help note your lack of . . . circumstance. 'Twould appear you can ill afford to lose aught that will provide for your table."

Abruptly he shoved her away. Then he began to pace, shaking his dark head. "It cannot be helped. I will take no chance with my plan. You will poison the well."

He had swallowed the bait. All she need do now was pull him in without getting herself killed in the process.

"I have already suffered the destitution of war," she said with determination. "Poverty is little recompense for killing a band of Normans. Your scheme reeks of penury and I'll not endure such again."

"You will lack nothing. The scroll will ensure that you prosper as my wife."

She crossed her arms over her chest. "If I have learned aught these weeks past, it is that men forget their bargains once they have gained their goals. Though I have come to regard you with more appreciation after dealing with the Norman pig, I have no need of you or your half of the scroll. I can rid Cyning of the Normans with no help from you, and I can enjoy the Danes' reward for my effort."

Before she could blink, he was upon her. Shoving her back against a tree, he pressed his forearm to her throat until she could scarce draw breath. "Greed has replaced your virtue," he snarled.

"My services will not be bought with promises," she wheezed.

He fair seethed with frustration. Removing his forearm, he gripped the neckline of her tunic. "You will hand over your half of the scroll and poison the well or, by all that is holy, I will kill Wulfwyn."

Success was at her fingertips. She could feel it. "As I said, I don't believe you hold my sister. Nor do I believe you possess the scroll."

He shook her and her head cracked against the tree behind her. "Tomorrow noon. You will meet me here and I will bring Wulfwyn." He shook her again. "Play me false and you will see your sister die before your eyes."

He released her then and jerked his head. "Begone with fair warning. One of my men guards this place night and day. I will know if you are not alone."

"What of Elswyth?" she inquired. "The woman bears no love of me and is like to spoil everything."

He smiled grimly. "You need not concern yourself with Elswyth. She will not trouble you again."

Gazing into his black eyes, she realized he'd had the brunette killed. The thought made her stomach lurch.

Had she not schemed to bring Elswyth and Cerdic to each other's throats, the woman might yet live.

Pushing herself away from the tree, she commanded

her wooden legs to carry her forward. She did not look back. Her tears would do naught but give lie to the impression she'd created for Cerdic's twisted imaginings.

Cerdic had Wulfwyn. She knew it in her heart and could think of nothing else as she made her way back to the manor.

Though several people called her name, she paid them no heed. Head bent, she swiped at the tears that muddled her vision. Eventually she made her way to the orchard, the barren trees reaching lifeless black limbs for the heavens.

She walked past them, her steps carrying her to her parents' graves.

Prithee, give me guidance, she beseeched her mother and father.

What was she to do?

The temptation to lay all her woes at Varin's feet was almost overpowering. He would know what to do, and he would help her. Yet how was she to explain the scroll?

Was it possible she could continue to keep its existence secret?

She stared at her father's headstone. Though Varin would unquestionably choose saving Wulfwyn over capturing a spy, would he make the same choice knowing that Cerdic held half of the invaluable scroll?

A document worth more than a fortune. A document that could destroy his king's hold on England and consequently Varin's hold on Cyning.

Doubtless, Varin would do his best to secure the document and save Wulfwyn. But what if he had to choose? Would he choose her sister over the scroll?

A hopeless breath trickled from her lips as she eyed the two carved slabs of stone. Nay, she was not willing to risk even the slightest chance of losing Wulfwyn. That was her mother's answer.

She frowned. So how was she to rescue her sister without Varin's help?

She sank to the ground, suddenly weak. Cerdic had at least ten liegemen, judging from the number of men who'd raided the village. At most, she might be able to kill one man.

Her thoughts spent the remainder of the afternoon leaping from one impossible scheme to another. Finally, as the sun began its descent, hunger growled in her belly.

The bones in her legs popped when she rose and her shoulders cramped. She had sat too long in one position.

Stiff and aching, she cast a final glance at her father's headstone, then started back toward the manor where she intended to visit the cook room. She could secure a blade without anyone being the wiser.

That was her father's answer to her troubles.

She bowed her head, the brown and gray of winter-frosted grass and leafless trees closing in upon her.

Would that she'd never heard of the scroll.

What had once held such promise was now but a curse. If she could succeed in killing Cerdic, she would take the entire document and burn it.

The smell of roasting meat made her mouth water as she neared the cook room. If Cerdic did not present Wulfwyn for her inspection on the morrow, she would follow him after their meeting.

Once she located his lair, she would wait until Cerdic and his men settled in for the night. Then she would free Wulfwyn and slit Cerdic's throat while he slept.

Entering the cook room, she approached Egric. "Have you any bones to spare for Poppit?" she inquired, her gaze landing on a butcher knife.

"Got one here." The cook nodded.

As he turned his back, Roscelyn swiped the blade, hiding it in the sleeve of her cloak.

"My thanks." She smiled at the rotund cook.

With that, she was out the door and on her way to the great hall. Upon entering, her gaze traveled over several liegemen who lounged at a table. Varin was not present, nor was Arnulf.

She hurried toward the curtained sleeping quarters. She would hide the knife in the one of her chests until the morrow.

At last she stepped from the curtain and headed for the tables. 'Twould be difficult to sit at the table and pretend all was well when she could think of naught but Wulfwyn.

Abruptly she was grabbed from behind and jerked backward. Without a word, Varin clutched her arm and dragged her toward the hall's entrance doors.

Her heart thundered at the sight of his visage, dark and burning with rage.

"Mi'lord, I would explain—"

"Not one word, or I will cut your lying tongue from your head."

SEVENTEEN

AFTER TRUSSING Roscelyn next to her lowly Saxon housecarl in the stables, Varin stalked to the dairy. Ignoring the wary looks and the hushed conversation of peasants who watched his every step, he fetched two pitchers of ale and made his way to the stream that ran behind the manor.

The deceitful bitch had played him well with her innocent looks and lying lips. Setting one of the pitchers on the ground, he drank straight from the other, praying he could wash away the foulness of her treachery.

He would have to question her, of course. But not now.

Not when his rage was so all-consuming he feared he would kill her.

'Twould hardly help him capture her husband if she were dead.

He drank deeply from the pitcher, refusing to acknowledge the painful wrenching that twisted his soul at the thought of her death.

'Twas death she deserved, a slow one to match the wretched depths of her vile betrayal.

He squinted as the setting sun broke from a cloud to reflect off the stream. For all its light, he could see nothing but darkness.

Draining the pitcher, he wiped his mouth with the back of his hand, then reached for the other. Had he not set Simon to guarding Roscelyn, he'd yet be wallowing in the poison of her seduction.

Not that he'd expected her to meet her husband. Rather, she'd so completely duped him that he'd wanted Simon to protect her should the lowly bastard threaten her.

He chugged more ale. Praise God's bloody bones he'd not told her about her guardian. 'Twas a thought he'd entertained and had decided against, feeling 'twould only make her anxious to know of his great fears for her.

The fears of a witless fool, he railed at himself.

"Varin," Arnulf's voice sounded behind him. "Time is wasting if 'tis your wish to question the lady."

He scowled. Would that Simon had been close enough to hear what was said between Roscelyn and her husband. Then he would have no need of questioning her. But the liegeman was forced to keep his distance lest he give himself away, and the forest absorbed sound like a sponge.

The only other person who could help was Elspen, but no one had been able to locate the wench.

He drained the remainder of the ale.

"Mayhap you should allow me to question her," Arnulf suggested.

Varin opened his mouth, prepared to decline the giant's offer, then changed his thinking. "Aye. You question the bitch. I am like to kill her if she presses me with any more of her wheedling lies."

ROSCELYN SHOOK her head at Gunderic in the dim twilight that spilled through the stable's doors.

"There is no need for quiet," she responded to his concern that a Norman guard stood just outside. "I care not who hears what I say. If I do not meet Cerdic on the morrow, he will kill Wulfwyn."

"Lord Cerdic would not harm Wulfwyn," the house-carl protested.

"Aye, Gunderic, he would. And he would take immense pleasure in it."

She'd just finished relating the tale of Cerdic's assault on Wulfwyn when the giant appeared carrying an oil lamp.

"Arnulf!" Hope charged through her breast. "You must hear me."

"I have come to do exactly that, mi'lady. But be forewarned, I will slit your throat ere I will allow you to again cause Varin such great pain."

She winced. "You must believe me, Arnulf. 'Twas not my intent to hurt anyone. My husband holds Wulfwyn hostage to make me do his bidding. I cannot let him kill her."

The giant listened patiently as she spoke, asking occasional questions, and when she'd finished, he slid his blade from its sheath.

Her breath caught. She'd failed. Arnulf knew when she was to meet Cerdic and had a good idea where the meeting would take place. Now he would kill her, and Wulfwyn would die.

"Slit my throat, giant, and I swear to dog your steps from beyond the grave. Neither you nor Varin will ever know peace."

Arnulf rolled his eyes. "If you would hold still that I may cut your bonds."

He sawed at the ropes that bound her to a post. "You have convinced me, mi'lady." He helped her to her feet. "But I am not certain you will find it so easy with Varin."

With that, he ushered her toward the hall. Silence descended over peasant and liegeman alike at their entrance and curious stares met them.

"Where is Varin?" the giant inquired of Walther.

The freckled man-at-arms gestured toward the bedchamber. "He is yon."

Arnulf led her forward and bid her wait while he entered the bedchamber alone. For a moment all was quiet, and her back felt hot with the burning gazes that surely regarded her from the hall.

Then Varin's voice thundered and she flinched. "The bitch has poisoned your thinking, man!"

Silence again fell and she rubbed the gooseflesh that had risen on her arms. His tone was as fearsome as the howl of a dragon.

She shuddered. She would make a run for it were it not for Wulfwyn.

At last the door opened and Arnulf beckoned her inside.

She forced her shaking legs to carry her forward. She must convince Varin that she spoke the truth or Wulfwyn would perish.

"Leave us," Varin rasped.

Arnulf cast her an encouraging look, then quit the room, closing the door behind him.

Before the light of a lone candle, Varin fixed her with a look that was rigid and cold as death.

"I will hear this incredible tale you have spun for Arnulf," he sneered, "and be forewarned. Simon followed you and heard every word that passed your deceitful lips. Lie, and I will know."

She stared. "You had me followed?"

The way he smiled, she would not be surprised to see the gleam of fangs protruding from his lips. "I have had you followed since the day I arrived at Cyning."

"But . . ." She frowned.

She should have known. How else would Varin have discovered her meeting with Cerdic?

"How could you marry a woman you so distrust?" she asked, scarce able to connect her thoughts.

"You have sullied yourself for naught, sweet slut. I never had any intention of marrying you. 'Twas your husband I sought."

Her insides shriveled against the sharp bite his

words inflicted and she turned her head that he would not see her pain.

She'd been a fool. Varin's charming manner, his interest in her person, his kindness toward her—all had been affected. He had only used her to gain information about Cerdic. How had she not seen it before?

It took all her strength to square her shoulders and return her gaze to him. Regardless of his cruel deception, she must somehow persuade him to help her free Wulfwyn. "Believe what you will, mi'lord. I only wish to get my sister from my husband's hands."

He advanced on her, his big body exuding menace. "Think you to fool me with such tales? You have schemed with your husband all along. I've known it since the moment he attacked the village."

She backed away.

"Oh, aye, mi'lady." He pursued her retreat. "Did you know your husband was recognized that night by a villager? I knew 'twas only a matter of time until the two of you gave yourselves away."

His hand shot out to capture her jaw, halting her backward flight. "You will wipe that doe-eyed look of innocence from your eyes. 'Twas at your behest that the stranger in the cart stole grain. 'Twas used to feed your husband and his men. When that failed, you had him attack the village, heedless of the lives of those people you claim to feel such loyalty toward."

She could almost smell the violence in him, could feel the scorch of his rage.

Her voice quivered. "You are wrong, mi'lord."

He pulled her face closer. "Think you I am stupid?" he hissed.

"Nay, mi'lord. You do not understand."

"I understand," he spat, giving her no chance to explain. Clutching her waist with his free hand, he jerked her body against his. "I understand your concern over food and supplies. Your husband shall have to eat once he recaptures Cyning."

She struggled against his hold.

"I understand how the sowing of crops delays the building of defensive works in favor of your husband."

He tightened his grip until she could scarce breathe. "I understand how you use your facile tongue to manipulate everyone at Cyning. Most of all, I understand your whorish lust for me. You sought only to gain my trust that I would swallow your lies without demur."

She gasped, both at the insult and for air. Curling her fingers, she slashed at his face with her nails. Her gaze instantly shifted to the ceiling when she drew blood.

"Bitch."

As if he would squeeze the life from her, he lifted her off the ground.

"You had best relate your husband's plans while you yet have breath."

Dear God. He was going to kill her. She drew back her foot and kicked him with all her might.

EIGHTEEN

❧❧

PAIN TORE THROUGH Varin's shin. How could he have forgotten the wench's deadly boots? He'd sported a bruise for a week from her clambering up his leg that day at the mill when he'd forced her to ride back to the manor.

Had she managed to break a bone this time?

Anxious for relief and more than fearful that she might strike again, he hauled her to the bed, tossing her on her back.

By all that was holy, he would have the truth from—

He frowned as a coughing fit seized her. Her small

white teeth bared, her eyes more red than gold, she clutched her throat.

Was she catching her breath or choking? Had he used more force than necessary or was she playing on his sympathies? Apprehension knotted his gut.

"Cease spluttering," he commanded.

When she continued to strangle, the knot moved from his gut to his chest.

"Cease, I say."

Without warning, she grunted and kicked at his groin. Though her aim went wide, she still managed a decent blow to his hip. 'Twas enough to send him backward a step, but not enough for her to escape.

She would not get a second opportunity, he vowed. He captured her legs and gripped her knees. Wrenching them apart, he stepped in between them. Let her try and kick him now.

His victory was short-lived.

A pillow slammed into his face.

Even as he reached to grab it with one hand, she twisted against his remaining grasp on her knee.

"Daughter of Satan," he gritted. How could one small woman wreak such havoc?

Linen rent and feathers flew where he tore the pillow from her hand. Tossing it aside, he again grabbed her other knee. When she continued to struggle, he jerked her hips against his.

At her shriek, he grabbed a handful of feathers. "Scream again, and you will find your mouth stuffed," he threatened, holding the handful of feathers near her mouth.

The wench closed her eyes and went still as death.

"Tell me of your husband's plans, mi'lady," he sneered. "Perchance, was the attack on the village made to draw me and my men out where we could be killed? Is there a specific day on which he will strike again?"

She did not move. Nor did she make any attempt to answer his questions.

"Forsooth, mi'lady," he quipped sarcastically. "Where is your facile tongue now?"

When still she made no response, his patience deserted him. "Damn your Saxon hide to hell. You will speak, or I will . . ."

The sudden realization of their positions struck him, rendering him incapable of speech or movement.

Feathers from the pillow had landed in the short wisps of golden hair that surrounded her face, one coming to rest on her cheek. His gaze dipped to the blue pulse that beat like thunder at the base of her slender throat. He could hear her breathing now, see the rapid rise and fall of her chest.

He looked lower. At the small, perfect hands that covered her womanhood. At the contrast between the seamed brown leather of his chausses and the gray of her soft tunic. At the manner in which the rumpled material retreated between her thighs, defeated by the invasion of his hips.

And now he could feel her legs trembling on either side of him.

Bloodygore. He straightened and shook the feathers from his hand where he held them near her mouth. The wench thought herself about to be raped.

Plague take him for a Sodomite. 'Twas not his intent and he would feel no shame over his treatment of her. He most certainly would not apologize for it. 'Twas she who'd kicked him, not once, but twice.

Her diminutive size mattered not. She deliberately used it to her advantage. Who knew how many men she'd duped into believing her helpless.

And innocent.

And pure, and sweet.

He snorted. What a dullard he'd been. He should have known something was amiss when she'd allowed him to have his way with her.

A sniff interrupted his baleful thoughts and he scowled. Now he supposed she would attempt to gain his sympathy with tears. Though her eyes remained closed and her long dark lashes were yet dry, her pert little nose wrinkled suspiciously.

He struggled to maintain his rage as the sniffing grew more labored. Her talent for manipulation was boundless, he reminded himself.

No virgin responded with such passion to a man's touch unless she sought to gain some end. For all he knew, her maidenhead was naught but a concoction of chicken's blood formulated by the witchwife.

His lip curled. How she must have laughed at his tender concern for her. She and her husband had doubtless been well entertained by his plans for marrying her.

Yet knowing her sniffles were a ploy could not save him. His anger dwindled with each shallow breath she took, and he slid toward the gaping maw of guilt that waited to swallow him.

Regardless of how he tried to deny his mean treatment of her, the evidence would not go away.

He was three times her size, perhaps more. She had

naught but boots and fingernails for protection against his might. He was a seasoned warrior, a man skilled at terrifying captives into divulging their secrets.

She was but a woman with no experience at such tactics.

Even as he squashed the sneaking impulse to console her, he reached out and tugged her up to sit.

Her eyes flew open and her shoulders heaved as she filled her lungs. When her hands shot upward, he captured her wrists, thinking she intended to claw him again.

"Ah-choo!"

Feathers flew, propelled by her sneeze.

Varin stared at them where they drifted to stick on his tunic.

She had not been about to cry, he thought stupidly.

Nor had she meant to claw him again.

She'd only meant to cover her mouth when the feathers had caused her to sneeze.

He loosed his hold on her wrists and stepped back, his rage at her deceit suddenly spent.

How was it that he e'er seemed to lose in his dealings with the wench?

Despite knowing the truth of her foul nature, there was a part of him that yet prayed there was some redeeming explanation for her treachery, that she'd not met her husband . . .

Hopeless fool, he chided himself.

Deny it all he would, he wanted to be the man to whom she would devote herself. That she'd chosen her husband over him left him feeling eviscerated, as if she'd actually carved the guts from his belly.

He ran a hand through his hair. Mayhap 'twould be best to drive his sword through his own chest and be done.

❧

THE CANDLE FLICKERED in its holder, casting shadows about the bedchamber. Swiping at her itching nose with a shaky hand, Roscelyn eyed Varin from where she sat on the bed.

Were it not for Wulfwyn, she would beg the man to kill her. 'Twould be a blessing to escape the misery that tore at her heart and soul.

As it was, she could not decide whether to throw herself at his feet and plead for mercy or try to reason with him. All that mattered now was Wulfwyn.

She bowed her head, staring at the dirt floor. Mayhap she could use her portion of the scroll to bargain with him.

Aye. His liegeman had heard every word spoken between her and Cerdic. While Varin could not yet know of its significance, he doubtless wondered about the scroll she and Cerdic had discussed.

She certainly need no longer fear that his discovery of the document would cause him to hate her. He already despised her.

Nay, she corrected herself. He did not hate her.

He felt nothing at all for her. Had never felt anything for her.

"Let us begin anew, mi'lady." Varin's harsh voice interrupted her thoughts. "You will tell me of your meeting with your husband."

She looked up. "I know not why—"

She caught herself before she finished the sentence. Why indeed?

What need had Varin of hearing aught from her if his liegeman knew every word that had passed between her and Cerdic?

What need had he of her at all?

His liegeman knew where she'd met Cerdic. He would know when she was to meet Cerdic on the morrow. 'Twould seem a simple enough matter for Varin and his men to surprise Cerdic and capture him.

"My patience wears thin, mi'lady," he prodded. "Speak."

Hope near overwhelmed her. Might she yet gain his aid?

She cleared her throat. "As you know, my husband holds Wulfwyn captive. Either I will do his bidding, or he will—"

Her voice broke. To speak aloud the terror that haunted her was near more than she could bear.

"Do not seek to gain my sympathy with pitiful tales of your sister's abuse at your husband's hands. Like as not, your husband was waiting for her when she arrived at the abbey."

Her breath caught at his icy disdain and she could only stare.

"Have you no heart?" she whispered at last.

"Heart?" He spat the word as if 'twere poison. "Your sister has suffered naught compared to the misery I have endured, mi'lady. Taunts and ridicule. Daily beatings by squires much older and bigger than me. Fighting with dogs for scraps of food, emptying the slop from chamber pots, kicked and cuffed by lord and lady alike for clumsiness."

Hatred for the Norman king rose hot in her chest to near choke her. Did the fat bastard sit before her, she would kill him for what he'd done to Varin.

Not that she would say as much to Varin. She searched his wasted features, unable to say aught that would soothe his bitterness.

His lip curled. "Admit it, mi'lady. You wanted your sister away from the manor that I would not use her as a hostage against you and your husband."

"You have lost your ability to reason, mi'lord."

He snorted. "Where any other Norman lord would have disgraced and defiled you, I have treated you fairly and with kindness. I have treated you like a lady, despite the fact that your sister stabbed me, despite the fact that your housecarl tried to kill my underlord, despite the fact that I have e'er been suspicious of you. Yet you scheme with your husband behind my back."

Unable to hold her anger in check another moment, she gave vent to her spleen. "What would you have me do?" she spat. "Place you and your perverse sense of loyalty to your king above my sister's life?"

She advanced on him, stabbing a finger at his chest. "Truth tell, had your man heard aught of what was said between Cerdic and me, you would not question my actions. You would know that my loyalty lies where it always has, and that is with my family and my people."

Jabbing her finger against his chest, her voice shook. "You would know that I hate my husband with every breath I take. You would know that he holds my sister hostage to force me to his will."

When he grabbed her hand, she fisted the other and slammed it against his chest. "If you believe for a moment that I would risk my sister's life on behalf of your repulsive king, you are wrong."

He clutched her fisted hand and held it immobile with the other.

"It matters not what you believe," she huffed, struggling against his hold. "Your king and your loyalty mean nothing to me. Nor does your honor."

Tears rose to sting her eyes when she could not free herself from his grip. "There is nothing and no one who will stop me from saving my sister. She is all I have in the world."

"Enough!" Varin bellowed, shaking her. "If you hate your husband, as you claim, and you long for your sister's release, why did you not enlist my aid?"

His demanding stare brought her up short. Breathing hard, her gaze darted over his harsh features. The dark stubble of beard that shadowed his square jaw, the angry draw of his lips, the cold blue of his eyes.

Did she dare tell him the truth?

Did she dare tell him that she would have confided in him, except for the scroll?

Would it save Wulfwyn if she told him the truth?

Or would it cost Wulfwyn her life?

She gritted her teeth.

What choice had she? To trust her sister to Cerdic, or trust Varin to be the man who'd e'er shown compassion to her and her people, who'd given her such pleasure, who'd charmed kisses from her . . .

And stolen her heart.

She took a deep breath. "There is a matter of which you are unaware, mi'lord."

Unable to look at his face, she lowered her gaze and spoke to his chest. "My husband holds a scroll. . . ."

His grip tightened on her hands until blood pulsed in her fingertips as she explained the scroll. But before she could relate how she'd sent the scroll to the abbey, he shoved her from him.

"Conniving bitch. Seek you to trick me with such lies?"

"You great fool!" she fair shrieked, heedless of the rage that darkened his face. " 'Tis no lie. While I would hope you would do your best to secure Wulfwyn's safe return, should you have to make a choice between Wulfwyn's life and the scroll—"

"Temper your tone, wench, or I will have you removed from my presence."

She clamped her teeth together and 'twas a moment before she could speak. "I had hoped," she finally gritted, "to rescue Wulfwyn myself before telling you what I knew."

She returned his burning gaze with one of her own as silence stretched between them.

At last he released his hold on her wrists.

"How many men does your husband command?" he demanded.

"I do not know."

"That is helpful."

"I only met him for the first time today."

"Is he camped in the place where you met him?"

"How should I know?"

A muscle twitched in his jaw. "Did you see tents, pallets, a fire?"

"Nay."

He heaved an exasperated sigh. "Are you to meet him again? Or is that, too, beyond your knowledge?"

She cast him a scathing look. "I am to meet him tomorrow at noon."

He glared in return. "At the same place?"

She nodded and her belly flip-flopped against a sudden spurt of fear. 'Twas too late to take back her words, and she prayed she'd done right in telling Varin of the scroll.

"Cerdic is to bring Wulfwyn for my inspection." Her voice quavered. "He warned me that there is a man who guards the place. If I do aught to betray him, he will kill Wulfwyn."

Abruptly Varin strode to the door and jerked it open. "Arnulf!" he bellowed, then turned back to her. "I must away if I am to reach the forest and position myself before daybreak. I have not the time to explain my plan twice, so you and Arnulf will listen together."

The giant scarce entered the bedchamber before Varin was issuing orders. "Rouse the men and select four to accompany us to the forest. Simon will have to be one of the four. He knows where we are going. The remainder will be armed and prepared to defend the manor."

Roscelyn listened with care as he outlined his plan and told her what he expected of her. When he'd finished and Arnulf had left, he called Adam to help him dress.

"Is there aught you can think of I have missed?" he

queried as the squire scurried about him with braies, chausses, undertunic, and boots.

Roscelyn shook her head, speechless with the fear that suddenly gripped her. What if Cerdic killed Varin?

"What if Cerdic has fifty men?" she asked as Adam rushed to fetch his sword from its standing place beside the bed.

Varin raised his arms so the squire could secure the blade about his hips. "If such were the case, he would have attacked the manor ere now. 'Twould not be in his favor to let us complete the defensive works."

Adam stepped back, finished with his tasks. "Leave us," Varin commanded.

Roscelyn watched the squire leave the room, then gave her attention to Varin.

His blazing gaze raked her. "Do not let doubts destroy your faith in me. To do so will cost you and your sister your lives."

He turned to leave, but she clutched his arm. "I will not fail you, but I have one request ere you go."

He turned back, his eyes dark and remote. "What is your wish?"

"When we are through, promise you will allow me and Wulfwyn to retreat to Dunstan Abbey."

His features hardened. "We will discuss this once Wulfwyn is safe. Get some sleep and I will have Adam awake you at the proper time."

With that, he was gone.

NINETEEN

ARIN FROWNED as he and Arnulf, along with four other men-at-arms, made their way toward the village. The improbability of succeeding at the task he'd set for himself already plagued him.

Without light, 'twas nigh impossible to see now. He could scarce imagine how they would find their way in the forest, and that while hoping to evade the watchful eyes of any Saxons who were guarding the meeting place.

But while the lack of light would make the going difficult, it also worked in his favor. Whoever stood guard in the forest would be unable to see him and his men.

And 'twas a cold night. That, too, was in his favor. Men who stood guard at night might well light a fire for warmth.

All was quiet when they reached the village, the peasants having sought their beds.

Varin halted long enough to explain the situation to Gilbert, who stood at his post in the lane. 'Twas a comfort to know his liegeman did not have a fire. Any who dared attack the village would not know Gilbert was there until 'twas too late.

Moving forward again, he whistled for his men to follow.

Far and away his greatest concern was that Roscelyn had lied. Though he longed to believe she'd spoken the truth, he and his men could well be walking into a trap of her making.

He shook his head. Whereas he'd advised Roscelyn to not allow her trust in him to waver, 'twas he who was filled with misgivings. In telling her to follow his instructions to the letter lest she and her sister be killed, he'd failed to mention that any failure on her part would likely cost the lives of him and his men.

An odor beyond bitter stung his nostrils where it wafted on a breeze and he wrinkled his nose. A cottage door stood ajar on his right, emitting shadowy light. The witchwife's hut.

How the old woman stood such noxious smells, he knew not. Like as not she used the same medicine for healing and poisoning alike.

The thought stirred his memory and he paused, signaling his men to do likewise.

'Twould be interesting to see if the old bird confirmed Roscelyn's story of her wedding day.

Not that the witchwife couldn't lie as well as Roscelyn. Rather, he knew for a fact that Roscelyn had not visited the witchwife since telling him how the old woman had prepared a sleeping potion for her. 'Twas not possible that the crone knew what Roscelyn had told him.

"Await me here," he ordered the giant. "And stay clear of the light."

Ducking inside the cottage, he swiped aside a dangling cluster of red leaves that hung from the rafters.

The old woman looked up from where she sat at a long table beyond the hearth fire. "Been expectin' ye, boy."

She'd been expecting him? Had he and his men so easily given away their approach that even an old woman had been alerted?

"How is that?" he asked, suspicion prickling his neck.

"Saw it in me runes."

He glanced about the ill-lit room, at the shelves of myriad bottles, at the cook pot that hung over a spitting fire. "I have need of your aid."

"Come and sits." She beckoned him.

Hunching his shoulders, he moved toward the stool she indicated on the opposite side of the table from her. "I have not time to sit," he said, eyeing the yellowed parchment scroll that lay unrolled before her.

"Me maps of the heavens," she remarked. "Wot is it that troubles ye?"

"I was wondering if you might know what occurred between Roscelyn and her husband on her wedding day."

"Wot makes ye think I knows aught of such?" She raised a bushy white brow.

He cast her a droll look. "There is naught in the village of which you are not aware."

"Ye are indeed a bright boy." She inclined her head. "So why shoulds I be tellin' ye of the troubles atween Ros and Cerdic?"

He rubbed his face as if it might staunch the flow of his fast bleeding patience. "Because I command you to tell me."

"That ar'nt no good reason." She scowled at him. "Ye'll have to do better than that."

His temper stirred at her baiting manner. "Hear me well, old woman. 'Tis by my goodwill that you abide in Cyning. You will tell me what you know of Roscelyn and her husband or I'll have your hide."

If his threat made any impression on the witchwife, she gave no indication. Instead she crossed her arms over her chest and narrowed her eyes. "Why does ye wishes to know?"

Spinning away, he stomped toward the door, swatting clumps of dried leaves from his path. What was he thinking to enlist the crone's help? 'Twas like talking to a deaf person.

"Ye will hie yerself back here, else ye will discover the full extent of me gramarye."

Varin ignored her. The old poseur wasn't about to frighten him. He'd had measure in full of her insolence.

Without warning, the door slammed shut in his face.

He took an involuntary backward step, his bones rattling even as the splintered door shook from the force of its closing.

Gathering his wits, he turned back to the witchwife and affected his most deadly tone. "Think you to intimidate me?"

The woman waggled splayed fingers at him, as if she were casting a hex. Absurd as 'twas, he could not prevent the chill of apprehension that crept up his spine.

He glared at her, his head bent before the rafters' low pitch. "Your manner is most grating to the senses."

"And ye are a fool if ye think I'll be tellin' tales on Roscelyn just acause ye says me to. Ye will tell me why ye wishes such information ere I'll say aught."

He rolled his shoulders uncomfortably. "The lady and I will be married and I—"

"Speak up, boy. Sometimes I have a bit o' trouble hearin'."

"The lady and I will be married," he thundered.

"Didn't say I was deaf," she screeched back.

Varin ran a hand through his hair and moderated his tone. "There is obviously some rift between the lady and her husband. The mere mention of him sends her into a panicked rage and I would not distress her by opening old wounds."

"Why did ye not say so?" the witchwife snapped.

"I did not come to argue," he grumbled.

"Bah," she sneered. "On the very day they was wed, Cerdic tried to force hisself on Wulfwyn, the muck-eating lover of sheep."

He scowled. Where he'd thought to ease his mistrust of Roscelyn, the guilt that stabbed him robbed him of any comfort.

How she must despise him. 'Twas no wonder she longed to reside in an abbey for the remainder of her days. Like as not, she would prefer the company of Satan to him.

Meanwhile, 'twould be his greatest pleasure to drive his sword through her husband's greasy heart.

Without thinking, he straightened.

"Bloodygore!" he spat when his head struck a rafter.

The witchwife rolled her eyes. "Clumsy oaf. Come and sits afore ye knocks the stuffing from yer head."

"I haven't the time," he repeated. "I am on my way to—"

"Given time," the witchwife interrupted as if he'd not spoken, "she would have kill't Cerdic."

He eyed the witchwife's wizened features. "Why are you telling me such?"

The old woman cocked her head, ignoring his question. "So ye loves the girl, do ye?"

"Love her?" He shook his head. "'Tis more like a wasting sickness. An insidious disease that taints the food I eat and the water I drink. Like a succubus, it steals the very air I breathe at night, and by day it robs me of coherent thought."

"That is good." The witchwife nodded sagely. "She is yer destiny. The two of ye were meant fer one another."

He caught himself ere he insulted her with comparisons of her daftness to mad dogs and full moons. Let the old woman think what she would. Though he would admit a great fondness for and attraction to Roscelyn, he did not love her.

And praise God he did not. He could well imagine the torture his heart would endure if such were the case.

"I must away. This Cerdic holds Wulfwyn hostage. Come dawn, my men and I must be well hidden in the forest."

He paused as the witchwife's spidery great-granddaughter rose from a pallet in a dark corner. How had he missed her presence?

A bean struck his forehead. "Ye've not heard a word I've said," the witchwife accused, her hand still raised from the action of throwing the bean.

"Your pardon."

"It seems yer thoughts wander easily, boy. I was sayin' that Golde here will accompany you."

He raised a hand and backed toward the door, banging his head again on a rafter. " 'Tis not necessary."

"Ar'nt none wot knows the forest like me Golde. She can guide ye wherever it is ye needs to go."

"Nay." He shook his head. " 'Tis far too dangerous for a young girl."

"Bah. She'll return the moment she sees ye settled."

At her fearless persistence, his thinking returned to mad dogs, inadvertently raising a question he could no longer resist asking. "Wulfwyn's pet—" He tilted his head. "—Poppit . . ."

Before he could decide how best to phrase his words, the witchwife pointed a finger at him.

"Best ye ties the lackwit cur afore ye leaves. The

beast's been knowd to follow them wot it loves to the grave and Wulfwyn won't take kindly to the animal's dyin'."

Varin eyed the old woman. *Lackwit?*

Following people to the grave?

Lack who'd ended up in a grave Varin had dug for him.

'Twas answer enough.

The witchwife's lips appeared to curl up at the corners in a smile, but before he could be certain, she turned her attention to the spider.

"Show's his lordship where he needs to go. Otherwise he's like to do naught but wander in circles the entire night long."

'Twas useless to argue.

Bunching his shoulders, he beckoned for the girl Golde to follow him. He would also rouse Ulric and send the man to restrain Poppit.

As Varin neared the cottage door, he paused and turned to narrow an eye at the witchwife. "Do not ever again slam a door in my face."

She raised a brow. " 'Twas naught but the wind."

TWENTY

ROSCELYN PACED the confines of the bed-chamber, ignoring Varin's directive to sleep. 'Twas not possible in her anxious state.

Was she doing right placing her trust in Varin?

What if he . . .

Nay, she would not let doubts nettle her.

She forced herself to concentrate on his plan, re-calling every word he'd said, and could find no fault with his reasoning.

At last, her restless feet carried her from the bed-chamber out into the great hall. All was quiet, the peas-ants asleep, the hearth fire banked for the night. The only difference between this night and any other was the lack of Normans, but 'twas a difference that made her shiver.

She moved on, out the side door and into the night. Without conscious volition, she made her way to the graveyard.

The bitter cold scarce made an impression on her while a three-quarter moon provided enough light to guide her steps.

Varin had given her no opportunity to explain her involvement in delivering the scroll to the pope. Which was just as well. 'Twould have only added to his distrust of her.

She knelt beside her father's headstone and began to dig. Her portion of the scroll would go to Varin in hopes that he would see her and Wulfwyn to the abbey.

A tear slipped down her cheek as her fingers struck the leather pouch that contained the scroll.

She could not stay at Cyning. She would always long for what she and Varin had shared before all the lies, the mistrust, the deceit.

'Twould tear her heart and soul in two each time she looked upon him, knowing he did not trust her, knowing he'd never intended to marry her.

Clutching the scroll to her chest, she huddled on the ground and stared at the stars.

Prithee, God, keep Wulfwyn safe. Do not let Varin die. Do not let Cerdic best him.

She repeated the prayers over and again.

By the time the sun rose, her eyes burned with exhaustion. As orange light spilled over the horizon, she returned to the hall where trestle tables were being set up for the morning meal.

Avoiding shrieking children and bustling peasants, she made her way to the curtained section of hall, glad to find it empty.

She selected a clean chainse and brown tunic, then tucked the leather pouch in the bottom of the chest.

Unbidden, visions of Cerdic and Varin battling one another with swords wormed their way into her thoughts. The scene unfolded in her imaginings, ending when Cerdic thrust his blade deep in Varin's chest.

Terror sent her digging for the knife she'd hidden yesterday and her hands shook as she dressed.

Where could she hide the knife that Cerdic would not find it should he search her? There was not a spot he had missed yesterday when he'd run his hands over her person.

Except one.

She snatched her braid loose and grabbed her comb. Yanking it through her hair, she set to rebraiding it, plaiting thick strands around the knife. The chore complete, she stepped beyond the curtain.

The odor of food made her stomach lurch and she hurried from the hall to pace the manor grounds. Four liegemen, armed and watchful, stood attendance at the manor's entrance, though their presence did nothing to calm her apprehension.

As the sun approached the noon hour, Adam found her. "Is there aught you require?" he asked.

She shook her head and adjusted her cloak, prepared to take leave.

"I bid you safe return." He bowed.

Her palms suddenly felt moist and hot, despite the cold. Her throat convulsed dryly when she swallowed.

Checking the leather thong that bound her hair, she squared her shoulders and strode determinedly from the manor.

She nodded at Gilbert, who stood beside the trestle bridge, and hurried down the hill to speed through the village and fields. The normalcy of the peasants going about their chores contrasted sharply with the fear that stole over her. Butterflies beat their wings in her belly, the fluttering growing in intensity the nearer she drew to the forest.

Breathing hard, she slowed her steps when she reached the first of the beech trees. She did not want to appear anxious when she met Cerdic. She must appear cool and aloof.

Counting her steps, she forced herself to a lazy pace. At last she reached the place where she'd met Cerdic yesterday, only to find it deserted.

Birds' calls echoed eerily and she glanced about. There was no sign of Varin and his men, and for a moment panic threatened to overwhelm her.

Cease, she chided herself. If she could see Varin, Cerdic would see him as well. Again she checked the thong that held her hair. Then the sound of approaching footsteps captured her attention.

One of Cerdic's brutish henchmen appeared. His gaze traveled over her and shifted to encompass the area.

"She is alone," he called over his shoulder.

Roscelyn's heart skipped a beat as a number of men filed from the forest—ten of them. Varin and his men numbered only six, she thought frantically.

In that instant, Cerdic appeared and her heart burst into thunderous rhythm as her gaze fell upon Wulfwyn.

Roscelyn ran forward but did not come close to reaching her sister ere she was grabbed from behind. Rough hands roamed over her body, reached inside her boots, and traveled up the insides of her thighs.

"No weapons," a voice announced from behind her.

Weak with relief that the knife remained undetected, she longed to scream at Varin to attack now. Instead she clamped her jaws shut, recalling his words. She was not to let doubt get the best of her.

Varin would know when to close the trap. She must do nothing to upset his plans.

She gazed stoically at Wulfwyn's matted auburn hair and feared her heart would break. Wulfwyn returned her look, her eyes round with fear and longing, unable to speak for the rag that was stuffed in her mouth. Her hands were bound behind her back.

Roscelyn choked back her rage and gave Cerdic a cold stare. "Am I not allowed to greet my sister?"

"You will come nowhere near her," Cerdic snapped. "Now that you can see her, we will discuss what is required of you."

"Can you not at least remove that filthy gag from her mouth that I may speak with her?"

"The child is besieged with demons," he spat. "She babbles constantly to dead people and spirits from hell and I'll not listen to such. 'Tis all I can do to have her near me."

A sick feeling stole over Roscelyn and she glanced

at her sister. Had the strain of the past weeks addled her wits?

Wulfwyn rolled her eyes heavenward and Roscelyn realized her sister was up to some clever scheme.

Without warning, Wulfwyn kicked Cerdic's shin and he drew his arm back to strike her. The girl jerked free of his grasp.

Suddenly men were dropping from trees, weapons drawn.

Shouts erupted all around.

Roscelyn raced forward to grab Wulfwyn, but she was too late. Cerdic had already captured her sister and backed against the dead oak tree. Snatching his sword from its sheath, he held the blade to Wulfwyn's throat.

"Hold!"

Roscelyn heard Varin's bellowed command and skidded to a halt. The silence that followed was broken only by the sound of harsh breathing.

"So, you have betrayed me to your Norman lover," Cerdic growled at her, then raised his voice. "Drop your weapons or I will slit the child's throat."

Roscelyn closed her eyes. The moment had arrived and even prayer deserted her. Varin and his men would never lay aside their weapons. Death awaited them if they did.

"I will agree to drop my sword if you will agree to a match of skill between you and I."

Roscelyn's eyes popped open at Varin's challenge. Cerdic was too intelligent to agree to such a thing. No sooner had she completed the thought than her husband laughed and confirmed her opinion.

"Even though you are outnumbered, I must decline. Not that the thought of tearing your head from your body does not have appeal."

"We will drop our weapons provided you will at least give me an opportunity to beat that smug look from your ugly face."

Cerdic's nostrils flared, as if he scented victory.

"What have you to lose, Saxon pig," Varin goaded, "unless you are afraid to face me? My men and I are dead, regardless of the outcome."

Was he daft? It mattered not what scheme he plotted at. There was no way Varin could win when he and his men were defenseless, no way to get Wulfwyn free.

"Done!" Cerdic snapped.

Desperate, Roscelyn came to a decision. She flung herself toward Cerdic. "Mi'lord," she whined. "The Norman forced me to do his bidding. He set a spy upon me yesterday when I met you. He knew everything by the time I returned to the manor."

Cerdic sneered. "Filthy bitch. I would not believe you if you wore wings and a halo."

"I beg you," she pleaded, dropping to her knees before him. "Spare my life."

He kicked her chest and she fell over backward. Instantly she scrambled to clutch his chausses. "I can help you gain entry to the manor grounds. The Norman has placed a heavily armed contingent to guard its entrance."

"Ungrateful whore!" Varin roared behind her. "I should have known better than to place my faith in your deceitful hide."

Cerdic's eyes shifted to regard Varin.

In one swift motion, she snatched the knife from her hair and lunged upward.

Wulfwyn tore from his grasp and Roscelyn shrieked her anger when the knife sunk in his raised forearm instead of his chest.

The clangor of swords rang in her ears.

Cerdic swung his sword at her and she leapt backward, but not far enough. The tip of the blade sliced across her chest.

Dazed, she glanced over her shoulder to see Wulfwyn at Arnulf's side.

Her sister was safe.

She turned back to Cerdic and raised the knife, heedless of the fact that his blade was plunging toward her heart.

She would kill him with the final beat of her heart, she vowed.

Abruptly Varin slammed his shoulder into Cerdic's belly and the blade fell from his grasp. Her hand halted mid-strike.

Her breath jammed in her throat as she realized she'd near stabbed Varin.

Dizziness assailed her and her body shook. She staggered backward. Faith, but her chest ached. Without thinking, she clutched her cloak.

At the sticky ooze of liquid, her legs gave way. Dropping to the ground, she sat staring at the blood that soaked her gray cloak and brown tunic. 'Twas amazing how much of it there was.

Indeed, she'd been dealt a fatal blow.

Swallowing bile, she glanced at Varin. She must wish him farewell ere she died. She would tell him she loved him as well.

She frowned. He was choking the life from Cerdic, whose face had turned blue.

"Varin." She tried to gain his attention, but her voice had not carried.

Gathering her strength, she struggled to her feet. "Varin."

When he did not hear her, she staggered toward him over ground that seemed to undulate beneath her feet. Reaching him, she tugged at his tunic.

His eyes were transfixed and his face was twisted with enraged hatred as he strangled Cerdic. If he was aware of her presence, he gave no indication.

Darkness encroached on her vision. 'Twas just like him to pay her no heed, she thought churlishly. By all that was holy, the great oaf would hear her farewell before she died at his feet.

Summoning the last of her strength, she pounded his back with her fist. "Varin!"

He turned a blistering look on her and she puckered her lips. "I am dying," she snapped.

His gaze focused and a look of horror crossed his features. He loosed his grip on Cerdic and clutched her to him.

The sounds of battle had ceased and his arms shook as he lifted her feet off the ground. Cradling her against his chest, he strode swiftly in the direction of the village.

"I but wished to say farewell," she whispered.

His features wavered before her eyes, then blackness engulfed her.

VARIN PACED the confines of the small bedchamber, scarce able to look at Roscelyn as the witchwife stitched her chest.

Well he could empathize with Roscelyn's sickness at the sight of blood. Though he would never admit it, the sight of the needle piercing her tender flesh made him ill. At least the potion the witchwife had given her had rendered her unconscious.

"Are ye listenin', boy?"

He glanced to see the witchwife gathering her basket.

"You are taking leave?" he demanded, incredulous.

The old woman scowled. "Course I'm leavin'. I gots work to do."

"You will remain and keep watch over Roscelyn," he snapped.

"Bah. She don't need no watchin'. I keeps tellin' ye 'tis little more than a scratch."

"If that were the case, she would not need stitches."

"Two," the witchwife huffed, "and like as not, she didn't need them. Just give her some of me potion if the discomfort bothers her when she wakes. I'll come check on her tomorrow."

"I know nothing of caring for the sick," he persisted. "And I have much to do."

"Well, call her sister to care fer her and get about yer business, boy."

With that, the old woman marched off, leaving him alone with Roscelyn.

He moved to sit beside her on the bed. She looked so small and pale, so lifeless.

He smoothed wisps of hair from her face. If she'd been killed, he would have never forgiven himself. Life without her would have been . . .

Cease, he chided himself. 'Twas little more than a scratch, he reminded himself. She was in no danger. He had many years ahead of him to make up for the terrible mistakes he'd made.

Indeed, he should fetch Wulfwyn and see to the saddling of Rok. He should be on his way to deliver Roscelyn's husband and the scroll to William. Best to gain the king's permission to wed Roscelyn ere she could recover from her wounds and protest.

Still, he reasoned, the hour was late. He and his men were exhausted from sitting awake in the forest treetops all night. A little sleep would not hurt. The Saxon bastard was well secured, as was the scroll.

Or rather, half the scroll.

He frowned. It did not sit well that half the document was missing. 'Twas imperative that it be found. Not that Roscelyn's husband could tell him aught. The man could not even whisper for the damage Varin had caused in strangling him. Nor would he trust the man to tell him the truth.

Mayhap Roscelyn would know of it.

Aye. He stared at her pallid countenance, a sharp contrast to the rich golden color of her unbound hair. He would stay the night and ask her on the morrow if she knew aught of the missing half.

The decision to remain the night made, he relaxed. Whether Roscelyn wanted him or not, she would be his wife.

A smile etched his lips as he eyed her upturned nose. What other man would have her? She could not cook, could not sew, could not care for battle wounds or sick folk. She was stubborn and clumsy and a danger to herself.

But she was clever and honest and loyal to Cyning. He need never fear leaving his holdings in her capable hands.

Every woman he'd ever known paled in comparison to her spirit, and her facile tongue was a joy—in more ways than one, he thought, wincing.

Knowing that she was naked beneath the bedcovers did naught but tantalize him. Though she was hardly an expert at kissing, never had he experienced such desire as her lips wrought. That she had not yet known the ultimate fulfillment a man's body could bring her only added fever to his blood. 'Twould be his greatest pleasure to watch her shudder with completeness.

As if Roscelyn sensed his thoughts, she stirred. A frown drew her brow and she sighed. Then her eyes opened.

Her gaze darted about the room before coming to rest on him. She immediately struggled to sit.

"Here, mi'lady. Do not exert yourself."

She stilled and stared at him, her golden eyes more hazy than usual.

"How do you feel?"

"I am fine."

He raised a brow. "That is what you always say."

"Cerdic and the scroll?" she asked, her voice sleepy.

"They are secure. I will leave to deliver them to William on the morrow."

Her eyes closed. "That is good."

A tap sounded at the door and he bid the person to enter.

"Dinner is served, mi'lord."

"Fetch me a tray. I will eat my meal here."

The squire nodded and in a short time Varin was filling his empty belly. The tray removed, he was next visited by Wulfwyn, who wished to see Roscelyn.

"Lufu says she is fine," the girl stated, her gaze roaming her sister. "Is she in pain?"

"She has been sleeping all evening."

Wulfwyn turned a green-eyed look on him. "My thanks for saving us from Cerdic."

"You . . ." He searched for the right words. "You were not mistreated?"

A cunning sparkle lit her eyes. "I pretended to speak with the dead and with all manner of demons. Cerdic was too scared to come near me, the dunghead."

He shook his head. "You are much like your sister with your cleverness."

"Do you think?" she asked in a hopeful tone.

"I am certain."

She squared her shoulders. "Shall I stay and care for her that you may seek your rest?"

"Nay. 'Tis you who needs to rest. I shall be gone tomorrow and you will have to care for her then."

She frowned. "Where will you sleep?"

"I will have Adam bring me a pallet and sleep here beside the bed."

And so it was until Roscelyn roused in the middle of the night. Pulling on a pair of braies to cover his nakedness, he lit a candle and moved to sit again on the bed.

"You are in pain?"

Her eyes were alert now, clear and wide and staring at his bare chest. "I . . . I am uncomfortable, but 'tis nothing terrible. Indeed, nothing would suit me so well as to rise and move about."

"Shall I fetch the witchwife's potion?"

She shook her head, then frowned. "Have you been sitting thus the entire day and night?"

"Nay." He nodded at the pallet on the floor. "I have been sleeping yon."

She blinked. "You must take your bed, mi'lord. I will do fine on my pallet in the hall."

"Shh. You will stay where you are."

She rose to sit. "But you have much to do on the morrow. You need your rest."

The covers slipped from her shoulders and he eyed the wound on her chest above the swell of breasts.

She jerked the covers to her chin. "Is it . . . does it look bad?"

He eyed her fearful countenance. "If you would lower the sheets that I might inspect it more closely . . ."

She edged the covers down and he affected a studious mien. "Lower."

She eased the sheets down a little more.

He shook his head. "Lower."

She scowled. "I cannot lower them any farther without exposing my . . ."

Her lips thinned. "Lecherous cur. You are incorrigible."

He shook his head at her. "You are very cute."

Her lips puckered and ere she could protest, he leaned forward. Though he meant only to steal a quick kiss, he could not resist lingering.

Within moments, he felt her arms go around his neck and felt her shiver. Like quicksilver, her mood shifted and she opened her mouth for his tongue.

The sheets slipped to her waist and he lowered his head to kiss her breasts, careful to not disturb her wound.

Her nipples hardened beneath his lips and he took one inside his mouth, running his tongue over the stiff bud. Her breathing quickened and the mattress rustled as she wiggled.

If only she weren't hurt, he thought raggedly. Taking a deep breath, he tried to draw away, but her hold on his neck tightened.

"Please, mi'lord. Finish what you have begun."

"'Twould not be safe. You are hurt. Lie back and go to sleep."

Ignoring his order, she clung to his neck and kissed him, her mouth hot and sweet and determined.

He groaned. "There is a point beyond which I will be unable to stop," he whispered against her lips.

"You have not yet reached that point?" she whispered in return.

"Bloodygore, wench. You are going to be the death of me."

With that, he eased her back on the bed and

stretched out beside her. Keeping as much space as possible between his chest and hers, he cradled her neck beneath his arm and trailed kisses over her mouth and down her soft neck.

"A saint on the cross could not resist you," he rasped, moving to capture a nipple in his mouth.

Her hands moved to the back of his head and he stroked the inside of her thighs with his free hand.

At her moan, he paused and raised his head. "You are hurt?"

"Nay." She regarded him with parted lips and eyes that smoldered.

He cast her a wolfish grin and again lowered his head to her breasts. Moving his hand upward, he grazed his knuckles over her woman's core, felt a deep sense of satisfaction at the moist heat there. He slipped a finger inside her and near wasted himself at her sharp intake of breath, at the way her hips rose for his touch.

Withdrawing, he rubbed her core again, his blood boiling hotter with each panting breath she took.

When next he slid his finger inside her, he raised his head to watch her. Swelled to near bursting at the sweet flush of pink color that bathed her face, at the dark sweep of her lashes where her eyes were closed, at the way her tongue licked her lips.

Pulling his arm from beneath her neck, he moved lower to kiss the inside of her thighs. She gasped when his lips closed over her core and she clasped the back of his head and spread her legs.

He could stand no more. Raising over her, he placed the tip of his arousal at her opening, then eased inside.

Sweet Blessed Virgin, never had he felt such intense pleasure. His movements slow and deliberate, he thrust and withdrew, waiting for her, waiting for the right moment.

It came not a moment too soon. She moaned and clutched at his hips, grinding herself against him, panting and straining.

When she shuddered, he could wait no longer.

He drew back once more, then buried himself to the hilt, his seed pumping from him.

In all his years, never had he experienced such a powerful release.

TWENTY-ONE

ROSCELYN WAS AWAKE when Adam arrived the next morn to rouse Varin.

Indeed, she'd never gone back to sleep after Varin had made love to her. The night's passion was what she'd wanted more than anything. The memory would have to last a lifetime, for she would never again see him.

She grimaced, though whether her pain was a result of her wound or her breaking heart she knew not.

Watching the squire lower Varin's short-sleeved byrnie over his head, she wondered if she had not made a terrible error in judgment.

Mayhap 'twould be best if she had no idea of the

pleasure Varin could bring her. Longing already encroached upon her and they'd not yet been parted.

"Go and see that Rok is saddled," he ordered once Adam had finished dressing him.

The squire bowed and took himself off and Varin turned to face her. "How are you feeling?"

He held up a hand and raised his voice to mimic her. "I am fine."

"How did you guess?" She forced a smile.

His look turned serious. "I have a question for you, mi'lady, one that I hope will not come between us. But William will ask."

She raised her brows. "Aye?"

"Your husband held but half the scroll. Have you any idea what might have become of the other half?"

She frowned and stared at him. "Only half? Are you certain?"

"Do not concern yourself. Whatever your husband did with it, he will say once . . ." He cleared his throat. "Once his voice is returned."

He said nothing of the torture that would be visited upon Cerdic to gain the truth from him, and for that she was grateful. Hate her husband though she did, 'twas not pleasant to think of his suffering.

Varin cupped her chin and raised her face. "I must be off. Meanwhile, you must rest and recover."

Leaning down, he kissed her. "Be well for me when I return."

She nodded and staunched the urge to cling to him. "Take care that your journey will be safe."

For a moment, he hesitated, as if there were more

he would say. His gaze roamed her features, then he sketched a bow and was gone.

Her shoulders slumped.

Never to see him again, never to know the heat of his kiss, the safety of his embrace, the joy of his teasing jests.

She pursed her lips against the tears that threatened. How ever would she live without him?

Her gaze traveled over the bed they'd shared, around the chamber she would never again see. Indeed, she would soon leave Cyning forever.

The moment Varin was away, she would approach Arnulf and convince him to escort her and Wulfwyn to the abbey.

Her anxious anticipation only made the minutes seem like hours. At last she wrapped a bedsheet around her shoulders and left the bedchamber for the curtained section of hall.

"Ros," Wulfwyn greeted her from a bench at a trestle table. "I was just coming to check on you. Varin said to give you time to sleep a little more."

The hall was empty and she motioned for her sister to join her. "Is he gone?"

Wulfwyn eyed her warily. "Aye. He is gone. Is all well?"

"Would you fetch Arnulf while I dress? I must speak with him."

The girl frowned. "Are you certain 'tis not something that can wait? You do not look well."

Roscelyn made a shooing motion with her hand. "Go and find the giant. I am fine."

Wulfwyn nodded, though she repeatedly glanced over her shoulder as she hurried to the hall's entrance doors. Once she was out of sight, Roscelyn entered the curtained section and moved to her chest.

She grabbed clean clothing and dressed as quickly as her wounds would allow, then reached for the leather pouch that held the scroll.

By the time Arnulf and Wulfwyn entered the great hall, she was sitting on a bench, the scroll on the table before her.

"Mi'lady." The giant shook his head as he approached. "What are you doing up? Varin would—"

"Varin would gladly slit my throat if he were aware of what I'm about to tell you. Sit and listen, if you would. I have a favor to ask of you, and I will make it worth your while."

She caught Wulfwyn's concerned look as the giant moved to a bench opposite her.

"Here is the other half of the scroll." She slid it across the table. "I could not bring myself to tell Varin of it, so I will leave it in your capable hands. In exchange, I would that you escort Wulfwyn and I to Saint Dunstan Abbey."

Wulfwyn gasped and Arnulf cast Roscelyn an incredulous look. "What . . . Why?" he stuttered. "How . . ."

She held up a hand. "'Twas I who originally possessed the document. I sent half of it with Wulfwyn that it would be delivered to the pope."

Arnulf said not a word as she told him everything that had occurred concerning the document. "'Tis the reason I did not trust Varin to rescue Wulfwyn. I feared he would place the scroll above her life."

The giant drew back, insulted. "I would never allow aught to happen to Wulfwyn."

Roscelyn took a deep breath. "Neither would Varin. It no longer matters. I will be the first to admit I was wrong. But I cannot remain here at Cyning."

Arnulf scowled. "Of course you shall remain here. Varin will understand. You need not fear."

"Whom do you seek to fool, Arnulf? 'Tis not something he will forgive, and I cannot blame him. He has worked hard to reach such a favored position with your king. Once I am gone . . ."

She paused to swallow the lump in her throat. "Once I am gone, Varin will be free to marry your king's niece. He will once again own the land that belonged to his family. Believe me, Arnulf, 'tis for the best."

Though it took another half hour of coaxing and cajoling, the giant finally leaned back from the table and crossed his arms. "Wait until Varin returns, and then I will take you if 'tis your wish. You have my word."

"Nay. Better for me to be gone when he returns. 'Twill save him the trouble of asking me to leave. I do not think I could bear such a thing."

Arnulf blew and exasperated breath. "Very well. When do you wish to leave?"

"Today."

"Today? But you are not well."

"I am fine, Arnulf. Ask Lufu. 'Tis but a scratch."

A FULL TWO WEEKS passed before Varin eagerly nudged Rok across the ford, then spurred him to a faster pace, leaving his liegemen behind.

'Twas not a good thing to do to a horse, to run him clear to the stables without giving the animal a chance to cool down, but he could hold himself back no longer.

Faith but 'twas good to be home and he could scarce wait to see Roscelyn.

Though it had taken great skill not to insult William when the king had offered his niece's hand in marriage, the king had finally agreed to his request to marry Roscelyn. In addition, William had fair bestowed a fortune on him for delivering the scroll to his hands.

Roscelyn certainly need never again fear a lack of provender. Indeed, he would be able to gift Roscelyn with his mother's jewelry.

Shouts of greeting met his ears and peasants cleared the way as he galloped down the village lane.

There was but one other matter he needed to attend to make amends to Roscelyn. If her housecarl agreed to swear fealty to him, he would free the man.

Urging Rok across the drawbridge, he was satisfied to see that the walls had near been completed in his absence. Raising a hand in greeting to Walther, he slowed Rok's pace ere he trampled one of the peasants that hurried about the manor yard.

Drawing rein at the stables, he dismounted, then strode briskly toward the hall. Bloodygore, but he'd awaited this moment for an entire fortnight.

While he surely had much scraping and begging to do to gain Roscelyn's forgiveness, 'twas a task he greatly anticipated.

Kissing the angry words from her mouth ere she could speak them, nibbling on her neck while she berated him for his cruelty, holding her close to keep her from smacking him. Stealing her boots that she could not kick him.

He deserved every curse she might heap on his head. And he fully intended to make the most of every curse until the lady forgave him.

Then he would—

"Varin!" Arnulf caught up to him as he neared the hall. "You are returned. How did things go with William?"

"We are invited to his coronation Christmas day in London. I will tell you more later. For now, I would see Roscelyn."

"A moment." Arnulf clutched his arm, drawing him to a halt.

"Well, what is it, man?" he prodded when the giant did not immediately speak.

Foreboding settled over him as his underlord's eyes shifted before his perusal.

Icy fear ran through his blood and his heart fair ceased to beat.

Had the witchwife been wrong? Had Roscelyn's wounds been more severe than the old woman had thought? Or had they perchance become infected?

He gripped Arnulf's arm to steady himself as the ground swayed beneath him.

"Roscelyn?" Her name was barely audible for his lack of breath.

"She is well," the giant assured him. "Calm yourself."

Varin bent forward and planted his hands on his knees, swallowing great lungfuls of air. "Christ's bloody bones, Arnulf. You scared me nigh unto death."

"My apologies. I did not mean to imply . . ."

Varin glanced up and the giant's gaze again darted away. Straightening, he raised a brow. "What has she done?"

"If you'll just allow me to explain before you start bellowing like a wounded bull."

"Where is she?"

Arnulf heaved a sigh. "She convinced me to escort her to her abbey."

"What?"

"She left you the other half of the scroll."

"I care not one whit for scrolls. Of all the . . . You let her go?"

"She was most persuasive."

Mayhap 'twas the fear that inspired his rage. Mayhap 'twas his utter disappointment at discovering Roscelyn gone.

Whatever the reason, Varin balled his fist and punched his underlord squarely on the nose.

❧❦❧

ROSCELYN SCRATCHED in the garden at the abbey. Her hands felt frozen because she'd removed her mittens to plant peas. Wulfwyn worked beside her, poking holes in the loose dirt for the seeds.

"Sister Hilde is going to teach me to recite Scripture," Wulfwyn remarked cheerfully.

Roscelyn smiled wistfully. Her only consolation in

living at the abbey was Wulfwyn's unexpected love of the place. Though it did little to warm her heart at night when she could think of naught save Varin, it eased her soul to know Wulfwyn was happy. Indeed, the nuns loved her sister and enjoyed her company.

Roscelyn smoothed the dirt over a seed and rose on her knees to rest her aching back. Would her soul never know peace for want of Varin? Would she ever pass a day or night without constantly thinking of him?

Abruptly a great weight struck her shoulders. Toppling facefirst into the furrow of freshly turned earth, she heard Wulfwyn laugh.

"Easy, Poppit. Easy. Where did you come from?"

"The wretched cur accompanied me."

Roscelyn came up spitting dirt and swiping at her face at the harsh sound of Varin's voice.

What was he doing here?

She blinked to clear her vision, only to have her eyes tear from the grit.

"Here." Varin took her by the arm and pulled her to her feet. "Bloodygore. You are as big a mess as ever."

He brushed at her face with the hem of his cloak. "Whatever makes me long to marry you, I know not."

Her heart thundered in her chest at his words. He longed to marry her? 'Twas not possible. He should be off to marry his king's niece.

She swatted at his hand. "You are rubbing the flesh from my face."

"Pff." He continued his ministrations. "I should be flaying the hide from your backside. 'Tis deceitful the way you turned Arnulf to your cause in my absence."

Finished with her face, he took her arm and pulled her toward the abbey's courtyard. "Telling him you would not wish to ruin my chances for a good marriage with the king's niece," he grumbled. "He is as dim-witted as you."

"You are not going to marry the king's niece?" she demanded.

"Nay. I will marry you."

Fearing that his words were false, she refused to give into the hope that near swamped her reason. To have it dashed would surely mean her death.

"But you will never own your family lands if you marry me."

He halted so abruptly that she stumbled. "You do not always know what is best for everyone and I'll hear no more arguments from you. You will wed me and there is the end to it."

She raised a brow. "And if I refuse?"

He shook his head at her. "You will not."

Puckering her lips, she was caught unaware by his kiss.

Embarrassment warmed her face and she struggled for release. 'Twas consecrated ground on which they stood.

"Say you love me," he murmured against her lips.

She shook her head as weakness stole over her senses.

His kiss grew more demanding. "Say you love me."

Her body trembled as he traced her lips with his tongue. "Say it."

"I love you," she breathed.

He drew away and scowled, brushing dirt from his mouth. "Must you e'er be so stubborn? I have likely swallowed enough dirt to fill a pigsty."

"Then you had best tell me of your great love for me. Otherwise I shall kiss you until you confess it."

He cast her a terrified look. "Nay, mi'lady. I will tell you I love you now. However, once you are cleaned up, you may rest assured that you will have much kissing to do ere you will again hear the words from my mouth."

About the Author

A native Floridian, Sandra Lee received a B.A. in elementary education, and promptly moved into the field of freelance writing without ever teaching a day of school. It has been Ms. Lee's experience that a twisted sense of humor goes a long way toward straightening out the dangerous curves on the highway of life, especially where romance and children are concerned. When she's not writing, Ms. Lee's time is spent with her husband and two daughters, none of whom appreciate her pointless lectures. Ms. Lee is also ruled by two dogs and three cats, none of which obey her commands.